SAFE HARBOR

The Inland Seas Series - Book 3

GWYN MCNAMEE

Safe Harbor
by Gwyn McNamee © 2019

Cover Design: Michelle Johnson at Blue Sky Designs
Cover Models: James Ramsey and Heidi Toporowski
Editing: Stephie Walls

"If you want the naked beauty of my vulnerability, you have to have the strength to share the burden of, the private pain, that makes me feel so tender and fragile. For I am as strong as I am weak. If you want me to come home to you, be the safe harbor, in which, I can seek refuge."

Jaeda DeWalt

Acknowledgments

Thank you to my wonderful team of alpha and beta readers, as well as all the experts I consulted to write this book. I am truly humbled by the love everyone has for these bad-boy pirates.

ONE

Preacher

I could have done without seeing Cutter's cock.

Catching a glimpse of Valentina naked is another story. I enjoy *my* cock and balls too much to attempt that, even if Cutter thought that's what I was doing. He would castrate me with his bare hands if I had been ogling his woman.

It may have been years since I last got laid, but that doesn't mean I'd resort to anything so underhanded just to get my rocks off. All I wanted was to make sure she was going to join us. This is important to everyone.

Potentially life or death.

It seems that's the constant state of our lives recently. Always someone worse than us breathing down our necks. First, *Il Padrone*, then Arturo. Now…this new threat banging at the door.

Footsteps pound down the hall toward my room, and Warwick, E, and Rion file in with an enraged Cutter and lust-dazed Valentina close behind. Milo trots in, looking annoyed at having his sleep interrupted. Cramming six people and a bulldog in here isn't exactly comfortable, but it *is* very necessary.

We need everyone on board and on the same page.

Cutter drags a T-shirt over his head and shoves his sunglasses on his face. He almost never wears them when he's alone with Valentina anymore, but habits are hard to break, and it's even harder to live without a mask you've hidden behind for so long. "What the hell is so important you had to drag us out of bed at three in the goddamn morning?"

Rion yawns.

Warwick brushes the sleep from his eyes. "Yeah, what's up? I have a very unhappy, pregnant girlfriend upstairs."

Not my fault.

I turn back to my wall of screens and throw one of the images onto the large TV monitor on the wall so they all can see it.

E narrows his eyes on it. "What are we looking at?"

"Potentially, big fucking trouble." I throw five more images up onto the screen with the first. "Someone has been trying to hack into my system for months."

Warwick stills, and his dark eyes snap over to mine. "What? Why the fuck didn't you tell me?"

"Because no one is going to get through my damn firewall. Hackers hack. It's what we do. I figured it was just some little shit in his mother's basement trying to get into what he thought might be a covert government ops group, given the amount of bandwidth I take up and my reputation on the web."

Rion smirks. "SAYYOURPRAYERS69?"

"Ha. Ha, asshole." I shove a hand through my hair and wave toward the screen. "Look, whoever this is definitely knows his stuff—"

"Or hers." Valentina glares at me and wraps her arms around herself, only emphasizing the fact that all she's wearing is one of Cutter's T-shirts. Her foot taps at the end of one long, tanned leg. Milo sits at her feet, staring at me like he's waiting for a response to her interjection, too.

I roll my eyes at her. "I'm not trying to be sexist here, Val.

Most hackers are men. It's a fact, not a damn issue for the women's suffrage movement."

E covers his amusement with his hand, where he leans against the wall. Rion barks out a laugh. Warwick fights a smile but doesn't open his mouth. He knows better than to comment on an argument with Val. Cutter just stands frozen in place, his signature sneer twisting his lips.

Valentina mimics his stance but bites her tongue. The woman may be the head of the Marconi crime family, but she's also the woman Cutter fucked so hard on the *Destiny* that her cries echoed through the warehouse while we all sat around listening. She might scare the men she controls and even her rivals in Chicago. Here, she's just another girl who has somehow managed to find her way into our world. When she's here, it doesn't matter that we work for her. Cutter would never let her try to throw around that weight when she's on our turf. It wouldn't end well for either of them.

I turn back to my computers and throw the map onto the screen. "As I was saying, this *person* knows what they're doing but is no match for my system. We're safe where that's concerned."

Warwick sighs. "I feel a *but* coming on."

There's always a but.

"But...I think it's more than just some bored kid. That concerns me."

Enough to drag them from their beds in the middle of the night.

Rion folds his massive arms over his chest and leans against the corner of my desk. "Why do you think that?"

"The prior half-dozen attempts were all somewhat inconsequential. Short. An hour tops before the person presumably either got bored or realized they were in over their head. But tonight...whoever this is has been banging at the door of my system for six hours with no signs of stopping."

"Shit." Warwick throws up his hands and paces. "Can you trace where it's coming from?"

"I've been trying ever since the first attack on the system. Like I said, whoever is doing this is good. They're hiding their tracks well. Even with this extended hack attempt, I haven't been able to pinpoint a location. It's dozens and dozens of redirects at this point."

No one says it, but we're all thinking it. It sounds an *awful* lot like the way the drugs were being shipped. But there's no way anyone could connect us to that. Even if Arturo had given our names to whoever was operating the *Marcella Marie* instead of just a general warning they were going to be boarded, we killed that entire crew, and even with our names, they can't connect *this* place to us and certainly not my system.

I'm just too jumpy. We all are after everything that's happened. It's been a rough six months.

I scrub a hand over my face and rub at my burning eyes. Six hours straight staring at these screens are starting to wear on me. "It may be nothing."

Rion snorts. "*May* doesn't instill a lot of confidence, bro."

"You think I don't know that?"

No one wants another *maybe* in our lives. The last few months have left us all on-edge. Taking out Arturo was a breath of fresh air, a weight off all our shoulders. It meant freedom from servitude. We're our own bosses now. We may still do jobs for Valentina to keep the lights on and ourselves from getting bored, but there's no longer a guillotine over our heads if we say no. Cutter's the only one who faces the back-lash from her. And frankly, they both seem to get off on it when they argue. It's foreplay to them. They've had angry sex against and on just about every surface in this place except the kitchen. And that's only because E would kill them if they tried that.

Literally.

Cutter wanders over to the screen and peers up at the map with all the dots indicating locations the hacker is relaying through. "So, what do we do now?"

I recline in my chair. "Not much we *can* do. I'll keep trying to track down this fucker and figure out if it's anything to worry about, but he…" I glance at Valentina, "or *she* isn't getting in, so the system is safe."

Warwick frowns, his dark eyes narrowing on me. "You're sure about that?"

He has no concept of the kinds of things I've done and can do. When Cutter brought Rion and me in to help him with this little pirate endeavor, we couldn't say no. Not when we saw how important it was to him. And over the years, we've become a brotherhood, with Warwick in command, but that doesn't mean we don't rebel or stand up for ourselves when he gets out of line or says something fucking stupid.

Like now.

"Fuck you, War. I've protected bigger secrets than you'll ever comprehend for this country and hacked into shit you don't even know exists. I can keep our damn system safe." Anger heats my skin, and I push up from my chair and go toe-to-toe with him. "If you have a fucking problem with how I do my job, just try to find someone else who can do it better. I'd love to see you fucking scramble."

Rion's massive arm shoves between us, and he pushes us both back a step. "You two, knock it off."

It's not like us to fight with each other. We're usually addressing all our frustrations toward the bad guys, but we thought they were all gone. A new, unknown threat is even worse than one we can see. At least then, we know who and what we're dealing with and can react accordingly.

Warwick holds up his hands. "I'm sorry. I just…don't want to end up looking over our goddamn shoulders again. I have enough to worry about."

No doubt.

Grace's pregnancy hasn't gone smoothly. While it appears she and the baby are healthy, she's experienced Braxton Hicks contractions already and has been off and on bed rest for weeks. Warwick isn't used to taking care of anyone, let alone a woman who's carrying his child. The stress is weighing on him. His dark eyes seem even darker lately, and the bags under them have doubled in size in just the last month.

I elbow Rion out of the way and grab War's biceps. Those worried eyes meet mine. I don't like seeing him like this. It makes all of us uneasy.

He needs reassurance.

"I got this, War. We're fine. I just wanted everyone to be aware of the situation. I'll figure out who we're dealing with. Everyone makes a mistake sometime."

We've made plenty.

The *Neptune's Daughter.*

Failing to eliminate Arturo earlier.

The *Marcella Marie.*

Although, the last one wasn't a mistake, per se. The guys got in and out clean, except for E getting hit. It's the only thing that could tie us to anything that went down on that ship. If he bled somewhere and the Coast Guard finds it and runs the DNA through CODIS, we're fucked. He's the only one of us who has ever done any prison time, and it's the one thing that could get us caught.

I've been following the investigation closely, watching for signs of anything that might point to E or any of us, and so far, nothing has appeared in any of the reports on the Coast Guard's digital system, but it doesn't mean I don't still worry about it.

Like I said, everyone makes a mistake, and it's only a matter of time before we make one that gets us caught. Yet, we can't seem to walk away from this life. The offer from Valentina to continue to work together for all our benefits was too good to pass up, and until we've secured nest eggs big enough to keep us living the good life until we croak, we're going to have to continue in the pirate business.

It fucking blows that all the hard work we've done for the

last five years hasn't been for our benefit at all, only to repay the debt to the Marconis. But times have changed, and now, we're in control of the jobs, and working with Valentina means we get a fair cut.

We won't be in the game for too much longer.

And this attempted hack is just another reminder of why we need to get out—sooner, rather than later. There's too much evidence on my system. Too much proof of every illegal and underhanded thing we've done for the last half-decade. It's enough to send us all away for life. Or worse.

I've come close enough to death already to know I don't want to face it again, whether it be at the barrel of a gun or with a damn IV in my arm in the death chamber. So, there's no way I'm letting whoever this little fucker is mess with us or find any information that could implicate us in any of the bad shit we've had our hands in.

Never.

I look from Warwick to Rion to E and then Cutter, finally ending on Valentina and letting my focus drop down to our four-legged friend. "Guys, I got this. Have I ever failed you before?"

They shake their heads. All but Cutter.

He stares me down through those shades. "There's a first time for everything. Maybe you should say a prayer for some divine intervention." He brushes past me with Valentina hot on his heels.

She offers me an apologetic half-smile before she disappears into the hallway after him, Milo close behind.

Fucking douchebag.

Warwick's hand lands on my shoulder. "He didn't mean that."

I shrug it off and return to my chair. "Yeah, he did. And you know it."

Rion moves over to examine the map. "He's just

concerned about security. It's in his blood. He doesn't know how to act any other way."

I chuckle and rap my knuckles on the desk. "You're preaching to the choir, man. I worked with Cutter enough before the attack to know exactly who and what he is, but he's only gotten worse since. We can all agree on that."

E, Warwick, and Rion all bob their heads silently.

"Even Valentina can't soften him, but that's not necessarily a bad thing. We need Cutter to be hard and vigilant. It's what he does best."

Rion's laugh booms around my small room. "I think he does asshole best."

"That, too."

Warwick steps up beside Rion and stares at the map. "So, what do we do in the meantime?"

"Let me do my job."

Sometimes easier said than done for War.

He nods and leaves my room. E slips out silently behind him, and Rion turns to me with a tight frown.

The big man has always been the one able to read me the best, and he senses my unease with the situation. "This could be really bad, couldn't it?"

"If whoever this is manages to get in…yes." I spread my hand out over my equipment. "But I don't intend to ever let that happen."

"You need a break sometime, Preacher. You look like shit. When's the last time you slept?"

Yesterday? No…two days ago.

He snorts. "You don't even remember, do you?" He doesn't wait for an answer, just claps his hand on my shoulder before strolling over to the door. "You need to sleep and then go do something to relax. Don't you have your appointment tomorrow?"

I do. But I had actually been considering blowing it off. "Yeah, I do."

"Go. You need to leave this damn cave of yours before you become a Gollum."

He turns the corner before I can retort.

He's right, though.

I need a break. Even if it's only for a few hours.

Ink therapy, here I come.

TWO

Everly

———————

The glass door closes behind me, and I twist the lock into place but don't turn to face the shop. If I do, the tears will come, and I can't have that. Instead of facing my new reality, I drop my forehead against the cool glass and struggle to take a deep breath.

You can do this, Everly. You have to.

I twist back around and scan the room. It's insane I've never set foot in here before, but that's just the strange reality of my life. If only I'd come earlier, forced Jimmy to offer me a job here, things would have been different. He would have told me, or I would have noticed something...

But *what-ifs* can drive you insane. And I already have far too many of them eating away at my brain to add another.

I push away from the door and drop my bag onto the low counter that separates the waiting area from the work stations. Two black chairs fill the other side even though Jimmy never had anyone else here with him.

"I'm a lone wolf, Everly."

His words echo through my brain just as clearly today as when he said them in an attempt to explain why he chose to live his life so isolated from everyone, including me lately.

I blink back the tears and wipe my nose. It's time to figure out what needs to be done around here. I flip open the appointment book. Nothing on today. That makes things a little easier.

The door rattles. My heart leaps into my throat.

It's okay. It's not him.

A closed sign still hangs on the glass, so whoever it is will eventually go away.

The door rattles again—harder this time—and a bearded man presses his face against the glass to peer in. His bourbon eyes meet mine and widen slightly. He points to the lock and raises a dark eyebrow at me.

Who the hell is this guy?

I slowly make my way over to the door, keeping my eyes on him, where he stands just beyond the thin pane of glass separating us. Thick muscles covered in beautiful ink bulge from his red T-shirt, and additional tats creep up his neck and across his knuckles where he has his hands dropped at his sides.

He must be one of Jimmy's clients.

I turn the lock and open the door a few inches. "Hi. I'm sorry. We're closed."

That same eyebrow wings up, and he glances over my shoulder into the shop. "Jimmy is expecting me."

That's odd.

I flip open the scheduling book to today. "There wasn't anything on the calendar."

The man's smoky eyes swim with confusion. "Jimmy and I have had a standing appointment on the first Friday of every month for almost five years."

Oh shit.

All the pieces click into place.

The attitude.

The impeccable artwork covering every inch of visible skin.

For some inexplicable reason, heat floods my cheeks. "You're Preacher."

A smile curls the corners of his lips, and humor flashes in his gaze. "I see my reputation precedes me. I don't know whether I should be flattered or worried. Especially since I have no idea who *you* are."

Right.

Awkward.

I hold open the door and motion for him to enter. He walks past me slowly as he assesses me. Having a man check me out so intently shouldn't bother me anymore. Not a day goes by when I'm not ogled by a dozen men. A woman with as much ink as I have can't just walk by unnoticed, as much as I wish I could sometimes. But something about the way *this* man does it sends goose bumps skittering across my skin.

It's been so long since I've had that reaction due to anything but absolute terror, it makes it hard to breathe.

He wanders over to the counter and examines the shop before turning to me. "So, where's Jimmy?"

I swallow past the lump in my throat and move to the other side of the counter across from him. "Jimmy…"

God, how do I even say this?

Preacher watches me expectantly.

Best to just rip off the Band-Aid, I guess. "Jimmy isn't coming back."

His brow furrows. "What do you mean he isn't coming back? Did something happen to him?"

"Cancer happened."

The broad shoulders of the man in front of me slump. "Well, shit. So…it's bad?"

I can't even form the words. I just nod.

"Shit." He shakes his head. "I can't believe it. I just saw him a month ago, and he seemed fine. A little run down, but not anything to raise concern."

Of course not.

Jimmy *would* continue to work while he was in agonizing pain as cancer spread throughout his body. He didn't have anything else and would never want to let down one of his customers, especially Preacher.

I close the appointment book on the counter. "I didn't know, either. I had no idea anything was wrong until he called me two days ago to tell me he needed me to come take care of the shop."

"You're a friend of his?"

How do I even answer that without getting into a long, complicated explanation?

"Yep." Keep it short and sweet.

His eyes roam appreciatively over my ink. "Are you a tattoo artist, too?"

"Yep." I search the shop for anything that needs to be cleaned up or taken care of immediately. Any excuse not to face him. The way his eyes bore into me strip me bare more than any man ever has with his hands.

He clears his throat and waits until I force myself to glance up at him again. A moment passes where he just stares at me, his too-knowing examination unraveling all the emotions I'm likely doing a shitty job at hiding.

The corner of his lips tip up in a lop-sided grin. "You know who I am. Did he tell you about me?"

I chuckle and lean against the counter toward him. "You have had more work done than any other client he's ever had. And, for some reason that hasn't become evident to me yet, he was very fond of you."

Preacher drops back his head, and deep laughter rumbles up from his gut and echoes through the shop. "Wow. You sure have some balls on you…" He waits for me to fill in the blank where my name should be. A few seconds pass. "You're going to play it that way, huh?"

Yes.

Because, for some reason, playing with this man is helping to relieve some of the pain tearing away at my heart.

He beams at me from across the counter. "Well, ma'am, I guess I don't need to know your name, but it will make having you work on me a lot less awkward."

"Work on you?"

"How else am I going to get this backpiece that Jimmy started finished? I'm not driving all the way to Milwaukee or Chicago to have someone else jump in at this point. You're here, and if Jimmy trusted you enough to ask you to look after his shop, you must be pretty fucking good."

My chest swells at the compliment I certainly haven't earned from him. He hasn't seen *any* of my work. For all he knows, I could be a total hack or a complete newbie. "That's a lot of faith to put into an artist you know absolutely nothing about." I lean slightly closer, over the counter, and fight a smile. "Not even my name."

He grins, and a dimple appears on his left cheek, right at the edge of his impeccably manicured, short beard. "I have complete and utter faith in Jimmy. He had faith in you. That's all I need."

I choke back the emotion threatening to steal my voice. "Everly. My name is Everly."

A large, tattooed hand extends over the counter. "Nice to meet you, Everly. James Davis."

"James?" I raise an eyebrow at him and place my hand in his.

He chuckles as his palm cocoons mine. The strong yet gentle pressure of his handshake sends shivers through me. "Preacher is just a nickname and what my friends call me. Only my parents call me James."

I pull back my hand. "Nice to meet you, Preacher. Now, do you really want me to work on you? Jimmy's been your guy for a long time."

Something dark and somber takes over the space between

us, and Preacher runs a hand over his short beard. "Well, if he's not coming back."

"He's not."

As much as I hate to admit it, Jimmy is never going to set foot in this place again. The next time he's here, it will be as ashes in an urn.

Preacher extends a sympathetic look. "I really need to have some work done today. It's…important."

He doesn't expand any further, but the way his eyes darken tells me all I need to know. He's one of *those*. One of the ones who need this, who need the pain to survive. It's his therapy. I recognize it and understand it because I'm one of them, too.

He holds out his hands in question. "What do you say? Are you up for doing some work on me today?"

Some would say it's a bad idea to ink while emotional, but for me, it's the best time to do it. It's when I can pour everything into my work—the pain, the longing, the fear and the need, and anything else I may be feeling at any given moment. Channeling that into my art is what keeps me sane, and I could *really* use a dose of that release right now.

"I'm up for it." I tap my fingers against the counter and point to one of the two chairs in the shop—the one that's obviously *not* Jimmy's.

Even though he's not coming back, I can't bear to work in his space.

Preacher examines it for a second before walking over to it with a slight limp. He grabs the hem of his T-shirt and yanks it off. The fabric falls to a heap on the tile floor, leaving his torso and all the stunning artwork covering it on full display.

A massive crucifix spreads across his chest, the familiar image of Jesus hanging from it, cut at his side and thorn of crowns adorning his head. Various scrollwork lettering surrounds it, along with dozens of smaller images and verses that all weave together to form a giant patchwork of art.

He clears his throat.

Shit. I just got caught staring at him like some thirsty whore.

"Beautiful work."

"Thank you. Jimmy did most of it over the last five years. I'm so glad I found him when I moved here."

That doesn't surprise me in the least. It looks like Jimmy's work. Detailed. Immaculate. Evocative. *Real.*

It has the anguish rising in my throat again, but I can't let it overtake me. I close the distance between Preacher and me. "What are we working on today?"

He turns slowly, and my breath catches.

The massive backpiece dominates his skin from shoulder to shoulder and down to the waistband of his jeans.

A familiar face stares back at me.

Lucifer.

The Dark Angel.

The Devil.

Satan.

Beelzebub.

There are a thousand names for him, but they all share the same face. The one that glowers back at me from between Preacher's massive, muscular shoulder blades.

Preacher arches his back, and the face ripples, sending the sinister grin of the Devil curling, making it come alive in a way that sends shivers through me.

"Wow."

Even partially finished, the piece is…breathtaking.

Jimmy truly was…no *is* an artist, unlike any other. His pieces aren't just art; they live and breathe. And the Devil on Preacher's back is, without a doubt, one of the single best examples I've ever seen.

I reach out and run my fingertips over the image, stopping where the forked tongue twists out from the sneering lips. "Shit, Preacher, I don't know if I'm comfortable working on this. This is…"

He glances over his shoulder. "It's important. To me. I need it finished. You're the one to do it if Jimmy can't."

It feels almost sacrilegious to be throwing ink into this thing when it isn't mine, but Preacher is right about one thing —having anyone else finish this would be an insult to Jimmy. The old man would *want* me to complete it. Something tells me it may be the very reason I got that call two days ago in the first place.

His schedule is almost wide open. He knew he was sick and hasn't been making many appointments on purpose— only a few here and there over the next couple weeks.

But he didn't tell Preacher.

This was a set-up.

I should be mad about it. Angry that he didn't bother to tell me what was going on, but I can't muster it up. The only thing I can manage is awe at the work and the faith both of them have put in me to finish it.

Don't let either of them down.

"Climb up and get comfortable. I need to get my machine and inks set up."

He turns to face me. "Thank you, Everly. You have no idea what you're doing for me."

And he has no idea what he's doing for me.

How badly I *need this, too.*

I grab my machine from the counter and begin pouring the inks necessary for the section of the tattoo we'll be working on today. Preacher's gaze follows my every move until I settle on the stool next to where he lies on his stomach.

"You ready?" I raise an eyebrow at him.

He grins and drops his head down onto his crossed hands beneath his chin. "As ready as I'll ever be."

I dip the needle into the deep burgundy ink and pause over his back. The yellow eye of the Devil glares up at me, and I fight a shudder. There's no room for unease or unsteady hands while doing this.

Preacher peeks up at me from the corner of his eye. "You okay?"

I bite my lip and nod. "Yeah, it's just…"

He pushes up onto his elbows. "Just what?"

"Well, why this tattoo? Why Satan? The rest of your ink and your nickname…"

I don't know how I intended to finish that thought or what my point actually is. It just seems so odd.

"Ever heard of the phrase *The Devil's riding your back*?"

I bob my head. I've heard it, but I can't say I've ever really thought about it.

"Well, it means man is constantly under the influence of a devil or an evil force riding on his back. I was raised to believe that's true, and given some of the things I've seen in my lifetime, I'm confident it is. This," he points to the tattoo, "is my constant reminder to *never* forget that."

Wow.

When I got that call from Jimmy, I thought my world couldn't be any more turned upside down. Between what's happened the last few months and learning of his impending death, everything I've known and come to rely on has been tossed out with the trash. But this man makes one statement, and it's like every single event leading up to today has been to prepare me to hear those words.

Everything makes sense now.

And yet, at the same time, I'm more confused than ever, mostly because of the handsome man with the kind smile, soft eyes, and deep words on my table.

THREE

Preacher

"What's that shit-eating grin for?" Rion's question booms across the warehouse almost the moment I walk in.

Fuck. Was I grinning?

That isn't good. Not good at all.

"Nothing." I steel my expression and beeline toward the kitchen. If I don't eat soon, I may drop. Hopefully, E is cooking up something good tonight.

Rion leans back in his chair at the table and watches me cross the concrete floor. "Doesn't look like nothing. Last time I saw that look on anyone's face…aww shit! Not you, too!"

I stop just outside the kitchen and turn back to him. "Not me too, what?"

Humor twinkles in his dark eyes, and he tips his beer toward me. "A woman. Only a damn woman leaves that look. Who the fuck is she?"

That's a good question.

The four hours I spent lying on that table today should have given me plenty of time to find out more about the stunning, inked woman, but flirting and digging into her past just seemed wrong.

It was clear from the moment she opened that door for me that Everly was emotionally exhausted—perhaps because of what's happening with Jimmy. Or it could be something else altogether. I don't know. And it doesn't matter. Either way, I didn't want to ruin the calm that seemed to settle over her face when she put that needle to my skin, by asking questions.

I was content to relax and watch her while she focused on the piece Jimmy has already spent so many hours on. Her green eyes flicked over to meet mine more times than I could count, and each time our gazes locked, my cock stirred and my heart leaped in a way it hasn't in a long fucking time.

Everly is an amazing artist and a gorgeous woman—all that dark hair flowing around her luminous, pale, inked skin.

So, where the hell did she come from, and who was she to Jimmy that he would trust her with his shop and to finish his work?

He wouldn't have handed off something he worked so hard for to just anyone. But he doesn't have children or any other family he ever spoke about. Which makes Everly an enigma.

It's one mystery I don't have time to solve. Just like I don't have time for a complication like Everly. Especially not when I have one huge unknown knocking at my firewalls, trying to get into my shit.

So even if Rion is right about my reaction to her, it can't happen. Not now. Not ever.

I grip the doorjamb and squeeze it until my knuckles whiten. "She's nobody."

Chair legs scrape against the concrete floor, and I duck into the kitchen before Rion can make his way over to me.

Shit. He's not letting this go.

E glances over his shoulder from his usual spot at the stove. "You're back. Hungry?"

I wander over and peer down into the various pots on the burners. "Depends on what you're making."

He snort-laughs. "Yeah, right. When have you ever *not* liked anything I've made?"

"Good point." I lean against the counter to wait for what is about to storm through that door—or should I say whom. He's like a goddamn pit bull with his prey. When he smells something brewing, he latches on and won't let go until he's annoyed every piece of information out of you.

Rion enters with a smug twist to his lips. "You think you can run away, man? I know where you live."

I roll my eyes and cross my arms over my chest. The motion pulls at the newly inked skin on my back, sending the familiar, pleasant burn through my body. "Ha ha. I'm not running. There's just nothing to tell."

E peeks at Rion while he stirs one of the pots. "What am I missing here?"

Rion being a total prick?

"Absolutely nothing." I shake my head. "Rion's just reading too much into something."

"It didn't look like nothing when you walked in." Rion reaches over, grabs a cookie from the Tupperware on the counter, and shoves it into his mouth.

We stare each other down as he chews. E grabs a bowl and fills it with rice and what smells like some kind of curry and hands it to me with a spoon sticking out.

I grit my teeth. "There's nothing to tell."

Rion finishes chewing and swallows. "Okay, buddy, if you want to play that game. Just don't come to me all torn up about some chick later. We've already had enough of that around here."

"Speaking of which, where is everybody?" I scoop a piping-hot spoonful of my dinner into my mouth.

"Cutter drove Valentina back to Chicago and took Milo. She has meetings the rest of the week, and Warwick took Grace crib shopping."

I snort and practically choke on the curry, sending red-hot spices up my sinuses. My eyes water, and I cough.

E and Rion both laugh, but E takes pity on me and hands me a paper towel.

With my face cleaned and tears wiped, I turn back to Rion. "You're shitting me, right?"

He relaxes his hip against the counter with an amused look. "Nope. Not shitting you."

Who would have thought our illustrious, hard-ass leader would be out shopping for onesies and itsy-bitsy furniture?

Sure as hell not me. I figured we were all bachelors for life. Now, he's going to be in charge of a new, little life. We're going to have a damn *baby* in the warehouse.

And Rion seems to be relishing in it.

I point at him with my spoon. "You shouldn't be grinning like that. You seem to love this baby shit as much as they do."

He shoves away from the counter and shrugs. "What can I say? I love other people's kids, but that baby bullshit isn't for me."

We all know it's true. The big beast of a man who can fly off in a rage with no warning is also the gentlest with the smallest of humans. When we were in Iraq, the way he used to talk to and treat the village children always belied the gruff attitude he sends out into the world.

But having his own kids?

Probably not.

That would require settling down, or at least seeing the same woman more than once. I don't think Rion has had a repeat in the almost decade I've known him. And he doesn't have any plans to change that anytime soon.

I snort, take my bowl, and follow him out of the kitchen. "See ya, E. I got work to do."

Rion turns back to me. "You still tracking the hacker?"

We make our way down the hall toward our respective rooms.

"The guy is good. I gotta give him that. But there are a lot of good hackers in the world, just not a lot of great ones."

"Let me guess. You're one of the greats?"

I grin and shrug even though it will bring that burn of pain. Maybe it's what I want. Self-penance. "I'm better than great."

"Arrogant much?"

"That's funny coming from you, asshole." I open my door, slip inside, and settle into my chair in front of the massive bank of monitors and keyboards occupying one wall.

This is my space. My sanctuary. The place I'm safe and no one and nothing can touch me. Although, having someone touch me today sure felt fucking good.

Her small, warm hands brushing over my skin…

My cock stirs to life, and I glance down at my crotch. "Knock it off. No time or place for her."

I dig into my food and chew as I pull up what I've managed to find on the hacker. This guy—or girl, if I need to appease Valentina—is using some majorly sophisticated shit to cover his tracks.

The first few attempts were nothing but momentary blips on my system's radar. And even though they show up as originating from all over the world, they share the same signature.

That's the nice thing about hackers. They leave a trail, a personal mark. Every single one is unique, just like a fingerprint. It's how people get caught, and one of the reasons I change up what I do every time I hack.

It's the reason I haven't been caught.

Well, since that first time. But that's long in my past. So much has happened since then. To the world. To me.

I'm not about to allow some little shit who thinks he's some sort of computer god ruin it by digging into things that aren't his fucking business—they're *our* fucking business only.

My fingers fly over the keyboard as my hunt continues through the Internet and the Dark Web. The guys get to go out on raids and physically track down and destroy anything and anyone who gets in their way. But I have this. My virtual pursuit.

All I need is one thread to follow.

A screen name.

An IP Address.

Anything to tell me exactly who or where he is.

It's not that I'm worried about him getting in. What I told the guys was true. My system is impenetrable, but know your enemy and all that. There's a lot to be said for it.

But what do I do when the biggest threat has beautiful green eyes, and colorful ink, and a smile that makes my heart race?

I was lying through my damn teeth when I told Rion and E nothing was going on. Between chasing down this hacker and meeting Everly, I've never felt more alive.

That's a very dangerous thing for someone in my profession, as Warwick and Cutter are quickly learning. Grace has never been cut out for this kind of life, but she was sucked in, unwittingly and kicking and screaming. Even when she tried to get away, her feelings for Warwick and the unplanned pregnancy dragged her right back.

And while Valentina chose this life, it doesn't mean Cutter doesn't worry about her constantly. She was also born for it and trained for it, in a way. Her role at the head of the Marconi family may be the polar opposite of her job as a police officer, but both required the same discipline and balls of steel. She was preparing to take over from her father before she even knew who she was.

Dragging Everly into this life wouldn't be fair, and she certainly wasn't born for it. The work covering her body may appear like a hard shield, but that woman feels deeply. It was written all over her soft face when she spoke about Jimmy and while she pressed the needle into my skin. Her art is her release, just like my *art* is mine. We may have different mediums, but we both desperately need our outlets.

And right now, hunting down this asshole has to be my primary focus. Protecting the guys. The girls. Me. It all has to come first, even if my cock wants something else.

Page after page, lines of code scroll past me in the dark. I reach for another bite of my dinner but find the bowl empty.

Shit. How long have I been working?

I peek at my watch.

10:30. I've been holed up in here for almost five hours already.

With nothing to show for it but a bunch of random pings on a map.

I stare at the red dots on the screen. The ones I've scrutinized for days, with the addition of the new one from just a day ago. They blur together, and I close my eyes and dig my palms into them. I reopen them to an unchanged screen.

But is it unchanged?

The dots…

The new one…

It's a pattern.

A subtle one.

One someone else might not see. But it's there…pointing to South America and the Caribbean. The same areas the drugs on the *Neptune's Daughter* and the *Marcella Marie* originated and shipped through.

This is about the shipments. It has to be.

There's no way it's a coincidence.

I grab my phone and call Cutter.

"Yeah, what's up?" His usual angry tone greets me.

"You need to warn Valentina. The hacker…it's all tied to Arturo."

FOUR

Everly

———

The bell on the door jingles, and I withdraw the needle from the skin of the girl in my chair and peek up. Familiar bourbon eyes meet mine, and my heart jumps as a slow grin spreads across his face.

"Preacher? What are you doing here?"

He strolls forward casually, a minor limp in his step, and leans over the counter. Humor dances in his gaze, almost as if he's asking himself the same question. "I made some progress on something I was working on and was in the area. I thought you might have some time for me." One of his dark eyebrows raises in question along with the corners of his mouth.

He's flirting with me. What the hell do I do with that?

A strange mix of excitement and fear tightens my throat. Things didn't end well with the last guy who flirted with me. And now it's been so long since someone has, I'm not even sure how to react.

Should I flirt back?

I duck my head down and pretend to examine my work to avoid having to make eye contact while I make this decision. But I've left him just standing there waiting for some response.

Awkward much?

It's time to make up an excuse. "I can't do any more work on your back. It's only been a week. It hasn't healed yet."

I peek up and see the knowing smirk on his face.

That's totally not true.

There are enough unfinished areas on that massive back piece that I could work on it for months and not go over the same area we worked on last week, but for some reason, the thought of having him shirtless on my table for hours and hours again has goose bumps breaking out across my skin.

"Besides," I point down to the girl on the table, "I have a client right now."

He leans over a little farther to see what I'm working on. A rose with a butterfly on her lower back. I bite my lip to keep from giggling. His judgment is written all over his handsome face.

Tramp stamp.

She literally could *not* have chosen a more cliché image or location. I tried to talk her into something a little more unique, but this is what she wanted. And I need to pay the bills somehow.

Jimmy left me control of all his accounts, and he's certainly not broke, but now paying for hospice, as well as his mortgage, and running the shop are going to put a strain on finances.

Especially considering the clientele, or should I say, lack thereof.

It makes me wish I could've brought my client book with me from Milwaukee. My wait was sometimes six months. Having all those clients here would make keeping this place afloat so much easier.

As it stands now, I have no idea what's going to happen.

Who knows how long Jim is going to hang on?

They told me it could be a day, or it could be months. His nurse, Betty, said the human body does strange things, and sometimes, the people they think will be gone end up holding on longer than anyone ever anticipated. And something tells me Jimmy is waiting for something. Though, I don't have any idea what.

He just can't seem to let go, and watching him suffer is getting harder and harder every day.

Keeping my head down and focusing on my art is the only break I get from the emotional gutting I receive every time I go to see him.

So, flirting with a hot guy who is smart enough to realize what a joke this tattoo is might not be such a bad thing.

Preacher shifts his attention from the tattoo up to me with an amused look. "It looks like you're almost done there."

The girl on the table lifts her head to glance up at him. Her eyes widen, and a strange little gasp slips from her lips. She's definitely checking him out, though why that causes heat to crawl up the back of my neck isn't something I'm ready to examine just yet.

I focus on the tattoo.

He's right.

I don't have more than ten or fifteen more minutes of work left.

Shit.

I had hoped he wouldn't inspect it.

Busted.

Humor dances in his kind eyes, and he wanders over to the leather couch in the corner and lowers himself onto the seat with his long arms spread out across the back. "I'll just wait."

Dammit.

And every second he's here watching me, I'll sense the heat of his gaze lingering on my skin. He might just be checking out my ink, but it seems like so much more. Like he's examining my soul, too.

Stop thinking about it…

I need to remain professional. I shouldn't be turning away any customers right now, even if sending away the tall, strong, handsome, and somewhat enigmatic Preacher would be the best for me personally.

There isn't really a choice. "All right, Preacher. What are you going to have done?"

He winks at me. "We'll figure that out."

I have to suck in a deep breath and steady my shaking hand before I return the needle to this girl's skin.

What was her name? Nicki?

Preacher unnerves me in a way no man ever has before. The fear flooding my system is so unlike anything I've ever experienced. Something tells me this man has the ability to hurt me worse than any fists ever could. And if I don't calm myself down, he's going to see what a mess I am.

That can't happen.

Two things matter right now: remaining professional and keeping my heart closed to Preacher.

I finish the last small portion of the girl's tat and wipe it down. "You're all done, sweetheart."

She smiles, bobs her white-blond head, and claps. "Yay! I'm so excited I finally got this done. I've wanted to do it for years, but you know…" Her eyes roam across my face, over the tattoo at my right temple and down over my exposed tattooed sternum and arms, "or maybe you don't."

"Nope." I yank off the plastic gloves and toss them into the trash. "Honey, I gave up caring about what anyone else thinks about me such a long time ago, I can't even remember a time when I did." Except for Preacher. For some reason, what *he* thinks seems to bother me. "You're still young. You should do the same. You have a chance to make your life a lot easier."

Preacher's chuckle floats across the room. "She's right."

The girl tosses a dark look over her shoulder at him.

Do they know each other?

She seems to have an issue with him, though I can't imagine what it would be. She rises to her feet and grabs her Coach purse off the table behind her. "What do I owe you?"

"One fifty."

She pulls out a wad of cash, breaks off a few bills, and hands them to me. "Thank you, Everly."

"You're very welcome. Just remember what I told you—wash it with antibacterial soap and use unscented lotion only on it. Don't scratch or pick when it starts to peel. If it itches, smack it."

She recoils slightly. "Excuse me?"

"Smack it." Preacher fights a laugh. "It works to help stop the itching."

The girl gives him an annoyed look. "I got it." She sashays toward the door, her tiny hips swinging back and forth in a pronounced fashion, though who she's doing it for, I'm not sure given the dirty look she tossed Preacher.

Quite an attitude on that one.

She jerks open the door and pauses to give Preacher another once-over. Her spine stiffens the longer she stares at him.

His eyes narrow. "Do I know you?"

The girl considers him for a moment, her plump, red lips pressed together in a hard line. "No. But I know you."

The door closes behind her, leaving both of us gawking at each other with bewilderment.

I cram the cash into the back pocket of my jeans. "Who was that girl? Do you know her?"

He pushes to his feet and makes his way to the counter. One of his shoulders rises and falls. "I don't recognize her, and to be honest, I don't get out a lot, so I doubt very much that we met before. Maybe she just doesn't like guys with tattoos."

Impossible.

Guys with ink—especially tall, hard, lean ones with gorgeous eyes and a bright smile—are simply irresistible.

I giggle and start cleaning up my station to reset everything for him. His gaze follows every movement I make—assessing me, unraveling me, stripping me bare of my defenses.

He raps his knuckles—the ones on his right hand that say HAIL—against the counter. "Is it all right if I come around?"

All right? What does that even mean?

I've never considered it before, not until this man somehow ended up in my life at the most inopportune time. But it's as "all right" as it will ever be. As *I* will ever be, considering everything that's happened.

No amount of time will pass that can ever erase what happened or the scars it left, but at some point, I need to pick myself up and live again. Preacher could be that opportunity, even though having him close feels very risky.

I nod, and he makes his way over to me slowly. His size and all that ink might be intimidating to another woman—hell, to a lot of men—but not me. Not with what I've seen. The ones you have to worry about don't have this kindness in their eyes. It's usually a darkness, one that draws you in and makes you want to heal them, save them, make them whole again.

Preacher has his secrets—we all do—but he doesn't bury them under anger the way so many men in my life have. He lays it all out there for the whole world to see—in his eyes. In the art on his skin.

My throat suddenly dries up like the Vegas desert, and it only gets worse the closer he comes. I swallow thickly. "So, Preacher…"

He sits on my table and grins. "So, Everly…"

Smartass.

A smile tugs at my lips. "What are we gonna do today?"

"Well," he runs a hand over his bearded jaw, "I've been

feeling adventurous. Your choice. Anywhere on my body that is open skin."

"You're fucking kidding me." I slap my hand over my mouth.

Did I just say that? So much for staying professional.

He shakes his head. "Nope. I trust you completely."

"How can you trust me? You barely know me."

Putting faith and trust into someone without truly knowing who they are at their core is what got me into the biggest trouble of my life. It's not something to throw around.

How can a man like Preacher be so willing to turn over complete control?

One of his wide shoulders rises and falls. "I've always been a very good judge of character."

I truly wish I could say the same, but my track record, especially as of late, has proven that not to be the case. Which is one of the reasons it's imperative that I keep Preacher at arm's length. A man like him could lead to devastating consequences.

"So, you're really gonna let me choose whatever I want, wherever I want?"

He loses the battle with the amusement pulling at his mouth. "I don't like the look in your eye. You're starting to make me think maybe I made a mistake in letting you do this."

I offer him a sweet smile. "Thought you said you trusted me."

"I did…until I saw the flash in your eyes and that devious smile."

"Nothing devious about it, just happy to have an open canvas. Don't worry, I'll give you something that's absolutely perfect for you."

The few hours we've spent together haven't given me long to get to unravel Preacher, but the ink on his body tells me all I need to make this choice. I know what he's getting and where it's going.

"Take off your shirt. Lie on your stomach on the table."

He drags his shirt up and over his head. "Promise not to hurt me too much, sweetheart."

I wink at him. "That's what they all say."

FIVE

Preacher

T he familiar smells of antiseptic and death fill my nostrils, and the constant beeping of machines follow me, the deeper I walk into the hospital.

I shake my head to try to rid myself of the inclination to run the opposite direction. With the amount of time I've spent in hospitals, just being here evokes the response almost immediately.

My chest tightens, and pain tears through parts of my body that it shouldn't. I've avoided places like this as much as possible since I was discharged. Which is strange because I always rather enjoyed going with Dad to visit parishioners. Giving comfort to people who are sick and dying always felt like doing God's work, but being here now is harder than I ever imagined it would be.

God, give me strength…

Going to see Jimmy's the right thing to do. It's not just some random stranger, some member of the church who needs comfort. Jimmy is the closest thing I have to a friend besides the guys, and he's also one of the only people on the planet who understands even half of what I've been through.

So, I need to see him so he knows I'm thinking about him

and praying for him. But I'm also here for selfish reasons. After another few hours on Everly's table, I'm more determined than ever to stay clear of her. I only returned in an attempt to relieve the desire drawing me back there. I thought I could get her out of my system. It didn't work, but maybe Jimmy can tell me something to seal the deal, to convince me I'm doing the right thing by keeping her away from this life I lead.

A middle-aged brunette watches me from behind the reception desk. Her eyes focus on the tattoos on my neck and hands.

I plaster on my best *I'm not a criminal* smile. "Hi. I'm here to see Jimmy McAllister in room 213."

It wasn't hard to track him down. There's only one major hospital within an hour of his shop, and it's the only place with a hospice wing. I also knew he would never want to go too far. Two minutes was all I needed to locate him.

The woman focuses on my knuckles, where HAIL and MARY are inked across the skin. "Are you family?"

"As close to it as he has."

Her mouth twists as she considers me. "Well, visiting hours are almost over. If you want to see Mr. McAllister tonight, you better hurry."

"Thank you." I rap my knuckles on the counter before turning to make my way down the hall.

There's a good chance he won't let me in. He's a prideful old man, and if he's anything like me, he doesn't want anyone seeing him like this. Having people visit me in the hospital and witness me at my worst and weakest was one of the hardest times of my life. I would understand if he acted the same way.

God, just let him be man enough to admit he needs a friend.

The door to his room stands ajar. I push it open slowly and brace myself for what I'm about to see. Everly didn't talk much about his illness or what shape he's in, but if they've moved him into the hospice wing, it isn't good.

A young blonde stands at his side, messing with something on his IV. She glances over her shoulder, smiles, and waves me in. I approach cautiously and focus on the man who's been my confidant for the last half a decade.

"Hey, old-timer."

His lids flutter open and tired blue eyes meet mine. "Preacher? What are you doing here?" His voice is low, soft, and raspy, not at all the strong, booming thing it used to be.

He's lost so much weight I might not have even recognized him if I'd seen him on the street.

How could he have gone downhill so fast?

I only saw him five weeks ago…

"You look like shit, old man."

He lets out a rattling chuckle that quickly devolves into a coughing fit. "Don't I know it."

I drag a chair over to the side of the bed, and the nurse helps him take a sip of water before retreating from the room. His wrinkled hand, one that was so strong only weeks ago, lies on the mattress in front of me. I reach out and clasp it, and he drops his head to the side toward me.

"What are you doing here, Preacher?"

The altruistic reason or the selfish one?

I sigh and run my free hand over my jaw. "I couldn't let you go without saying goodbye."

Humor glints in his tired gaze. "You met her."

Awww. Hell.

Everly showing up wasn't by accident. If it were, she wouldn't be the thing he mentioned. "This is feeling an awful lot like a set-up, Jimmy."

He shrugs, a feeble movement that seems to cost him more energy than he has left. "No set-up. Just a hope that the two people closest to me in my life might hit it off."

"Who is she, Jimmy? Your daughter?"

It's the only connection that explains why he trusts her so much. But it doesn't jibe with what I know about him. We didn't share our whole lives, but we talked about a lot of important stuff during our sessions—our service overseas and what happened there. It's strange that he wouldn't have brought her up if he had a daughter.

Jimmy clutches my hand. "As close to one as I ever had." He lets out another wheezy cough and sags back onto the mattress.

Even the little bit of talking we've done has wiped him out.

His lips part slowly, and he sucks in a shaky breath. "We didn't talk much for a long time. Then…" his head shakes back and forth slightly, "she needs someone like you, Preacher."

Just the fucking words I didn't want to hear.

I squeeze his hand again and lean closer. "Jimmy. What's going on with her? Why does she need me?"

A light snore is the only response Jimmy offers. Soft breaths puff from his lips, and his hand goes limp in mine.

Shit.

Tears burn my eyes, and I use my free hand to wipe them away. I never thought I'd be back in this position again, at least, not anytime so soon. Losing another friend. Having to say goodbye. I've done enough of that already.

I wrap his hand in mine, close my eyes, and drop my head. "God, thank you for being with us right now. We confess that we don't understand why things happen the way they do. We don't understand why illness comes into our lives, but we do know that you walk every path of life with us. Remind Jimmy that you are walking with him right now. Remind him that you love him, no matter what he is going through. God, we thank you that you never leave us, that you never forsake us, but you love us. Amen."

There are times when faith is tested. Far too many times in most people's lives, including my own. This is just one in a long line.

Everly is a mystery I don't need to solve. Yet, Jimmy's words won't leave my head. *She needs someone like you.*

Jimmy has no idea what kind of man I am, what I'm involved in. I'm the last person he should want anywhere near that girl if he really cares about her, which he obviously does.

If he only knew…he'd want me far away from that inked beauty.

———

The door to my room flies open, and Rion strolls in with a beer in hand. "What are you doing?"

"I'm doing what I always do. I'm covering everyone's asses and making sure we don't get caught and thrown in prison… or worse."

"You figure anything else out?"

No. And it's driving me fucking mad.

I stare at the map I've left up on the monitor to our left. "Just the Caribbean and South American connection. I'm positive that's where the source is despite his best efforts to throw me off track by routing through servers all over the world. I've got some feelers out, and I've left some bread-crumbs in a few places to see if he's gonna bite."

If I'm lucky, he's not going to be able to resist what I've dropped, and the more times he tries to get in, the more infor-mation I'll gather. It will eventually lead me right to the bastard.

Rion grunts. "Is that a good idea? Baiting him?"

I run a hand back through my hair as I consider the options. "I need to do something, or we're never going to know who this is."

"Do we need to?" He takes a drink from his beer. "You said he can never get in, right? So, if he can never get in, he'll never be a threat, right?"

"Until he is. Even if he can't get into our system, that

doesn't mean whoever this is can't track us down some other way. With what we do, it could be any number of enemies we've made over the years. You know we'll never be safe. The most important thing we can do is be vigilant."

He tips his bottle toward me. "You're right." His hand tightens around the brown glass, and he sits on the edge of the desk and takes a swig. "Where the fuck have you been all day, anyway? Protecting our asses?"

I glare at him. Rion runs so hot and cold that I can truly see why Grace calls him The Hulk. One minute, he's grinning and joking, and the next, he's an angry, green, raging monster. Right now, he's somewhere in between, probably inching toward the one we want to avoid, likely because we've spent far more time cooped up in here worrying about our fucking lives during the last six months than we did in the last five years. He's the one who needs to get out, to get laid, to have a taste of what they call the nightlife around here, though it does nothing for me. I still tag along occasionally, mostly to make sure he doesn't do something stupid…again.

My computer pings, and I turn back and check the notice. Nothing important, but he doesn't need to know that. "I was out doing something for myself so I could focus better when I'm here. And I have work to do."

"Something for yourself?" A slow grin spreads across his face. "You saw her again, didn't you?"

"None of your fucking business."

He points the bottle at me again. "That's a yes."

"Let it go."

A slow smirk slants his lips. "Not gonna happen, buddy. No way I'm dropping it."

And he won't.

He'll probe and poke at me until I eventually come clean. It's one of his many talents.

I sigh and lean back in my chair. "She's pretty incredible, Rion."

He crosses his arms and dangles the bottle from his fingers. "I don't doubt it. I've never seen you like this. But to be fair, you really haven't given yourself much of an opportunity to meet anybody since we moved here, have you?"

I haven't. Other than going to see Jimmy and going for an occasional drink at one of the townie bars with Rion, I spend all my time in here holed up, hacking to find information we need to plan our jobs. Women were the last thing on my list. "Nope. I haven't."

"She's working for Jimmy?"

"Kind of." My throat tightens, and I swallow through the rock lodged there. "Jimmy has terminal cancer."

Rion's eyes soften. "Aww, shit, man. I'm sorry. I know how much you like the dude."

"Yeah. Well, he apparently left the business in her hands."

His brows rise. "She's an artist, too?"

I lean forward to drop my elbows onto my desk. "A really damn good one."

Beyond good, actually. She could set up shop in any major city and make bank. So, the fact that she's slumming it in this tiny shithole of a town in the middle of nowhere says a lot. She's running from something. I didn't see it before, but especially after what Jimmy said to me, it's become clear. She may be here to deal with Jimmy and his business during his illness, but there's more going on there.

Why wouldn't they have spoken for a while? What the hell happened to that girl?

Rion sips at his beer and watches me intently like he's expecting me to continue. He circles his free hand in front of him. "So…did she work on your back?"

I shake my head. "No. She did last week. Today was something new."

"I want to see."

No doubt, he does.

I hesitate for a moment. I don't want to deal with Rion's

43

inevitable reaction when he sees it. But he'll harp until I give in. I push to my feet and lower my pants, exposing the top of my left ass cheek and the fresh ink Everly just put there.

He barks out a laugh and almost spills his beer. "Holy shit. You chose that?"

Hell no.

It was all in good fun, letting her make the choice of tat and placement, but not knowing what she was permanently etching onto my skin was a bit unnerving.

Now that I've seen it, it's hard to decide if I totally hate it or just hate how easily she picked something so perfect for me.

I chuckle. "No, I told her she could do whatever she wanted, wherever she wanted."

Rion's eyes widen. "Dude. That was pretty fucking stupid."

No shit.

"Nah." I drag my pants back into place and sit. "I like it."

"You would." He snorts and drains his beer. "You really like this girl, huh?"

Yes.

The answer in my head comes far too quickly for comfort. There's no room for *liking* someone in my life. Not now. Maybe not ever.

"I don't know."

"Yeah, you do. You just don't want to admit it." He shoves off the desk and wanders toward the door. "I'm gonna head over to Murphy's in a few. Why don't you come with me and invite her?"

Because the more time I spend with that woman, the more time I'll *want* to spend with her. Time I don't have. Not if I'm going to continue to keep these fuckers safe. Cutter may be the deadly one with firearms, but I'm just as deadly, if not more so, with my keyboards.

Any distractions could be disastrous for all of us.

I wave absently at my computers. "I really should work on this."

He claps me on the shoulder. "Preacher, you need to get your dick wet, and it sounds like this girl is just the one who can do it for you. You deserve to have a life outside these four walls, outside the warehouse. I may not be happy about all the estrogen ending up in this place, but just because you fuck her doesn't mean she has to become more than that."

That's easy for him to say. He wasn't raised the same way I was. He doesn't have the same ethics and morals. The same Catholic guilt that eats away at him. The same compass directing him which way to follow.

Flee from sexual immorality. All other sins a person commits are outside the body, but whoever sins sexually, sins against their own body.

He'll fuck anything that moves. Me...I can count the number of women I've been with on one hand—hell, with half of one hand. For me, sex has always been sacred, something meant for someone I love. Not just somebody I want to get balls deep in.

But Rion could be right. Maybe I need to reassess the situation with Everly and try to brush off that layer of lingering guilt.

Just because I want to fuck her doesn't mean it has to be anything more than that. I'm a grown-ass man who has seen and done things most people can't even imagine. I can be with a girl and not have it mean more...

Can't I?

Rion pauses at the door and turns back. "Seriously, man. Come with me. Call her. Have her join us."

"I'll think about it."

He chuckles and waves me off. "Don't pretend you haven't already made the decision. We leave in half an hour."

SIX

Everly

T*hey call this a bar?*
 The small, one-story building looks more like a hunting lodge than a place to hang out and drink. Though, I guess that's what happens at hunting lodges, anyway, or so I've been told. I can't say I've ever hunted or really known anyone who did, so whether it's just abandoned wives making the claim or an actual fact is beyond me.

I glance down at my phone, to the message Preacher sent me containing the name and address of where to meet him.

Yep. This is the place.

That tall, tattooed man is waiting inside for me. Meanwhile, I'm standing out here, trying not to throw up.

I almost said no. In fact, I almost texted to say I couldn't make it three times after my initial yes. But...I chickened out on chickening out.

He said to meet him and a friend.

This isn't a date. It's just a drink.

Dating a client isn't okay; having a drink with him...that's client development. It's just good business.

I think...

I will need to learn how to manage a business if I am

going to stay here and run Jimmy's place. But that's so far from being decided that I don't even want to think about it. Going back to Milwaukee isn't an option, but I can always return to Minneapolis, or go somewhere completely new where he can't find me. Somewhere safe. That's all I need. And I don't know if this is that place yet, if it ever can be.

Right now, my focus is spending time with Jimmy during his final days and getting his affairs in order. I can't get ahead of myself. Jimmy is still here, so I'm still here.

Doing some client development.

I pull open the door and step into the dim townie bar. It's exactly how I imagined it would look inside when I saw the outside. Barely there lighting, dark wood walls, dartboards and a pool table in one corner, and an old jukebox in the other. It's like stepping back in time to the 70s.

Things change slowly around here. And that's not necessarily a bad thing.

I find a familiar set of broad shoulders at the long bar. I draw in a breath. "Here we go."

Because talking to yourself is a sure sign of mental stability.

The guy sitting next to Preacher is the kind of big I don't think I've ever witnessed in real life. He should play one of those big guys in a superhero movie. Because he could definitely snap a human in half without even trying.

I approach slowly, taking the time to appreciate Preacher's strong profile and all that beautiful ink on display on his arms and neck. The man is hot. There's absolutely *no* denying it— no matter how hard I might want to fight my attraction to him.

The closer I get, the more uncertainty eats away at my decision to come tonight.

Don't do that, Everly.

They both turn toward me like they sense me getting near. Preacher grins, and his friend's dark eyes widen slightly as they scan me from head to toe.

I had no idea what to wear to a place like this out here. Most of the outfits I would've worn going out in Milwaukee just seems completely inappropriate, so I toned it way down. I would've looked like an idiot or, at the very least, a prostitute if I had worn one of those. Yet, even in my more conservative choice of a black miniskirt and loose-fitting tank top, all eyes are still on the tattooed girl making her way across the floor to the bar.

My appearance has always drawn attention, but once I added this much ink to my body and face, it brings a whole other level of scrutiny. One I have never minded before, but after what happened, being assessed so closely leaves a lingering little chill in my spine.

Shake it off, Everly. No one knows you here. No one knows him *here.*

I give Preacher and his friend a return smile, and Preacher slides off the high bar stool and waves for me to take the seat he just vacated. He stands against the bar to my left, so I'm between his friend and him.

Preacher's arm brushes mine as he leans toward me, and a smirk sexy enough to melt off a woman's panties tilts his lips. "I am so glad you could make it." He points to the big guy. "This is my friend Rion."

The big guy holds out a large hand, and I place my tiny one inside it.

He squeezes firmly. "Now, I can see why Preacher has gotten so much new ink recently."

Wow.

I can't fight the smile that statement brings, and Preacher slaps the back of Rion's head before he takes the seat next to me.

"So," I take in the bar, "you guys come here often?"

Don't know why anyone would unless they enjoy hanging out at total dives.

Preacher chuckles and shakes his head. "Not if I can help it. This one," he motions toward Rion, "is the guy who enjoys the nightlife and gets out whenever he can, but he's got a couple places he likes to frequent."

I scan the rest of the place. "It's definitely got a vibe, doesn't it?"

Rion's boom of a laugh resonates from somewhere deep inside his massive chest. I wouldn't have expected a sound like that to come from a guy as huge as him. I wouldn't have expected him to laugh…period. But the sound is genuine, as is his accompanying smile.

Don't judge a book by its cover, Everly. You, of all people, should know that.

I scan the ink on his arms and hands. "You have some nice work."

He glances down at it. "Thanks."

"Where do you have it done?" If it's around here, then I have more competition than I thought. It would be the final nail on the coffin of whether to stay or not.

A look gets exchanged between Rion and Preacher over my shoulder.

What's that about?

Rion stares at the ink on his hand around his beer. "Here and there. I was in the military for a while, so I moved around a bit."

The military?

None of Preacher's tattoos suggested any sort of military connection that I saw, but it would certainly explain the way he carries himself and why Jimmy took such a liking to him. After his service in Nam, Jimmy developed unbending respect for anyone who ever served any time.

I turn to Preacher. "Were you in the military, too?"

He shrugs—very non-committal. "Something like that. What can I get you to drink?"

Well, that's vague. Why won't he just answer my question?

Just another thing I'll have to wonder about with Preacher. He hasn't volunteered much information during our sessions.

Usually, that would have me keeping him at arm's length. Mysterious isn't always good. Sometimes, it's just a precursor for the dark shit that's about to come.

But I've never felt anything but safe with Preacher around—even in an unfamiliar town and about to lose the most important person in my life. I should feel adrift, but when I'm around him, it's the opposite. Almost like I'm being anchored in place with his quick smile. Even the unease I had early has evaporated, despite Preacher's cagey answer to my question.

He waits patiently for my response, the corners of his lips twitching.

I peek down at the pint glass in front of him. "I'll have whatever you're having."

Rion smacks the top of the bar. "A girl who likes beer? Well, A-fucking-men."

I gawk at him. "What, women don't drink beer?"

"Most I know don't. They drink gin and tonics and rum and Coke when they're trying to look cool and fruity, girly drinks otherwise." He winks. "I like a woman who can drink like a man."

I hold up a hand. "I wouldn't say I can drink like a man. My tolerance is pretty shitty, actually. I just enjoy a nice beer."

Preacher snorts as he waves over the bartender. "So does Rion.'"

Rion grunts at him and gives him a sneer.

These two certainly seem to know each other well and clearly enjoy ribbing each other.

"How do you two know each other?"

They exchange another look.

Preacher takes a drink of his beer and licks his lips. "We worked together years ago. And now, I do security for the company Rion works for."

"Security?" Not really what I was picturing. "What kind of security?"

He points to his beer and holds up two fingers to the bartender. "Cybersecurity."

"You're a computer nerd?"

It's the last thing I would've expected. Given his muscles and tattoos and arrogant swagger, I can't imagine him behind a desk all day. Most of my clients who work on computers are shy or awkward. The complete opposite of what I'm finding with Preacher.

He laughs and wiggles his tattooed fingers. "Yep, total nerd. I spend most of my time in front of the wall of computer screens."

"Wow."

One of his dark eyebrows rises. "Wow, what?"

"Just not how I pictured you spending your time."

He tosses me that smirk that starts a low burn in my belly. "So, you've been picturing how I spend my time?"

The heat of blush creeps across my cheeks.

Shit.

I shouldn't have admitted that. So much for staying cool and keeping things friendly. But I can't deny to myself—or apparently to Preacher—that I've thought about him. A lot. Ever since he first stepped foot into the shop, I've wondered what other ink he might have hidden below the belt, and I've imagined *other things* down that way, too.

Definitely not the appropriate way to think about your client. Stay cool. Nonchalant.

I clear my throat and try to sound non-committal and smooth. "Maybe."

Preacher's eyes dance with amusement. He didn't buy my attempt to brush it off.

The bartender sets a beer on the bar top, and I take three long gulps of the cool ale to keep myself from saying something else stupid. It's *too* late to save myself from my prior word vomit incident, but I can at least *try* to prevent another one.

Rion glances down to the end of the bar where two blondes sit, whispering to each other and inspecting us. He raps his knuckles against his beer glass. "I'm gonna go make some new friends."

He swaggers over to the girls and leans against the bar next to them. Both of them swoon and flip their hair back. Girlish giggles float across the space from the MENSA candidates.

I snort before I take a sip of my beer.

"What's so funny?"

I refocus on Preacher, who wears an amused grin. "Your friend. Can he always just walk up to any girl and get her?"

Preacher's shoulders rise and fall nonchalantly. "Pretty much." He takes a swig of his beer and rolls the bottle between his fingers.

The idea that Preacher might be able to do the same thing just as easily hits me, and a strange tingle of jealousy spreads throughout my body. I swallow more of the cold beer and watch him watch me. "What about you?"

The corners of his lips curve up. "What about me, what?"

"Can you just walk up to any girl like that and get her?"

He roars with laughter, drawing the attention of half the bar, and the vibration of it rolls through his arm where it brushes against mine. "I wouldn't know. I've never tried."

Never tried? Yeah. Right.

"You never tried to pick up a girl in a bar before?"

He shakes his head with the most serious darkening of his bourbon eyes.

"How the hell is that even possible?"

It's like…the most basic guy move of all time.

How would you even meet someone otherwise?

Unless he uses one of those hook-up apps, but something tells me that isn't Preacher's style, either.

He shrugs. "It just wasn't ever on my radar. I was in

school, and I stayed super focused on my studies and…other activities. Then, I worked a lot, and then I came here."

There's more to it than that. Nobody has that boring a life. But whatever Preacher's hiding, I don't think it's that he's a player. He seems genuine—something that's very rare in this world, something I thought I had once but was sorely mistaken about.

I sip my beer and finally take a second to savor it instead of just using it as an excuse to cover for something. The familiar hoppy flavor reminds me so much of Jimmy, I almost can't swallow it. I force it down and play with the condensation on the outside of the pint glass.

For some reason that hasn't become apparent to me yet, Preacher makes me say and do things I wouldn't have ever thought possible. Like right now, the truth of my struggle over coming tonight sits heavy at the tip of my tongue. "You know, I wasn't going to come tonight. I almost talked myself out of it several times."

He leans in until his lips brush against my ear. "I almost didn't invite you. I almost texted you to cancel several times."

The flutter of his hot breath and the low timbre of his voice vibrating against my sensitive skin send a shudder rolling through me—a very good one, one that awakens something deep in my core I thought long dead.

I turn my head to the side until our lips are mere centimeters away from each other. His dark eyes dart down to my mouth, and mine do the same to his before our gazes meet again.

My tongue slips out across my bottom lip. "So, why didn't you cancel?"

"Why didn't you?"

"Touché."

The sexual tension building between us is the kind that leads to ripped clothing and that heavy, post-orgasmic haze that wraps around you for days.

It's exhilarating and terrifying at the same time. The feeling of truly being *alive* again fills my veins.

God, does it feel good.

He leans in and presses his lips to mine. It's slow and gentle yet filled with a kind of passion I haven't experienced before. One that says he really, truly wants this. That here is where he wants to be, for no other reason than me.

No one's ever wanted me without having ulterior motives or holding back something that would have changed how I felt about them or the situation. No one's ever just *wanted* me before. And knowing Preacher does sends a rush of joy and lust through me.

My head swims in the feel of his lips brushing over mine, in the flick of his tongue, the tightening of his hand on my upper arm.

But he backs away just when I almost forget where we are. I groan in frustration and open my eyes.

A smug grin now occupies the lips that were just on mine. "You can always go home if you don't want to be here."

Arrogant.

It should be a massive turn off, but the playful way he says the words have my body yearning for him to kiss me again. And so much more. "Oh, I want to be here."

His dark eyebrows rise. "Are you sure?"

"Uh-huh."

Totally sure.

And his mischievous tone invites me to shift forward and kiss him. The same slow, lingering kiss he just gave me.

His large, strong hands wrap around my back, and he drags me off my stool to stand between his spread legs so he can deepen our kiss. That same hazy cloud surrounds us, blocking out the 80s hair band music playing from the juke-box, the stale beer smell, and the low rumble of voices from the other patrons.

We're in our own world. I'm losing myself in something other than despair for the first time in a long fucking time.

Someone clearing their throat drags us away from each other. We both glance toward the other side of the bar.

The bartender eyes us with a hint of annoyance mixed with amusement. "If you two are gonna do that, you need to take it somewhere else. This isn't a brothel."

My jaw drops. "And I'm not a hooker."

The bartender chuckles and taps the bar with his fist. "Good to know."

Preacher's hand slides down and squeezes my ass, and his lips find my ear again. "That is very important information to know."

I swipe playfully at his hand and grab my beer to finish it off. The two blondes still occupy Rion on the other side of the room. He's totally oblivious to what's happening over here.

The cool drink doesn't do anything to quell the inferno raging through me from Preacher's touch and kiss.

He angles his head toward the door. "You want to head outside?"

The question and promise in his eyes have butterflies rising in my stomach. They're not the usual ones of fear, though; they're of anticipation of what's to come.

"God, yes."

SEVEN

Preacher

The longer I sit next to Everly at the bar, the more I think about what Rion said about being able to keep things casual. I really like this girl, but maybe sex can just be sex. Despite everything I was raised to believe…

Better to ask forgiveness than permission, right?

It's been years since I went to confession, but if God can forgive all sins, He can certainly forgive my giving in to my desire for Everly. In the grand scale of sins, it's pretty low on the rankings. And who could blame me while looking at her?

She's gorgeous, funny, smart, and I respond to her in a way I haven't to a woman in a very long time. Despite all the stress weighing down on my shoulders because of everything going on with the crew, when I'm with her, it seems to disappear into the ether of my brain. It doesn't exist when she's smiling at me and flashing those big, green eyes.

It's like she's a respite. An escape. A place to hide away, even if only briefly, from all the turmoil in my life, from all the threats and responsibility.

This doesn't have to be anything serious. I can do casual.

At least, that's what I try to convince myself as I hold the door open for her and follow her out into the crisp fall

Wisconsin night air. The warmer weather of the Indian Summer we've been having has finally passed. The colors of the leaves will be changing soon—one of my favorite times of the year. It's when I can really see and appreciate the beauty of God's touch in the world.

Even though the big man upstairs and I have had our differences, there's no denying His hand's role when you see the first rays of a sunrise strike the oranges and reds of the forest along the lakeshore. And I get to see it every day. One of the perks of the warehouse location.

We may be remote and lack some amenities, but you can't beat the fucking views. Even the dead of winter is beautiful here. The crystal-clear ice along the shore, the sunlight reflecting off it, and the snow covering the beach and trees…it takes your breath away.

And while the real cold hasn't descended yet, it's coming soon. Until then, we'll enjoy *this*. The perfect night to sit outside with a stunning woman like Everly.

Her strange mix of shyness and spunk has me twisted up in knots. It keeps me moving toward her when, in all reality, I should be backing away to protect Everly and me. But if what Rion said is true, and we can keep this casual, it will be good for both of us.

A release. A connection. A coming together of two people who share an undeniable attraction.

There isn't anything wrong with that.

I just need to convince my Catholic guilt to agree with me.

In the past, I've managed to justify my actions with the fact that I loved the women I was with. I was dedicated to them. Committed. We may not have been married, but it wasn't a fling. It wasn't meaningless, animal sex. But this, with Everly, will be something different. I can't let it become more. It can *never* become *that*.

I motion for her to head toward the back of the building and place my hand on her lower back. She shudders beneath my palm. My cock twitches and comes to attention. It's been a long fucking time since it has stirred to life from something so simple as a beautiful woman's ass swaying in front of me and her reacting to my touch.

Down boy.

Rushing things is completely unnecessary. I don't want to scare her off. But there's no denying the vibe between us in there. The heat that radiated and built when we kissed. The desire for each other lingered in the air so thickly, the damn bartender noticed it.

So, I don't think I misread her. And I know what I *want.*

HER.

She peeks at me over her shoulder and smiles. It's so warm and genuine, flames lick across my skin despite the cool air. We turn the corner around the back of the building to where a few benches and chairs sit around small tables on a cement slab with a fire pit.

Rion has dragged me back here a handful of times over the years. And despite it not really being my scene, I have to admit, I enjoyed it. "It's great to relax out back here in the summer. Have some beers. A nice fire."

She bobs her head as she sets her purse onto one of the small tables. "I bet. It's a nice night, though." Her hand waves through the air. "Not cold at all."

I grab her wrist to stop her forward momentum and turn her to face me. "If you're not cold," I run my hands up and down her bare, tattooed arms, "then why did you shudder before and why do you have goose bumps now?"

A tiny grin plays on her perfect bow lips. "The honest answer?"

I nod. I always prefer honesty to any other option. Though, in my profession, honesty isn't always possible. I lied a lot for many years in order to do my job. And now, what I'm doing with the guys, well…it's all lies, all the time.

At least before, my actions were sanctioned by the U.S.

Government. What the crew does could land us on death row if Wisconsin had one. As it stands, we're facing federal piracy charges. If we were convicted there, we would never see the light of day again, especially after what happened on the *Marcella Marie.* It won't matter that I wasn't there and didn't pull any of the triggers. I'm just as guilty as the rest of the guys in the conspiracy.

I may have survived Iraq, but I don't think I'd make it in prison. I'm too soft. Too ethical. Too much of a good guy to do the things needed to make it there. Things I'm sure E had to endure during his stint. Plus, I'm too pretty. I chuckle to myself.

But not as pretty as this woman.

Everly stares up at me in the moonlight, her green eyes twinkling with amusement. "Your touch, just being close to you, it…makes me want things I wasn't sure I ever would again."

Christ.

The absolute sincerity of her words unravels me. Something happened to this girl. No one makes a statement like that unless they've been hurt in the past. But instead of turning me away, her confession removes any reservations about pursuing her. It means she feels the same attraction I do. One we can't deny for another minute.

I drop my head and press my lips to hers softly. A tiny little gasp slips from her mouth into mine, and her hands clutch at my T-shirt. I growl and drag her fully against me. My cock presses into her belly. One of her small hands slides down across my abs and grabs me through my pants.

"Fuck." The mumbled word against her lips seems to fill the silent night air around us. But it doesn't matter. We're alone out here. No one to hear us. No one to witness the scalding desire ignite between us.

Her hand tightens on my cock. "I'm glad I came tonight, Preacher Davis."

I grin and kiss her again. "Me too, Everly…"

Christ, I don't even know her last name.

"Webster."

"Everly Webster." I crash my lips to hers, this time, harder, more demanding. There's no question here, just a statement about what I want from her.

She has every right to stop. To say, "no, I barely know you, and I'm not that kind of girl," but instead, she whimpers and runs her small hand up and down my jean-clad length.

If she keeps that up, this is going to end before it even gets interesting. It's been so long since I've experienced a woman's touch, I almost forgot how incredible it is.

Her small, tight, willing body in my arms. Her eager mouth pressed against mine. Her hand gently massaging my cock.

I lower one of my hands down and under her skirt to clutch her ass. She groans and shifts to give me better access. The warm globe fits perfectly in my palm, and I clasp it hard. My fingers brush against silky panties—ones that are very wet already.

Christ, she's ready for me.

But we can't do this here. I may be willing to bend my morals to be with Everly tonight, but I'm not going to do it at the back of a dive bar. That would be too crass. Too dirty. Too…everything I've always tried to avoid.

"Let's go back to your place." My words are harsh, low, and a lot harsher than I intended them. More of a demand than a question. Not at all how I would normally act with a woman, but Everly Webster has already proven she can throw my world into a complete tailspin with a single look.

She shakes her head and clutches my cock harder. "No. We can't. Here."

I tear my head back from hers and search her face for the truth of what she wants. "You don't mean that."

Determination settles in her eyes, and she nods. "I do. I *do* mean that."

She can't be serious.

But when I peer down into her glittering eyes and her soft face in the moonlight, I find she is very serious.

The lust soaking her gaze and the heat of her body and her hands all over me only emphasize her desire. She wants this just as badly as I do. Enough to do something stupid and reckless.

I grab her hips and lift her easily from the ground. She wraps her legs around my waist and crosses her feet at my back, digging her heels into me. The position places her pussy right against my cock.

"Fuck, Everly." I walk us the three steps to the side of the building and press her back against the rough brick exterior.

She groans and uses her new leverage to grind herself along my shaft.

Jesus. That's incredible.

There are so many damn things wrong about this, but it feels so fucking right. This is the type of temptation I was warned about my entire life. Everly is a walking sin. One I can't deny myself.

I capture her mouth, thrusting my tongue between her lips, demanding entrance, willing her to give herself over to this completely. Begging her to feel what I do. She opens for me and responds in kind, a desperate tangle of need, of desire, of pent-up whatever this is that's been building between us during the time we've spent together.

Has it really only been a handful of hours?

It's pure insanity how in such a short span, I've become so comfortable with her. So content. So invested. This is so damn real, even though we barely know each other.

Real and dangerous.

I can't think about anything but the physical need now. If I do…if I dare consider something more…we'll both end up somewhere we shouldn't venture. Somewhere that only leads to anger, hurt, and potentially worse.

Her hands move to my belt buckle, and she deftly releases it and slides the zipper of my pants down. A warm palm finds my cock, and she works my jeans down far enough to free me. Small fingers wrap around the base of my shaft and stroke up in one smooth motion.

"Sweet Jesus, Everly. You sure you want to do this here?"

The corner of her kiss-swollen lips twists up into a sultry smile. "Stop questioning it and enjoy it, Preacher."

Well, hell.

With one hand firmly on her ass, helping to support her weight, I tear her panties with my other hand. Her eyes widen slightly, and she grips my cock and drags the head through her arousal.

Fuck.

Her eagerness and absolute readiness for me is the biggest fucking turn-on. A shudder of anticipation crawls up my spine. I grasp her firmly with both hands, vibrating with the need to drive into her.

She digs her nails into the skin at the back of my neck and angles her hips to allow me to push inside her welcoming heat.

"Fuck." I've never been so inarticulate in my life, but being buried in Everly Webster is a whole different kind of experience. Her warm, wet walls tightening around me send all rational thought fleeing from my brain.

There have only been a few times in my life I sensed God had touched me, that His hands played a role in the happenings around me and absolutely proved His existence. One was Iraq. This is another.

The fucking existential experience of being with Everly.

She presses her heels into my lower back and grinds down against my cock with every thrust I make. Her nails claw at the skin exposed above the collar of my shirt, and she drops her head back against the brick, exposing her neck.

I lean forward to press my lips against her collarbone and work my way up until I find her mouth, just as eager as the rest of her. Her pussy clenches around me, and I groan into her mouth. I shift her up slightly to adjust the angle of our connection, and she gasps and clamps down even harder.

"Fuck yes, right there, Preacher!"

Christ...yes. Right fucking there.

I've done a lot of things in my life I thought were going to send me to Hell, but fucking Everly against a wall outside a bar has to be at the top of the list of the ones that are well worth it.

EIGHT

Everly

———————

The scrape of the cool brick against my back juxtaposed with Preacher's warm hands gripping me and hard cock driving into me throw my world into an overwhelming tailspin.

He's everywhere.

Inside me.

Surrounding me.

Enveloping me.

His taste on my lips and my tongue.

His scent invading my every breath.

His grunts and moans and curses filling my ears.

The feeling of contentment I never thought I'd find again filling my heart.

It's too much and not enough at the same time.

I knew what would happen if I came outside with Preacher. The way he looked at me, touched me, the sexy tilt of his lips…we wanted the same thing. And despite my reservations about getting involved with anyone, let alone someone like him, I need this opportunity to be carefree again. To not think about the past or my bad decisions. To live in the moment with a beautiful man who wants the same thing as I do.

Even if it's just for one night.

Even if Jimmy is gone next week and I leave with what's left of his belongings that are now mine, I can at least say I had this.

This man.

This experience.

This reckless abandon. His cock stretching me and filling a void in my chest I hadn't even realized was there. The pleasure surging through my veins.

With every thrust of his hips, he drives me back against the wall and helps rebuild a little piece of me that was broken so badly.

This man I barely know has managed to restore something I thought could never be fixed.

And I can't examine why that is.

There are too many questions in that. Too many things I'm not ready to explore. Because it means reliving things better left in the past and studying parts of my mind and myself better forgotten.

All that's gone with Preacher. At this moment. In this most unexpected of places. None of it exists.

He shifts slightly, and the head of his cock drags against my G spot. "Oh, my God. Preacher! Fuck! Right there! Please!"

His strong hands hold me in place as he pounds into me.

This isn't love-making. This is craving release. Two people attracted to each other who, despite the reasons against it, decided they just needed to forget themselves for a while.

We both have secrets. Ones we may not be willing to share, but we can share this.

And in the future…

Nothing seems impossible at this second, with us

connected like this. The possibility of *more* encroaches on the part of my mind that insists this is a one-time thing.

But I push it away, deep down with the other thoughts and memories that will only get in the way of just *feeling* this. Feeling *him*.

A slow burn starts to spread through my body—the sign an earth-shattering orgasm is about to descend over me. That tidal wave of absolute bliss has been missing from my life for so long, I almost don't recognize it knocking on the door. This is the time to give in to him and this fully. The time to embrace the craziness and passion. To release anything holding me back.

I clutch at his neck and roll my hips to meet every snap of his. He reaches between us and finds my clit. His thumb circles it in time with the rhythm he's set for us.

It's all I need to send me skyrocketing away from this tiny town in the middle of nowhere and into the great, wide universe I wish so much I had the guts to explore.

The explosion of pleasure rattles my limbs, and my pussy clenches around his dick. His thrusts continue through my release until he grunts my name and buries his face against my neck as he shoots his hot cum inside me.

My orgasm finally ebbs, and I sag against him. If he didn't still have me pinned against the wall, I would collapse into a pool on the concrete beneath us.

"Fuck, Everly." His hot, heavy breaths tickle the hair on my neck, and the rough scrape of his beard against the sensitive skin there has a little shiver shooting through my limbs.

Fuck, indeed.

I chuckle. "Isn't that what we just did?"

He pulls back his head slowly and watches me with half-hooded hazy eyes. A slow smirk spreads across his lips. "We sure did." His mouth finds mine, and a slow, lingering kiss spins my head and heats my body again. He makes his way across my cheek to my ear. "That was brilliant, babe."

Those whispered words send my soul fluttering.

His lips return to mine with a slow, sweet, gentle kiss. "I want you to know, I don't normally do this. I'm not like Rion in there. When I'm with someone, it means something."

The wall around my heart squeezes and vibrates, threatening to shatter. It's the last thing I expected him to say at this moment. "You're a true mystery, Preacher Davis."

"Not really." He shrugs slightly and tries to hide his amusement.

"Oh, but you are. One I would very much love to unravel."

Where the hell did that come from?

The last thing I should be doing is making plans with a guy who is all wrong for me in a town I have absolutely no solid plans to remain in. But the words ring true deep in my soul. I *do* want to unravel the mystery spiraling around him. The tattoos. The vague answers to my questions. The apparent contradiction that is Preacher Davis.

He doesn't acknowledge my comment—but whether he didn't hear me or is just ignoring it is another question—and leans back enough to withdraw his still hard cock from inside me. We both groan at the loss of connection, and he reaches in his back pocket and hands me a handkerchief.

Who still carries a handkerchief?

Apparently, Preacher Davis.

I accept it and brush my fingers over the monogrammed material. Like some gentleman from the last century. Though, they probably didn't give it to women to use to clean up with after a quick romp. I do my best to remove the evidence of what we just did while he rights his pants and secures his belt.

"Sorry." His single word apology is low and almost inaudible.

I glance up at him. "About what?"

He motions between my legs. "That. We should have used a condom. It's my fault."

We should have. If we were smart and careful. But it seems like being reckless was on the menu tonight—though it's the furthest from how I should be living my life right now. I've been there and done that, to dire consequences.

I shake my head to try to assuage the worry furrowing his brow. "It's okay. I've been getting the shot for years. I probably couldn't get pregnant now if I wanted to, and I'm clean."

At least physically.

Mentally and emotionally are another story.

His amber eyes darken with concern like he doesn't quite believe when I say I'm not worried. "Me too."

"I trust you. I would never have let you anywhere near me, let alone had sex with you if I didn't." The words bring the unexpected burn of tears to my eyes.

Oh, no. I am so not crying right now.

Instead, I suck in a breath and try to shove away how truly important saying that was. "And saying I trust you is actually saying a lot for me."

One of his dark eyebrows rises. "Why is that?"

Shit. I shouldn't have said anything.

Preacher isn't the type to let comments like that go.

I wad up the handkerchief and toss it in an old trashcan a few feet over from us. "It's a long, painful story you don't want to hear."

He considers me for a moment in the silence of the night.

I shift awkwardly and adjust my skirt back into place. There's no way I'm tearing open those old wounds. So, it's time to redirect the attention away from what I let slip. "What about you? You going to tell me your story?"

I've already stupidly admitted I want to know. Why not just come out and ask?

Even with only the moonlight illuminating his face, the struggle in his eyes is plain as day. His lips press together. It's like he wants to ask about what I said, but he's either afraid because of what I might say or afraid because of where it may lead—to finding out more about each other. And he doesn't offer an answer to my question, either.

The butterflies of anticipation I had before are quickly replaced by ones of unease.

It's not that I thought this was going anywhere. I don't even know how long I'll be here. But what was just a magical moment has suddenly turned uneasy. Maybe I misjudged him.

I wave a hand at him. "You're right. Maybe we should keep things more casual and this a one-time thing."

The words tighten my throat, but I still manage to say them. Better to rip off the Band-Aid than to wait and have him tell me he doesn't want to see me again. I can't let this lust get worked up or confused for something else.

After all I've been through, it's obvious I'm a shitty judge of a person's true intentions. I may have misread this entire thing with him.

"Everly," his voice comes low and gravelly, "it's not like that."

"It's not? We barely know each other." I shove a hand through my disheveled hair. Not that there's anyone out here to see me looking like I just got fucked, but I'm suddenly suffocating under self-consciousness I haven't felt in years. "I barely even know myself anymore." I clench my eyes shut. "And I just let you fuck me against the wall of the dive bar."

Shit. What the hell did I do?

I press my fingers into my temples and study the night sky. There are so many more stars here than in Milwaukee, where the city lights block them out. Out here, there's nothing *but* stars and the vast expanse of the endlessness of space. It's beautiful and daunting. It also reminds me there's so much in the world I want to see, and this town is the last place I want to settle down.

It's far too close to things I almost died to escape from.

"Everly, please don't get upset." Preacher takes a step toward me.

No.

My hand shoots up to stop him. "I'm not. I promise. It's just been a long week sorting through Jimmy's stuff, and I need to get home and go to bed."

You think I would have learned after what Axle did. You would think I'd be a better judge of character and that I would do more to protect myself. But not only did I open myself up to Preacher, but I also just had unprotected sex with him in public.

That's so not like me.

Although, the me I was with Axle was a lot different than the me I am now or the one I was before I met him. I let him take over my life. I let him control me and use me. And now, I'm about to let Preacher do the same thing by allowing him to work his way under my skin.

I need to get out of here.

The only way to stop this from going any further, from opening myself up to any more pain, is to walk away.

I finish righting my clothes and make my way toward the front of the building. Without glancing back, I snatch my purse off the table and dig for my keys.

Preacher's heavy footsteps follow behind me. "Everly, please wait."

"There's nothing to discuss, Preacher. This was fun, but it is what it is. We shouldn't pretend it's something more by sharing anything meaningful with each other."

"Shit. That's not what I meant. There are things you don't know. Things I can't tell you."

I spin to face him.

He stops a few feet away from me, concern lacing his dark eyes. But he doesn't say anything, just watches me, like he's waiting for me to say something that will make his reluctance okay.

"Can't or won't, Preacher?"

During the time we've spent together, he's been very

careful not to discuss his past or even anything about his current life. Other than meeting Rion tonight and getting a tiny glimpse at one friendship—one that is itself heavy with vague comments and knowing looks—he's a complete mystery.

He's hiding something. We all do. But I can't risk getting myself emotionally involved with someone who isn't completely open with me, even if it's only temporary.

The easiest way to face this is head-on. It's what I should've done with Axle instead of cowering and letting him walk all over me. "I'll be leaving soon." I take a deep, shaky breath. "As soon as Jimmy finally passes." Something chokes my throat, and I shake my head to clear the images suddenly flashing before my eyes. "So, let's not pretend there's anything more here. Goodnight, Preacher."

An immense relief mixes with disappointment as I turn away from him and storm across the parking lot toward my car. There's no point in looking back.

You can't look back. You can only move forward.

If I continue to reflect on everything Axle did to me, what *they* did to me, I will never be able to function, never be able to get out of bed every day, but what just happened with Preacher proves very much that I'm still damaged goods.

Someone stable doesn't fuck a guy she barely knows outside a bar.

God, what the hell is happening to me?

NINE

Preacher

The two dots on my radar screen inch closer to the target location. The *Calista* and the *Destiny* aren't the most impressive boats on the water, but they do what we need them to. The *Calista* is sleek and fast and acts as a decoy to get ships to stop and offer assistance, while the *Destiny* is a workhorse with a deck and hold large enough to transport whatever we're out there to steal in the first place.

Watching them approach the ship that's the object of our next raid has acid churning in my stomach and crawling up my throat. You would think I'd be used to it after five years of sending the guys out on missions without me. But every single time they board those boats still feels like the first. It's the exact same anxiety whenever they go out onto that water.

Not being there. Not being able to help…it's an impossible position to be in. And it has nothing to do with the desire to get my hands dirty.

I'm not like Cutter. I don't need to be in on the action. I don't need to be the one pulling the trigger. I'm not cold and disconnected. I can't turn my emotions off and point a gun at someone, let alone end someone's life without a second thought.

Hell, I couldn't even turn my emotions off enough to have meaning-less sex with Everly.

Of course, my required training at The Farm prepared me to take a life, but the hope was I would never need to use it. Computer analysts never anticipate being dropped into war zones. Little did I know how often working for the CIA in computer forensics, cyber-warfare, and offensive and defensive cyber collection would embed me in some very dangerous situations.

Including one that changed my life drastically and brought me to where I am today. After the attack, I don't even know if I can bring myself to pull the trigger again. It's something I've never had to do—take a life—and it would be hard for me to morally justify it in most circumstances.

Though, there are definitely jobs that make the guys' decisions to end lives a bit easier. When the guys went out to the *Marcella Marie* and killed *that* crew, they did it to protect themselves. They did it because the crew was ready and waiting for them with heavy weaponry. They fought back. And even though we're still not one hundred percent sure if it was a set-up by Arturo or if the true owner of the drugs just anticipated it, either way, that crew was anything but innocent.

That isn't always the case. The *Neptune's Daughter* crew were all just caught in the wrong place at the wrong time. They were ignorant of what was in their cargo. If the guys had been forced to kill any of them, our lives would be a hell of a lot different today.

No Grace.

No baby.

No Valentina.

We'd still be working for *Il Padrone* or Arturo.

That would have sucked balls.

Working for her is night and day different from our role under the previous Marconis. We can pick and choose our missions and get an even fifty-fifty split of anything we take.

It's a new world. One where we're not doing someone else's dirty work because we're forced to. Now, we do it because we want to.

Maybe, for a quick minute, I thought that would be an ethical dilemma for me. It was easy to justify doing it when we needed to because of Warwick's debt and the ax over our heads from the Marconis, but now, it's a conscious choice to be a criminal, to continue raiding ships and working for the mob.

But things have gone so smoothly and been so quiet since Valentina took power, there hasn't been anything to worry about. That makes me even more uneasy.

Letting down your guard is a sure-fire way to have something important slip through the cracks. To make mistakes that cost someone their lives. Let's just hope today goes as well as those other missions.

Put on the whole armor of God, that they may be able to stand against the schemes of the Devil.

Our target today may not be the Devil, especially compared to some of the others we come up against, but the prayer I've said before every mission has almost become routine.

And that ship isn't transporting something innocuous. It belongs to a rival group of Northern Italians trying to muscle their way into Marconi territory in Chicago. Valentina doesn't even care what the cargo is. She just wanted it gone—dropped to the bottom of the lake.

Seems like a waste to "disappear" something that could be so valuable, but she's the boss when it comes to these jobs, and if we ignored her wishes, Cutter would be the one who pays. As much fun as that might be to witness, there's no point in crossing that woman intentionally.

They'll get on board, get the crew controlled, drop whatever it is off the side, then head home. That's the plan, anyway.

I shouldn't be nervous about it, but after the *Marcella Marie* fiasco, it's hard to control the dread that settles over me every single time they go out on that water. Especially since I'm here and helpless to assist if anything bad goes down.

But it won't. God willing…

As the two dots on the screen approach the one representing the target ship, my headset crackles to life.

"I can see them." Warwick's familiar voice comes over the radio. "Won't be long before we're on board."

Tension coils through my limbs. Any minute now. I press the button to talk to the crew. "*Destiny* ready?"

"Affirmative." Cutter's one-word answer comes loud and clear, the typical response from the man of few words.

He's more of a man of action. God knows, he'd much rather be on the *Calista* and be first on board to control the crew, but people are too suspicious and uncomfortable around him. He's never been able to dispel the vibe he puts off—and it sure as shit isn't innocent and friendly. The glasses covering his eyes and the scars he can never conceal don't help matters. He could never be the decoy. They'd know something was wrong immediately and either sound the alarm or start shooting before we could.

Warwick and Rion can charm their way on board without anyone suspecting a thing while the *Destiny* and Cutter and E hang back. By the time the crew of the target ship realizes what's happening, it'll be too late.

Assuming everything goes as planned.

And we did plan. Just like we do with *every* job. Every last detail mapped and plotted. A Plan *A*, *B*, *C*, *D*, and then some, should things go south.

I click the red button on my screen. "Activating jammer."

We don't need the cargo ship to be able to call for help. The sophisticated tech allows me to block all their signals while still giving us a secure one so I can talk to the guys. One thing my job afforded me was access to the best of the best of the newest technology, stuff average citizens wouldn't even believe exists. And while I may be out of the game for the government, it doesn't mean I don't still have friends in high places. Friends who can procure certain items for me. Like the NODS goggles Cutter needs to help make up for the injuries he suffered.

The larger dot representing the ship we're about to take down approaches the stationary one that is the *Calista*.

Only another few minutes.

I wish we were already done, though. Because even a few minutes to think is too many, at the moment. Every time I'm not doing something, every second my mind isn't occupied completely, all I do is think about Everly and what happened the other night.

It's not like I could tell her that I wouldn't be able to see her for a couple days because we're pirates and we're going out to raid a ship for the Italian mob in Chicago. It's not like I can explain to her what we do. There wasn't any way to tell her "my story" without revealing all the dark and sordid things I'm involved with.

I didn't want to hurt her, but I also can't expose her to what goes on here. It's bad enough that Grace is pregnant and knee-deep in it. We don't need another innocent involved.

Keep her out of it, Preacher. It's for the best.

I tell myself that over and over as I watch the dots finally converge.

My radio crackles. "Going in."

I hold my breath and wait for an update.

Come on, guys.

This is about the time I always imagine the crack of gunfire and a hail of bullets. Sometimes, the memory of the explosions rock me, and I can still feel the heat of the flames and weight of what came after it.

I press my palms into my closed eyes to clear my thoughts. I have to be one hundred percent focused during these things, or something could go wrong. There are too many things to go sideways. I'm not going to add to that list by being distracted.

A boat could pass by and see something.

I scan the radar. No one else around. Which is precisely why we chose this spot to stage the raid.

The Coast Guard could somehow get a call from the victim ship despite my jamming device.

Nothing on the Coast Guard's feed. The nearest boat is thirty miles away. Way too far to get there in time to do anything now.

It's exactly how we planned it.

We hit in the most remote parts of the shipping lanes of the lakes. Places where we're sure there won't be anyone else around. Of course, there's always a chance a small pleasure craft might happen by but not this time of year. November isn't prime boating season in the Midwest. That water is ice cold, and so are the winds at this point.

We've put ourselves in the best position to succeed, but there's one thing we can't know for sure. One thing we can plan for but pray it never happens.

Someone on the crew could fight back…

It's the most likely problem. And it's the thing that has unease tightening its fingers around my spine now and every time they go on board.

The ten minutes I wait in silence for an update from War and Rion might as well be ten hours. I clench my hands where they hover over the keyboard.

Let's do this fast, guys.

But it isn't fast. It never is. Rounding up and controlling a crew takes longer than any of us are comfortable with.

My radio finally crackles. "All clear."

The sound of Rion's voice releases the tension from my body.

Cutter's voice cuts through any lingering concern. "Coming in."

Once he's there, things are golden. He won't let anything happen to the guys. If anyone is stupid enough to try to fight back now, Cutter will end them without thought.

I watch the *Destiny* move in on the other two dots and stop. Cutter and E will be on board in seconds.

The line crackles. Warwick's voice comes through loud and clear. "They're on. Cargo bay open. We should be outta here in a few hours."

A few hours is a long time. And everyone knows it.

Usually, when we do jobs, we're just taking a few pallets. We're in and out as fast as possible. But on this one, Valentina wants it *all* gone. Whatever's in that fucking hold is a danger to the family. And if nothing else, she's loyal. She may have only stepped up as head recently, but her father trained her well. If she says whatever's on board needs to disappear, then she's likely right.

It's another waiting game for me. Monitoring radar and radio channels. Watching for anything that could interrupt the guys and put them in any danger.

The Coast Guard line comes to life. "Report of disabled boat…"

I hold my breath as the coordinates are rattled off. Every second is agony.

Whew.

I release my held breath.

Nowhere near our guys.

That's good. It means resources will be pulled in that direction, away from our crew and even farther from their avenue of escape when they do head back this way.

My chair creaks as I lean back and relax for a few seconds. I haven't balanced this strange combination of fear, longing, and desire in my entire life. And it has nothing to do with the guys being out there and everything to do with Everly. I just keep coming back to her, even when my focus should be elsewhere.

There's something sad and broken in her eyes despite the effort she puts out to appear strong. Originally, I thought it was just that Jimmy is dying. They're obviously close, and losing someone like that can break anyone. But after what went down the other night, I'm convinced there's more to it.

She alluded to having trust issues, and that typically stems from some sort of betrayal. I could've learned what happened and gotten a glimpse of what scares her so much if things wouldn't have gone to shit the other night, but there's nothing I can do about it now.

And it's for the best, anyway.

A thousand reasons exist why I should stay away from her. And only one to keep seeing her. That one is selfish. That's the one I have to push away so I can concentrate on this. Keeping the guys safe, it's all that matters right now. And once this raid is complete, I'll go straight back to finding this hacker and anyone else who wants to harm us.

It's my job to protect the team, and I'll do it with my own life if I have to.

TEN

Everly

———————

"Ev? Where the hell have you been? I've been calling you for days. I was worried." Her voice floats through the phone, her concern evident.

Liz has every right to be worried. After what happened. After what she knows was done to me. After witnessing the aftermath.

She lets out a frustrated sigh. "Don't ever do that to me. I thought maybe he…"

"No. I'm okay. I'm sorry I scared you." I rub at my tired eyes and look around the guest room at Jimmy's house. "Things have just been a little tough. I needed some time."

Tough is an understatement, but there's no need to drag her down into the depths of my anguish right now.

"Aww, I'm sorry, Ev. Are you still in Wisconsin?"

I fall back onto the bed, surrounded by the boxes of old photos and the rest of Jimmy's personal possessions he stored in here and stare at the off-white popcorn ceiling. "Yeah."

A momentary silence precedes the question I know is coming and I don't want to face. "How is Jimmy doing?"

I swipe at the tears that trickle down my temples and onto the pillow. "Not good. Really not good."

Today at the hospice facility, he appeared dead already, like he was barely hanging on. A living corpse and a mere shell of the man I love so much. Sitting there with him had taken more out of me than I thought possible, yet when I came back to the house, I still sought out things that would break my heart more. The boxes of photos were on a closet shelf. Each and every one brought more tears.

Images of Jimmy's life.

My life.

A life I never would have had without him.

"Oh, honey." Liz sniffles. "I'm so sorry. I would come up there if I could."

She would be here in a heartbeat if her job afforded her the opportunity to take some time off, but she can't. Finding someone to take the graveyard shift at an inner-city hospital was nearly impossible. And Liz is the only person I ever let close enough to me to know everything.

Which means I'm totally alone in this misery with no one to hold me or comfort me, and when Jimmy is gone, I'll basically be totally alone in life except for her.

I choke back a sob and shake my head at the absurdity of the situation. "He's such an idiot. Why didn't he tell me sooner? We could've had so much more time together."

Time I desperately need.

"I know, sweetie, but he probably didn't tell you because of everything that was going on with you."

That doesn't make me feel any better. In fact, that realization only tightens the vise around my heart more and has tears free-flowing. She's probably right. Jimmy has always been so damn selfless. He wouldn't have wanted to cause me any more stress or pain. He waited until he knew the end was close to call me to tell me because there was nothing either of us could do to stop the inevitable. He suffered alone to make my life easier for a few weeks.

Dammit, Jimmy.

"You're there with him now, Ev. That's all that matters."

"I guess." At least I got to see him again before he dies. I got to tell him how much I love him and how much he means to me. Not everyone gets that. I should be thankful for that instead of being bitter about his not telling me sooner.

"How are things going there with the shop? Are his clients okay with you working on them?"

I laugh, but it lacks any humor.

How do I answer that question?

The few regulars he had seem okay with me, and it's not like he gets a lot of walk-ins. The only even remotely interesting thing that's happened since I've been here is Preacher, but if I tell Liz about what happened with him, I'll get an earful.

Time to dance around the truth. "It's fairly quiet here. Nothing to report."

Silence fills the line for a second, then Liz *tsks* at me. "Why are you lying to me, Ev?"

Busted. Shit. Shit. Shit.

I clear my throat. "Uh, what do you mean? I'm not lying to you about anything."

"Ev, I'm your best friend. You really think I can't tell something is going on? I can hear it in your voice."

Just like she could when the shit was hitting the fan with Axle. She must have asked me a thousand times what was wrong and demanded I tell her, but I kept her in the dark when I should have been running to her for help.

I sigh and drop my forearm over my eyes. There is no use fighting her. She's relentless in nagging me. "There's this client of his."

"Who? A guy client? A hot guy client?"

Her mouth is undoubtedly watering right now. Liz loves dick. There's no other way to say it. Give her a hot guy with a decent package, and she's in Heaven. People have given her a hard time about it in the past, but I can't really blame her for being so promiscuous and loving the cock. Not when she's just living her best life and loving it.

Not when I fucked Preacher the other night so shamelessly in public.

My body heats at the memory of his body pressed against mine. The scrape of the wall against my back. His cock filling me... "Yes. A very hot guy. He was one of Jimmy's regulars."

"*Ohh*, lots of tattoos?"

The colorful ink over every inch of his skin flashes before my eyes. "Covering just about all of him. At least, the parts I've seen."

She laughs. "And what parts are those?"

The insinuation is there, but she doesn't come right out and say it. If I don't want to spill the beans about what went down between us, now would be the time to fake a reason to hang up. But she might be able to help me sort out what went down.

A neutral party to bounce my concerns off and get a detached view of the situation.

"He's been shirtless on my table a few times and..." I trial off intentionally, leaving the silence hanging long enough for her to get the gist.

"Oh, my God. Did you sleep with him?"

"Well? That depends on your definition of sleep."

"Oh, my fucking God! Did you guys stay up all night banging?"

Visions of just that flit through my head. It certainly wouldn't be a bad thing. "Ha. I wish. But no, actually, things kind of went south after we...you know."

"What do you mean?"

The words to explain what happened with Preacher fail me. It was so *damn* good. And then, in an instant, it changed so much. Maybe she can help me organize the jumble of emotions clouding my judgment here.

"Well, we met at a bar for a drink, and we went outside to talk and..."

"Jesus, Ev, did you have sex with him at the bar?" Her incredulity clings to every word.

So not like me…and she knows it.

I cringe before I even say the words. "Technically, outside the bar."

"Girl, when did you become me?"

"I don't know, and why is that such a bad thing?"

I sometimes envy the way Liz lives her life. She's carefree and happy. If she wants to be with someone, she is. If she doesn't, she says no. There are no games. There's just Liz being herself.

After everything that's happened, I don't think I can ever be like that. I don't believe it's possible for me anymore, even if I really tried for it.

"Shit. I didn't mean it like that, Ev. It's easy for me to just fuck a guy because I want to have sex, but I know what Axle did to you and how much it fucked you up. If you want to go out and have random sex with some tattooed guy, you have every right to do that without feeling bad about it."

"I know, it's just…" I struggle with a way to explain what happened. "Things with Preacher are just complicated. We didn't exactly part on good terms."

"Why the hell not? You didn't come?"

I snort, and my core clenches at the memory of the orgasm that shattered me so completely. "Oh no, I definitely came. Harder than I ever have in my entire life. But afterward, he got really cagey about telling me anything about himself, and I don't know; it just weirded me out and made me think he must be hiding something."

"The way Axle was?"

Axle never hid anything from me. Not really. I wish I could say I was tricked, that somehow, I had been conned into believing he was someone else when I fell for him, but it was always there.

The signs.

The evidence of what was going on.

The proof of who and what he was.

I should have known he wasn't going to be my white knight or Prince Charming.

I should have anticipated what might come.

But I didn't.

I couldn't.

I was blind to it all.

And by the time I realized what he was, it was too late.

Preacher doesn't exactly look like the kind of guy your mother would be thrilled for you to bring home for dinner, either. And if Mom were still alive, she would probably tell me I should have learned my lesson. But there's something about him, something that connects with me on a deeper level than I've ever experienced. Something that tells me he is different.

I've been wrong before, though.

Terribly wrong.

And I paid for it.

I shift back and recline against the headboard. "I think I just have a habit of making shitty choices with men."

"That's not true. Axle was a fluke. A one-off. He's gotten into your head. You're still messed up from everything he did to you, and you're not seeing things straight. The guys you dated before him weren't so bad. They weren't *the one*, but they weren't terrible, either. What did this Preacher guy say that got you so upset?"

I wrack my brain for the words we exchanged that night. "Honestly…I don't even remember. All I know is that he wasn't telling me something. Something important. And it felt like he was trying to brush me off and avoid learning anything real about each other. It was just kind of a red flag."

"Do you *want* more from him? Was this something that you expected to turn into more than a fling?"

It's a good question. One I've been bouncing around in

my head since I walked away from him that night. One I don't have an answer for.

"I don't really know what I expected. It just sent up a warning for me. Maybe I'm just paranoid after everything that happened."

"Was he an asshole to you? Did he treat you like trash?"

I snort. "God, no. He seems like a really nice guy. Very down to Earth. Wicked smart. He's some sort of computer whizz. Lots of religious tattoos, too. But he definitely has a secret."

"Don't you? Does he know your whole history?"

"Well…no." And I wasn't willing to offer it to him that night, either. I wanted to learn more about him, but I wasn't going to give him the dark, dirty details of my own had he asked. I would have made an excuse and changed the subject. Without question.

Hypocrite much, Everly?

"So, don't you think you should maybe cut him a little slack? I mean, you guys fucked outside a dive bar in middle-of-nowhere, Wisconsin, right. It doesn't exactly spell long-term relationship material, does it? Maybe he just didn't want to get into things any further because he didn't know where you guys stood."

I hadn't thought about it that way. Maybe she's right. Maybe I should have given him a chance to explain his reluctance. He said there were things he couldn't tell me, but maybe if we sat down and hashed it out, I would understand and this awful feeling that's filled me since that night would ease.

"Ev, you should text him. Tell him you want to talk."

"And then what?"

She lets out an annoyed sigh. "Fucking talk to him, you idiot. Find out what happened the other night and where this thing between you guys is going, if anywhere. I mean, are you even planning on staying up there?"

Thankfully, she doesn't say after Jimmy dies, but it's implied.

It's another unknown.

Another thing I've been thinking about constantly.

I shrug even though she can't see it. "I don't know. Bumblefuck isn't my scene."

And it's too close to certain people I would rather not find me.

But I don't need to say that. Liz knows all too well why I didn't come up here to be with Jimmy before.

Her light chuckle tinkles through the phone. "I'm sure you stand out like a sore thumb up there."

That's putting it mildly. In this super conservative area, a woman with tattoos covering every inch of skin is an anomaly. One that draws attention, most of it unwanted.

"You could say that. So do Preacher and his friend."

"Whoa, whoa, whoa. You never mentioned a friend. Is he hot?"

There's no need to even consider my response to her question. "Oh, yeah. Rion is definitely hot, but given what I saw the other night, it's probably from various venereal diseases raging and eating away at his body."

She laughs so hard, it vibrates through the phone, and I find myself clutching at my stomach with laughter. It feels damn good. I haven't done enough of it in the last six months. Though I did find myself smiling and laughing with Preacher…

"Ev, girl, hang up with me and text him. And don't go so long without calling me again. Really, I worry."

Guilt at causing her distress claws at me. It's not fair. She's been through Hell with me, and making her worry again is tantamount to torture.

"Liz, he's not gonna find me up here."

I've been saying those words to myself over and over again since I arrived. The more I say them, the more convinced I become that they're true.

Liz releases another sigh, one I know all too well. "I know, Ev, but still, I'm a worrier."

"It's one of the reasons I love you."

"Love you, too, girl. Let me know what happens with the tattooed bad boy."

"I will."

If I ever muster up the courage to contact him. I stare at the wall across from the bed. A photo of Jimmy and Mom hangs in a frame there.

I remember the day I took it. Right before she died. We were all so happy. So content to just be with each other.

Jimmy wasn't the type of guy you'd expect to find your happily ever after with, and Mom didn't, but he was *there*. For her. For me. Whenever we needed him. For anything.

I shouldn't be so quick to judge Preacher and his reluctance. Being careful is good. But being closed-off to any possibilities isn't a way to live.

My finger hovers over his name on my phone. I pull up the last message we exchanged—the address and time to meet at the bar. Neither of us has tried to contact the other since that night.

Though, I have no idea what that means…

I need to stop reading so much into everything, but it's hard not to over-analyze when I've been so damaged by not analyzing enough in the past. It's time to at least give him a chance to explain. I can walk away once I know. I type out the message with shaking fingers.

I'm sorry about the way things ended the other night. I'd like to get together. Can we talk?

My phone drops onto the bed next to me, and I close my eyes, letting the almost silent night envelop me. I'm so used to the sound of the streets, the honking horns, people yelling, all the hustle and bustle. The silence up here is almost deafening.

It leaves too much silence in my head to fill with other things.

My phone dings, and a smile crosses my lips.

That was fast.

Maybe he's not as angry with me as I thought.

I swipe to open the message, and blood chills my veins. I don't recognize the number, but there's no question who sent it.

I miss you, Evermore. It's been far too long.

ELEVEN

Preacher

———————

The bright lights of the warehouse practically blind me. I cover my eyes for a second and blink away the glowing orbs in my vision. When I reopen my eyes to the offensive light, it's not nearly as bad, but fuck…

I've been in there too long.

After three days being holed up in my room messing with this damn hacker with only bathroom and food breaks, it's taking far too long for my vision to adjust. A dark room with only computer screens to light it isn't good for my eyes either.

I yawn and stretch, gripping the door jamb for leverage. Every joint I have aches and pops. Sitting in that position for so long is so damn horrible for you. But I'm not about to stop until I get this fucker.

And I need a distraction anyway, from what happened with Everly the other night. It…*she*…still haunts my thoughts. And would my dreams if I'd gotten any sleep the last few days.

No matter how many times I go over our conversation outside behind the bar, I still can't figure out why she snapped. One moment, I was deep inside her and she was coming all over my dick, and the next, she was running away like her ass was on fire and I was the one who lit it.

I get that my unwillingness to reveal more personal information may have given her the wrong impression, but that couldn't be it. She couldn't have been expecting more.

Could she?

It would be a terrible lie if I said I hadn't considered it myself. Because Christ knows, I like her, but even if there weren't a million reasons why my life doesn't jibe with having a woman in it, she's leaving this piece of shit town eventually. She had to understand this couldn't be more than just sex.

Right?

It couldn't. And convincing ourselves otherwise would only hurt both of us in the end. So, while it may have hurt to see that look gracing her beautiful face when she left that night, it was the way things had to end.

No matter how much it hurts or how many times I relive our time together.

I wander into the kitchen and grab a box of cereal from the pantry. My body protests as I reach up to snag a bowl from the shelf. Muscles ache that I'd completely forgotten I even have.

Christ, I'm getting too old for these marathons.

I pour a huge bowl and grab the milk and a spoon. Not quite one of E's gourmet meals, but it will do in a pinch. I'm lucky he's been bringing me sustenance the last few days, or I would have collapsed long ago.

Still might.

At least I finally have something to show for it, though. All the work and stress and long hours. They paid off. Big. And it couldn't have come soon enough.

I rest my hip against the counter while I eat. It's still early enough that no one else is up.

Or should I say late? Shit. I don't even know.

I've lost all sense of time. But I just can't kick the nagging sense this hacker wants more than just getting into our system.

Ever since we took the drugs from the *Neptune's Daughter*, I've been waiting for something big to happen.

And then, we took more from the *Marcella Marie*. Probably pretty fucking stupid since we know both shipments were connected to the same shell company. Someone lost millions in heroin. Someone who undoubtedly isn't too happy about it. Which begs the question…

Why haven't they done anything about it yet?

Now that I have a better idea who is behind the hack, that question might have an answer, but I need to discuss it with the guys. We made a pact when this crazy band got together that we wouldn't make decisions alone. We wouldn't go off half-cocked or make rash choices without discussing it with the entire crew. It's an agreement that has worked well over the years and protected us from doing some very stupid shit during some very tense situations. And the guys need to know what I found so we can figure out how to address it.

E strolls into the kitchen, scrubbing a hand over his face.

I swallow the bite of sugary cereal in my mouth and watch him walk around the counter without even realizing I'm here. "Morning."

He jerks and glances my direction, surprised someone is up and in here before him. "Oh, you finally decided to grace us with your presence?"

I flash him a grin. "I knew you fuckers missed me."

"Yeah, yeah." He waves me off, and his gaze drops to my almost-empty bowl. "Want me to make you a real breakfast?"

My stomach rumbles in response. Eggs, bacon, French toast…one of E's spreads would hit the spot right now if there weren't other things going on. "I can't believe I'm going to say this, but no."

His cooking is the fucking bomb and turning it down physically hurts.

Who would've thought a prison cook would be such a badass chef now?

I set my bowl onto the counter. "As much as I'd love a massive pile of home-cooked goodness right now, we need to call a meeting."

He glances over from where he's starting the coffee maker and narrows his blue eyes on me. "This about your hacker?"

I nod and shift to alleviate the tweak of pain in my lower back. "Yep."

He's ready to ask another question, but Rion trudges through the door in nothing but a pair of boxer briefs that leave very little to the imagination.

Rion raises his eyebrows at me and dives right in. "You gonna tell me what happened?"

I scowl at him. "I don't know what you're talking about."

"The other night with Everly. You two were looking awfully cozy when you disappeared outside together, but when you came back in to tell me you were leaving, you looked pretty fucking pissed off."

My hands lock around the counter lip, and I grip it tightly to keep myself from going off on him. The asshole has been stopping by my damn room to annoy me with this shit so much since that night at the bar, I locked him out. "Nothing happened. I don't want to talk about it."

He gives me a knowing smirk. "What's there to talk about if nothing happened?"

Smartass.

I don't have the time or patience for him right now. "Just leave it alone. We have bigger problems."

He nudges E out of the way to grab the coffee pot. "I don't have any problems. I had a threesome with those two gorgeous blondes."

Which I already knew and have zero desire to hear the details about. When Everly left and I made my way back inside to round up Rion, it was clear where he was headed— home with the two girls hanging all over him.

I'd say he's a lucky bastard, but I don't think the man has

had one meaningful sexual experience in his life. I don't get how he does it. What happened with Everly was supposed to be that...completely meaningless. Just sex. But I haven't been able to stop thinking about it or her or the way she reacted afterward since.

And I certainly don't want to talk about it with these douchebags. "Go wake up the guys and meet me in my room. I've got information no one's going to want to hear, but they need to."

Rion holds up his hands and shakes his head. "Fine. Fine. Whatever you want." He takes his coffee and wanders out of the kitchen.

E pours himself a cup of joe and watches me. "Want to tell *me* what happened?"

If there were any one of the guys I would talk to about it, it would be E. He's the only one with any kind of *real* experience when it comes to relationships, but I don't even understand what happened, and like I told Rion, we have other things to worry about now.

I shake my head and rub my jaw. "Just join us in my room."

He bobs his head and takes a sip of his coffee. "I will."

I make my way back down the hallway as Warwick thunders down the stairs. He follows me in, with Cutter, Rion, and E not far behind him. Milo wanders behind the guys, seemingly annoyed with the early arousal.

Our illustrious leader, who just left a warm bed with his pregnant girlfriend, scans everyone. "What's going on?"

I lock gazes with him and tilt my head toward computer monitors. "I got him."

His eyes widen. "You know who's hacking us?"

"Not exactly who, but I have a pretty good guess. And I know *where* it's coming from...Colombia."

Warwick sighs. "Which makes sense considering the heroin."

Exactly what I thought.

"Yep. It has to be one of the cartels." I twist my chair to face my screens. "And I've done some research. The one with the biggest operation, the one that seems to be using the same shipping lanes the cargo on the *Neptune's Daughter* and the *Marcella Marie* came through, is The Blood Rose Cartel."

Really nasty fuckers, too. Reading up on them has left more than a bad taste in my mouth. It left a chill in my blood.

We thought the Marconis were a threat. These guys make the Italians look like fucking nuns.

"I haven't been able to pinpoint the city yet, so I can't guarantee it's them, but it's the most logical deduction based on what I do have."

Cutter grunts. "Is there any way to know for sure?"

I glance back at him. "I could leave him something he couldn't resist."

Rion drops down onto my bed.

Asshole.

I wave my hand at him. "Make yourself at home, fucker."

He blows me a kiss. "I will." He tucks his hands behind his head and leans back against the wall. "What would you leave him?"

"An open door."

Warwick snarls. "You mean let them into the system?"

It may sound insane, but it might be the only way to get this guy. "I could create a mirror drive, one that he thinks is a real system when our real stuff is actually protected. I can make it look like part of my firewall crashed. It would be too much to pass up. This guy has been trying to get in for a long time, so I can't see him passing up an opportunity to do just that."

If I were in his shoes, I'd probably fall for it.

"And once he's in, finding him will be easy as pie because his exact location will be revealed."

War doesn't seem convinced. He drums his fingers on my desk while he considers my suggestion. "Is it safe?"

All I can do is shrug. "The way I would do it would be."

Hopefully.

In theory. And it's worked a hundred other times when I worked for The Company. It helped us take down a lot of really bad guys over the years.

Cutter crosses his arms over his chest. "What other options do we have?"

"None that I can think of." And I've been thinking about how to catch this guy for a long time. I've attempted every avenue I can think of to track him down, but I've hit a brick wall. There aren't a lot of options at this point.

Warwick leans against my desk. "I don't like this. But the only other thing I can think of would be to contact them."

Cutter hisses. "Are you fucking insane?"

I have the same question.

War holds up a hand. "Just hear me out. If it is The Blood Rose Cartel and they're trying to hack our system, they're probably trying to find us because they figured out we were connected to the stolen drugs, right?"

Everyone nods because it's the only logical connection.

"So," he drops his hand and paces, "if we contacted them and told them it was all Arturo's doing and that he is dead, maybe we open a line of communication with them and figure out a way to resolve things peacefully."

Rion lets out an incredulous laugh. "You really think a cartel is gonna want to negotiate with people who stole millions of dollars of heroin from them?"

War's gaze darts between all of us, and he stops. "Maybe if we offer them something in return."

Cutter appears unimpressed. "Like what?"

One of War's shoulders rises and falls nonchalantly, but the tension in his stance gives away how nervous he really is about whatever he's about to suggest. "Like part of the Marconi territory."

"No fucking way, man." Cutter's fists clench at his sides, and his jaw tics. "Valentina's not giving those scumbags any of her territory, and I'm not going to let them anywhere near her."

War holds up his hands in resignation. "It's just a suggestion. I'm just tossing out ideas here. It's not like *we* have a lot to negotiate with. Anyone else have anything better?"

Everyone exchanges glances, and I tap my knuckles against the desk. "Setting a digital trap is a lot safer than opening ourselves up to these guys."

It's also a lot safer than suggesting Cutter's girlfriend turn over part of her territory.

Rion pushes off the bed. "But what do we do if we find out it is them? Are we going to go down to Colombia and take out an entire fucking cartel so they can't do it to us first?"

He has a point.

It wouldn't be the first time Cutter and Rion did something like that, but when Cutter went on missions before, he had the well-oiled, well-trained, well-gunned machine of Delta Force behind him. We can't accomplish anything like that, and everyone here knows it. We're a rag-tag team of guys with some training and some skills. It's gotten us this far, but taking on an entire cartel would be walking into our deaths.

Warwick kicks the desk. His frustration radiates off him. "I think we need to know who we are dealing with before we make any decisions. Set the trap, Preacher, and we'll go from there."

Cutter glowers. "I'm calling Valentina to tell her the fuckwad suggestion you just made. You better watch your fucking ass the next time she's up here because she's gonna kick it."

I snort-laugh and nod because he's totally right. Valentina

is a force to be reckoned with, and he's the only man on the planet who can handle her.

Warwick doesn't stand a chance.

I already have one angry woman to worry about. I don't need a second one, so I'm staying mum on War's suggestion.

War holds up his hands in surrender. "Don't tell her. It was just an idea. She doesn't need to know."

"Then you shouldn't have made that suggestion, fuck-wad." Cutter storms out of the office while Milo stays on the floor where his owner just stood, his face planted on his paws. He slowly lifts his head and looks at the door before lumbering to his feet and trudging after Cutter.

E and War follow after him.

Rion lingers and watches me for a second from my bed.

I raise an eyebrow at him. "What? What's the fucking look for?"

"Nothing, dude. But you know where I am when you're ready to spill the beans."

"There are no beans to spill."

I'm not the kiss-and-tell type, and I'm certainly not the fuck-and-tell type. Rion can march around with notches on his belt, letting everyone know what a player he is, but it's not my style.

And what happened with Everly shook me more than I care to admit. I'm not going to let him turn it into a fucking joke.

"Get out of here so I can work."

He shifts off the bed and chuckles to himself as he walks toward the door. "You're a fucking mess, dude."

"Oh, yeah, and you're not?"

"At least I admit I am." He winks before he closes the door behind him.

Asshole.

The man can't mind his own fucking business. My phone vibrates, and I grab it from the desk.

Everly?

I wasn't expecting her to contact me. Not after what happened and how many days have passed.

I'm sorry about the way things ended the other night. I'd like to get together. Can we talk?

It might be wise to consider my response, to think about the pros and cons of trying to smooth out things with her. But for as smart as I am, sometimes, I'm not so wise.

Yes.

I should say no. I should be letting Everly go. But I can't let things end the way they did. If nothing else, we need to end things on better terms for my sanity's sake.

I'm tied up with work for the next couple of days, but I'll text you when I'm available to meet. Okay?

No response.

She probably sees my reply as a blow-off, but I'm not in any shape to see her right now, and this cartel bullshit is more pressing at the moment.

TWELVE

Everly

I should be used to this by now. The constant beeping and whirring of the machines. The smell of antiseptic and death in the air. The sad looks employees give me. The deathly hallows of the hospice.

Yet, after weeks of coming to visit Jimmy and seeing him like this, it still chokes me up. This place still gets to me, and so does seeing him.

This isn't Jimmy. This isn't the strong man I've known my entire life. This isn't how things should end for him, connected to tubes and machines and in agony.

But it is.

And according to the nurse, he's not going to make it much longer.

He hasn't opened his eyes in hours, and she told me not to expect too much. He may not be able to anymore. Though, she swears he can hear me even if he can't talk and that he knows I'm here with him. Anything I say can offer him comfort in his final moments. At least, that's what she claims.

I don't know if I truly believe that, but I do know I'll never leave this man when he needs me. Not after everything he's done for me.

So fucking much.

I'll be here every second until he's gone. Even when it tears me apart.

A tear trickles down my cheek, and I swipe it away and clasp his hand between mine. "I hope you can hear me. I need you to know how much I love you." My voice cracks and breaks, and I bite back a sob. "You're the only one who ever truly took care of me, and for that, I will be eternally grateful." I choke on the emotion blocking my throat and have to take a second to find my breath. "I don't know what I'll do without you. I'll be all alone."

His frail fingers tighten around my hand. I jerk up my head, and his eyes flutter open. Pale blue. Familiar. Still full of the love I've always seen there. Yet, lacking the spark of life they've always held.

"Jimmy?"

He offers me a weak smile, one that appears more painful than anything. "That's what I'm told my name is…" He devolves into a coughing fit that has him wincing and his hand tightening around mine. "I love you, little girl."

"I love you, too." I can't say that enough. Even if he did hear me before. It can *never* be said enough to the people who matter.

"And…you're not alone, Ev." His words are low, barely audible, but they claw at my heart all the same.

"What do you mean?"

He coughs again, and this time, it takes even longer for him to regain his breath. Each second is agonizing. Watching him in so much pain. Seeing him struggle with the most basic of bodily functions.

The nurse was right. He's not going to be here much longer. Please, God, not much longer…

But he finally settles, and his gaze meets mine. "I knew exactly what I was doing when I called you here."

Late. At the last minute. He waited until it was too fucking late, and I had no time left.

But I can't be angry with him now. Not now… "You aren't alone, either, Jimmy. You have someone who loves you. You're the only father I've ever had. I'm a big girl. I can take care of myself."

He nods slightly. "I know you can, but there are some monsters in this world, as you've learned, ones who masquerade as something else."

Even though Axle didn't exactly hide who he was, Jimmy couldn't be more right about that. People put on masks. They hide what lies deep inside them, who they truly are. A girl with a smile can be broken inside. And a bad-boy renegade can be the fucking Devil.

"Preacher…" The single word is whispered so quietly…

Did I hear him right?

"You want me to get a priest in here?"

I never knew Jimmy was so religious. It must be something new, something he found recently as he approached death.

He shakes his head and raises his hand. "No. Preacher…James."

My chest tightens.

Why is he bringing him up?

Preacher was too busy to see me. Or at least, he used that as a shitty excuse to blow me off. I was stupid to believe he might want to clear the air between us. Apparently, I'm the only one who hated how we left things. I'm the stupid girl who has been obsessing about it since I left him that night instead of concentrating on what's going on in my life and getting it back on some sort of forward track.

I lean over the bed and rest my elbow on the mattress. This isn't the time to dump my baggage about Preacher on Jimmy. "What about him, Jimmy?"

He swallows thickly and sucks in a wheezing breath. "He can protect you. He can give you what you need."

"Jimmy…" I squeeze his hand.

He means well. He really does.

"We barely know each other."

And what I do know has done nothing but twist me up in knots and confuse me.

A tiny smile curves the corners of his dry lips. "*I* know enough. I've spent a lot of time with him. Trust…trust him with you."

Every word is agonizing for him. A use of energy his body no longer has. He should rest, but his words have raised a question I hadn't even considered before.

"Is that why you asked me to come here?"

He manages a sly grin I didn't even think he was still capable of. "Would I do something like that?"

I laugh as tears stream down my face. It's impossible to tell if they're from his comment or my anguish.

Yes. He would.

He's always looking out for me. And now, knowing he's going to be gone soon, he wants to make sure I'm not alone. He wants to make sure I'm protected. That what happened can never happen again. That I won't have to spend my life looking over my shoulder and jumping at every tiny sound.

I choke back a sob and drop my face over his heart. The uneven rise and fall and the slight rattle in his chest shatter me.

The end is close now.

His hand comes up and settles across my shoulder. "Trust me. And him. If you ever need help, go to him. Promise."

It seems so important to him. Like a last wish of sorts. I can't deny him anything at this moment, even though I don't believe it's anything that will ever be a reality.

Preacher and I are a fantasy. He isn't a knight in shining armor or a Prince Charming. In most stories, he would be the villain.

And I won't be staying much longer.

But I'll let Jimmy believe whatever he wants if it will give him comfort.

"I promise, Jimmy."

He releases a relieved sigh and pats my shoulder. Being in his arms one last time feels like the beginning of the end. Though, I'm not sure of what.

I lie against him for what might be hours, listening to his ragged breathing and holding his bony hand. His chest stops moving.

No.

I jerk away and search his face. Though it's now gaunt and pale, it's still my Jimmy. He's so serene. Almost as if he's just sleeping. No longer in pain. No longer in this world. He's finally at peace.

"Goodbye, Jimmy."

Even though hours have passed, I still can't bring myself to accept that he's truly gone. I sit in his living room, staring at his things, the photos on the walls.

Me. Mom. Jimmy. All of us together. So many memories, good ones. The ones I *want* to remember. I wish I could just forget the last six months, wipe them completely from my memory, go back to a time when my life was relatively simple. I wasn't happy, but I wasn't this…

Alone.

Warm tears flow down my face, and I wipe them away only to have more take their place.

"You're not alone." Jimmy's words echo in my head.

I pull out my phone, and my fingers hover over Preacher's name and number.

He said he wasn't available for a few days. I should leave him alone. Just ignore what Jimmy said and remember the pain I suffered that night when Preacher blew me off and acted like I was nothing more than a quick fuck.

But my mind keeps drifting back to him. Despite everything that's happened. I press the call button.

The phone rings. Once. Twice. Three times.

"Everly?"

The sound of his voice sends an unexpected warmth through my body despite the uncertainty surrounding him. "Hi." My voice cracks, and I clear my throat. "Preacher?"

"Yeah, Everly, what's wrong?"

Everything.

"Jimmy is gone."

Saying those words twists a knife in my heart. Admitting it's true is more than I can handle.

"Shit, Everly. I'm sorry."

I can't fight back the sob that climbs my throat. "I know you cared about him, too. Can I see you?"

A litany of curses floats over the line. "Everly, I'm sorry. You have no idea how much I wish I could be there right now, but I'm in the middle of something for work. Something that can't wait. And I'm going to be tied up for a couple of days. I will do my best to get there soon as I can."

The pain that hits me is unexpected. I thought I had prepared myself for rejection from Preacher. But being blown off stings ten times worse than the last time. Because I need him ten times more now.

He's not coming.

I really am alone.

"Okay. I understand." I end the call before he can come up with another bullshit excuse.

Jimmy may have had good intentions in trying to introduce us, and he could have thought he knew who Preacher really is, but he should have heeded his own advice. Everyone wears a mask.

I stare at the ceiling. Since moving here, it's become my

favorite pastime. Counting lumps and holes in the uneven texture.

It reminds me of my life. Ugly and haphazard, covered in bumps along the way. That's all Preacher was. Just a stupid bump. One that I obviously need to forget. I'm only going to hurt myself more wondering what the hell happened.

I close my eyes and try to forget the horrible day. Sleep always makes things better.

Pounding at the door jerks me awake, and I blink off the sleep.

What? No one should know I'm here.

Ice seeps into my veins. The message I got the other day…

Did he find me?

My heart thunders, and blood rushes in my ears. I don't even have a weapon. I'm sure Jim has a gun somewhere, but I have no fucking clue where he keeps it.

Shit. Shit. Shit.

I grab a lamp off the end table and peek through the window at the front of the house. "Preacher."

Thank God.

A tremendous wave of relief floods my system as I yank open the door. "Preacher, what are you…"

He steps in and takes me in his arms before I can say another word. "I'm so sorry about everything. I can't stay long. Work is…complicated right now." He pulls back and peers down at me with warmth softening his gaze. "But I just couldn't stand the thought of you being alone."

"You didn't have to come."

Warm palms cradle my face, and he brushes the tears from my cheeks with his thumbs. "Yes. I did."

His admission drags a wretched sob from my throat, and I crumble into his arms. He scoops me up, carries me into the house, and uses his hip to push the door shut behind him.

He settles on the couch, drapes me across his lap, and holds me close to his strong body. "It's so hard for us to understand death. For us to comprehend why God would take something, someone we love so much from us. But I believe He has a plan, Everly, and Jimmy was somehow part of it. He needed him now, even though we thought we deserved more time with him."

Who is this guy?

Preacher couldn't be more of a contradiction if he intentionally tried. Yet something tells me he's not trying. He's a true mix of strength and softness. Passion and patience. Faith and uncertainty.

I pull back from him, still clutching his neck, and stare at the face of the man I'm trying so hard to stay closed off to. "Where did you come from?"

The corner of his mouth ticks up into a grin, and he shrugs. "Ohio."

THIRTEEN

Preacher

"What smells so good?"

I turn from my spot at the stove to find Everly leaning against the door jamb of the kitchen. I flash her a grin and glance down at the pan on the stove. "Breakfast, though, I am definitely not what anyone would call a gourmet, so I apologize in advance for the quality of the food."

She laughs and waves a hand at the stove. "I'm sure it's fine."

One of her hands moves back through her disheveled hair, and she yawns and wanders into the kitchen. After a quick peek at the stove, she drops into one of the seats at the table behind me.

It was a long night, with a lot of tears and apologies for something I had no control over.

I eventually fell asleep with her wrapped in my arms, but I have no way of knowing if she got any shuteye. "Did you sleep okay?"

She watches me for a second before she bobs her head slowly. "Yes. Actually, I slept better than I have in years."

That confession has an ache forming in my chest. "Why

haven't you been sleeping? Because you knew Jimmy was sick?"

It's the logical reason, but I don't miss the slight recoil and the way she chews on her bottom lip and averts her eyes, as if taking time to consider how to answer.

There it is. The more I've been sensing.

She finally meets my gaze. "No. I didn't know about his illness until very recently."

"So, what was keeping you awake, then?"

Sleepless nights aren't anything new to me. After Iraq, I think I could count on one hand the number of hours I've slept in a week. And once I started working with the crew, I had other priorities. But now that she mentions it…I slept pretty damn well last night with her in my arms.

I don't even want to begin to examine why that is.

She sighs and fiddles with a napkin on the table. "You really want to know?"

I pile the two plates next to the stove with eggs and bacon. She watches me bring them over to the table, and I set one in front of her and settle across from her.

Even though it's likely a horrible idea to delve into each other's pasts, I can't deny the burning desire inside me to understand. "Yes. I really want to know."

Her eyes narrow skeptically. "Really? Because it didn't seem like you were interested in sharing anything personal the other night."

She takes a bite of her eggs and waits for my response.

I rest my elbows on the table. "It's not that I wasn't interested."

One of her eyebrows rises.

"It's just that…my job is complicated."

To say the least. How do you explain to someone that you're a pirate?

She takes a sip of the juice I poured earlier and swallows. "What were you doing last night that you didn't think you'd be able to come?"

Trying to track down a hacker who may be part of a vicious South American cartel that might be after us because we stole a bunch of heroin.

"Something complicated."

That eyebrow wings up again in a challenge.

"Something *very* complicated."

Her fork hits the table, and she leans forward, a flash of annoyance darkening the green of her eyes. "You already told me you do security work and mess around with computers. I don't understand what's so complicated about that."

You would understand if I did tell you.

"It's better that you don't know. My job isn't something you want to get involved in."

She grabs her fork but just pushes her food around on her plate, clearly still agitated over my unwillingness to divulge all the sordid details of my life. But part of me is convinced she's only angry because she doesn't want to reveal what she's hiding and realizes how hypocritical it is.

I sip my coffee and wait for her to answer my question, but all she does is avoid my gaze. "Are you going to tell me what keeps you up at night?"

Everly is a complicated woman, but if there's something dark in her past, I want to know what that is. This *thing* between us may not be able to go anywhere, but that doesn't mean I won't try to help her if I can. She puts on a brave front and wears the tattoos like a shield, but what's underneath is what interests me and keeps *me* awake as much as everything else going on right now with the crew.

She takes a bite of her food, but it doesn't appear it's because she's hungry, more as another distraction from answering. She swallows. "How much did Jimmy tell you about his life?"

"Not much. I know he served in Nam and had the shop here for half a decade and was in Minneapolis before that, but neither one of us are particularly chatty about our pasts."

That was always by design. It was one of the reasons I

enjoyed having him work on me so much. He didn't ask a lot of questions. We talked, but neither of us pressed. We offered what we felt comfortable with while respecting the fact that some secrets should stay buried. Some artists need to chat constantly, to fill any dead air with mindless nonsense, but Jimmy just settled into his work and plowed ahead.

She sets down her fork again and clutches her hands together on top of the table. "Well, Jimmy had reason to not talk about his past. Did he ever tell you he was a member of the Devil Brothers in Milwaukee?"

"What?" That wasn't the secret I was expecting her to reveal. "Jimmy was a biker?"

He had a rough edge and the appearance to match, but he was always so chill. I never imagined he'd be involved with a criminal organization known for being so brutal and dangerous.

The corner of Everly's mouth curls up. "Yeah. I think when he got back from the war, he was disillusioned like so many were and found a brotherhood there that was similar to what he had in the service."

"But the Devil Brothers are pretty bad fucking dudes."

To put it mildly.

The rumors about what they're involved with, not to mention the actual charges and convictions handed down against their members over the last several decades, are enough to make most people want to stay clear.

"Yep. And I'm sure there are a lot of things Jimmy did that he wishes he could take back. But it led to him doing something that changed my life forever."

"How did you get tied up with them?"

I can't see Everly getting involved with the Devil Brothers. Definitely not her scene.

She shakes her head. "It was my mom. Years ago."

Which brings up the question I've been dying to ask since I first saw Everly at the shop…"Is Jimmy your father?"

"No." She gives me a sad smile. "But he was the only father I ever knew. My mom was the old lady of one of the bikers. He was a real dickhead. He beat the shit out of her all the time, fucked cut bunnies right in front of her at parties… he was a real asshole. And then, she got pregnant. And I think she hoped the abuse would stop, but it only got worse."

My hands clench on the table, but I let her continue. This doesn't seem like the type of story you interrupt even though anger over what happened to her mother makes me want to slam my fist through the wood underneath it.

"He accused her of cheating on him and said the baby wasn't his, but he wouldn't let her leave. She gave birth to me and went back to the clubhouse with him." She twists her napkin around her shaking fingers. "She was back in the hospital within a week with a broken cheekbone."

Jesus.

Rage simmers in my veins.

What kind of asshole would treat a woman, the mother of his child, like that?

A single tear trickles down Everly's right cheek. "Jimmy knew my father was going to kill her eventually. He had to do something. I know it was a hard decision for him. Those guys were his brothers, and even though they all did some bad shit, Jimmy was loyal to them to the core until that moment."

How could anyone be loyal to a bunch of criminal thugs?

That's exactly what the guys and I are. But we would never treat a woman like that. Ever. We may hurt people. We may kill them, when necessary. But there's a line we never cross.

Apparently, the members of the Devil Brothers don't carry the same ethics.

I force myself to unclench my fists. There's no need to scare Everly by letting her see my ire. "So…he chose to turn his back on the club in order to protect you and your mom?"

"Basically." She shrugs like it was nothing, but it is *far* from nothing to take a stand against men like that. "He took us in the middle of the night and left town."

"Where did you go?"

"Minneapolis. I think he figured with the entire state of Wisconsin between us and the Devil Brothers and the Rebel Chasers chapter in Minneapolis not wanting the Devil Brothers in their territory, he never thought they would come after us. He set up a new tattoo shop there and supported us."

"Were they together?" I suspect I already know the answer to that question, but the way she's talking about Jimmy, I'm starting to wonder if she really knew who he was.

She gives a sad smile. "No. Although, I never understood why. It was clear she loved him, and he loved her. They genuinely cared about each other."

"I have no doubt about that. Jimmy was a good guy, even if he does have a dark past. But it doesn't surprise me in the least that they weren't romantically involved."

Her eyebrows shoot up. "Really? Why not?"

She really doesn't know?

It isn't something I would usually tell anyone, but given the circumstances, it's something I think Everly deserves to know to help her understand her past.

I clear my throat and hold her gaze to gauge her reaction. "Because Jimmy was gay."

She freezes, and the napkin she's been fidgeting with falls to the table. "What? No, he wasn't."

I sigh and run a hand over my beard. This is awkward. "Yeah, Everly, he was."

Her mouth opens and closes a few times before she finds her words. "Did he tell you that? I've known that man my entire life. I think I would have noticed if he was gay."

"No, he never told me. But that's not something he would tell you or me. What do you think would have happened in the 60s to a gay biker? Or even the 70s or 80s or today?"

She considers me, but her eyes give away her disbelief.

He may never have come out and told me explicitly, but it was pretty clear based on what he *did* say. "I caught on to a few things over the years he worked on me. The way he spoke about one of the guys from his unit back in Nam. The insinuation was there that they were a lot more than friends."

"Wow." Her wide eyes show her confusion. "How could I have not noticed?"

"Think about it. You probably did; you just didn't know what it meant."

"You think you know someone, and then…things change so fast."

I get the distinct feeling we aren't talking about Jimmy anymore. She drops her face into her hands and settles back in her chair.

When her eyes meet mine again, the pain there is completely different than the one they held last night. "My mom died when I was almost eighteen. She never told me much about my father, and I always wondered. About two years ago, I decided I needed to try to find him." She releases a huffy, humorless laugh. "I don't know why. It was stupid and pointless. I just couldn't see that Jimmy was the only father I needed at that moment. There was just part of me that needed to know where I came from, where my roots were."

"So, what did you do?"

"I went to Milwaukee. I went to the Devil Brothers' clubhouse."

I snort. "You just waltzed right in there?"

A tiny smile tugs at her lips. "More or less. Looking like I do, nobody questioned me when I showed up at a party."

Now *that* I can easily believe. Everly is stunning, and with all that ink, she would have fit right in with those guys.

"My birth father was long dead. Which I didn't know when I got there. I asked a few questions, trying to keep things light and not give anyone any reason to suspect I was there for any ulterior motive."

"What happened?" I take a drink of my coffee, suddenly feeling the exhaustion of the work and lack of sleep. I don't want her to see my yawning and think I'm not interested.

Her eyes water as she shrugs. "I fell in love."

I practically choke, and I cough a few times to clear my throat. "Please tell me it wasn't one of the bikers."

She glances down at her plate, sheepishly. "I wish I could. His name was Axle. Or at least, that's what they called him."

I already don't like where this story is going.

The acidic coffee churns in my stomach while I wait for her to continue.

"Things started out great. We were hot and heavy for a while, and he worked me into a false sense of security with him. I felt like I had found a younger version of Jimmy."

Oh shit.

My heart aches for her. She went looking for her father and found a guy she thought was her version of the only father figure she ever had. Knowing what I do about the Devil Brothers, I can already tell that whatever is coming, it isn't anything good.

She sniffles and focuses her gaze down at her hands. "It was a good couple of months before I realize what a horrible mistake I had made."

I almost don't want to ask the question, but I need to. "What happened?"

If that douchebag laid a fucking finger on her, I'll fucking kill him.

She sits back in her chair and watches me for a moment. Probably too afraid to answer. "At first, I just caught him with other women. Cut bunnies who came to parties at the clubhouse while I was at work. I got a job at a parlor in Milwaukee that was really busy, and I worked a lot. I should've known he was doing it the whole time. I think I was just turning a blind eye and hoping it wasn't true. But it's kind of hard to ignore when you walk in and find your boyfriend with his dick in another woman."

"Jesus, Everly, I'm sorry." My hand tightens around the knife next to my plate without me even thinking about it.

"So am I." She drags in a deep breath. "But it is what it is."

What kind of asshole would cheat on a woman like Everly?

He must have been insane. I twist my knife in my hand. There are so many things I would do with this thing if I ever meet this guy. I'm not a violent person by nature, but her story is bringing up feelings in me that make me question that.

But honestly, hearing he just cheated on her gives me a little relief. It's a lot better than what I was imagining. "So, you left?"

She freezes, and her eyes slowly drift up to meet mine. "I wish I could say I did. It would've saved me a lot of anguish if I had taken off that very day. In retrospect, I should have. I should've known it was just a precursor to something much worse."

My hand tightens on my knife, and I have to drop it before I do something stupid like stab the table or myself in anger. There are very few things that are worse than walking into your boyfriend banging another chick. And all the ones I can think of make me want to kill the guy with my bare hands.

Her sad, tear-soaked gaze holds mine. "You sure you want me to tell you this?"

I grit my teeth and nod.

I need to know.

Even though it's hurting her to tell me. Even though it's killing me to hear it. I have to understand what she went through.

She runs a shaky hand through her sleep-rumpled hair. "I confronted him about the cheating. We argued. Hard. There was a lot of yelling and screaming. And then…" She sucks in a deep breath. "He got physical."

I clench my jaw to keep from saying or doing something

insanely stupid in this moment, like rushing over and taking her into my arms or taking off to find this fucker.

"He beat the shit out of me and then threw me onto the bed and raped me."

A low growl slips from my lips before I can contain it. The pure sound of my fury leaving my body is more animal than human.

Everly gives me a tight smile. "I told you it wasn't pretty."

She had warned me. I just hadn't expected that.

"That was just the start of it, though."

Jesus. How can it get worse?

I thought I was prepared for whatever she had to tell me, but if that was just the *start*, this man was truly the Devil personified.

"After that…he was a different person. Or maybe he was the same person he always had been and I just never recognized it or overlooked it and pretended it wasn't true because I wanted so badly to believe I had found somebody to take care of me and love me."

Everyone deserves that. She shouldn't beat herself up for wanting something every single human being needs.

"He lost any compassion or good feelings he had toward me, and if he ever did love me, it was long gone. I just became a plaything to him. Something to use and abuse and treat like garbage." She swallows quickly and reaches out to take a drink from her glass of juice. Her hand trembles so badly when she sets it back down, it almost splashes over the side. "He started sharing me with his friends."

I shove up from the table, rattling the plates and glasses, and start pacing. Wrath rages inside me. I thought I had seen the worst of humanity during the war, but this…

If I had tried to sit through any more of this story, I might explode.

She watches me with apprehension. "They took turns with me. Watched while others did things. It became a kind of game at the club. Though, I know not everyone participated in it. There are stand-up guys there, whether you believe it or not. Guys like Jimmy. Axle knew he could never get away with what he was doing if it were publicly known. He knew they would kick him out or worse if they found out. So, they did it in secret."

Because that's what depraved fuckers do.

They hide away in the dark recesses of society. They try to cover up the dirty deeds they do by putting on a different face for the world.

She shakes her head but doesn't look at me. "I never thought it would come to that. I never thought people could be so heartless and so cruel. But I learned my lesson the hard way. People aren't who they seem, and they will let you down."

I breathe deeply through my nose and try not to let my anger seep into my words. None of this was Everly's fault, and I don't want her misunderstanding why I'm upset. "How long did this go on?"

"Six months."

Six months? She endured that *for six fucking months?*

My hands fist at my sides. It's the wrong question to ask, but it's the only one running through my head right now. "Why didn't you leave? Why didn't you get help?"

She finally glances over at me. Tears stream down her face in earnest now. "It wasn't that easy. There was always someone at the clubhouse keeping an eye on me, and even if there hadn't been, I didn't have anywhere to go. I had moved in with him at the clubhouse almost immediately, and all my stuff was there. I only had a few friends in Milwaukee, and nobody I considered close enough to actually stand up to people like that. If I had asked, they would've been risking their lives just to help me get out. And I couldn't do that."

She was protecting her friends at her own expense. That doesn't surprise me at all.

Yet, there was one person who would've walked through fire for her. "Why didn't you call Jimmy?"

That man would have done *anything* for her. Even confront the new generation of the club he escaped from with her.

She shrugs. "Because I was embarrassed. I let it happen. I couldn't stop it."

"Jesus, Everly," I clasp my hands at the back of my neck and pull at the tension there, "none of that is your fault. You didn't do anything wrong. You're the victim. Don't convince yourself otherwise."

She nods, but I'm not entirely convinced she believes me. I know enough about PTSD to recognize it. I've seen people blame themselves over and over again for things that happened beyond their control. She's doing just that and doesn't even realize it.

"Eventually," she sniffles and wipes her nose on her napkin, "I couldn't take it anymore. I was nearing the point of breaking. I was this close," she holds her fingers just millimeters apart, "from killing myself just to make it stop."

My fingers curl around the counter and tighten. The thought of anyone doing this to her, of her thinking that…it's enough to drive me to do something that would very much be considered a sin.

Thou shalt not kill.

Except when it's a monster motherfucker like Axle.

A genuine smile graces her lips. "But then, I found something at the clubhouse."

"What?"

"It was an old picture of Jimmy. They had a wall with pictures of former members. Because of the way he left, they had removed all references to him. But one day, Axle told me to clean up the place, and when I moved one of the pictures, I saw another one tucked underneath it."

"Jimmy?"

"Yes. He looked so young and strong and tough, and it

made me remember who he really was. That it didn't matter what I did or what I got myself into, he would always, always, always come for me. I managed to steal a cell phone from one of the guys during a party when they were too drunk to know what was going on. And I called him."

"What did he do?"

I can't even imagine how Jimmy would've reacted to having someone he loved so much be in that position. Especially after he'd rescued her mother from almost the exact same fate.

"He was already living up here, and he was in Milwaukee to get me within two hours."

"And they just let him take you?"

"He didn't give them a choice. He came in guns loaded and pointed at them. Apparently, there's a back door that has always been easy to get open even when locked. The club was too lazy to ever do anything about it. He took me, and we left."

God.

I would have loved to see that. Jimmy storming the place, ready to blast anyone who got in his way. I wish I had been with him.

"You lost all your stuff?"

She nods, and another tear floats down her cheek. "Yes, but I got away with my life."

I walk over and drag her up into my arms. All I want is to feel her body pressed against mine, to breathe her in and know she's okay. I bury my face into her hair, and the soft scent of her shampoo still lingers there from yesterday. "I'm so sorry that happened to you."

"It's not your fault."

I draw my head back and capture her face in my palms, angling her face up so she's forced to see the sincerity in my eyes. "I know it's not, but when a man does that to a woman, when *men* do that to a woman, it makes me feel like our entire gender is at fault."

She shakes her head. "You're not like them, Preacher."

I'm not so sure about that. I would never physically hurt a woman, but I've certainly hurt a lot of people—directly and indirectly—through my job. "Where's the asshole now?"

Because I'm going to fucking kill him.

"Probably still with the crew. Jimmy rented me an apartment back in Minneapolis. He originally wanted me to move up here with him, so he could make sure I was safe, but I didn't want to be this close to Axle, and he knew I was right about that."

The asshole is only two hours away. That's way too fucking close for my liking.

"And this guy never tried to contact you?"

She freezes in my arms and directs her focus away from me.

Shit.

I turn her face back to me. "Everly, did this fucker try to get in touch with you?"

"Not back then." She bites her lip. "But...I think he did recently."

"What do you mean, you *think*?"

"I got a text the other night. After I sent you the text. It was from a number I didn't know. But it had to be him."

My stomach coils into a knot, fear mixing with anger to form a tight ball of volatility. "Why do you say that?"

"Because he called me the nickname no one else ever did. Evermore. It was a reference to Edgar Allan Poe's 'The Raven.'"

"I don't get it."

"I didn't at first, either and found it charming. But once I realized what Axle meant by it, it left me with a chill every time I heard it. The poem is about the undying devotion of a man who refused to give up his love even after her death. It was a way of telling me he was never going to let me go. That I was his…forever. Even after death."

Christ. He truly is a fuckwad.

"Everly, I promise this asshole will never touch you again. I'll make sure of that."

A sad smile crosses her lips. "Don't make promises you can't keep, Preacher. These are dangerous guys. Guys you shouldn't tangle with."

There are so many things I want to tell her about me, about the crew, to put her at ease, but I can't. "Trust me when I say this, Everly. He will not fucking touch you again."

He won't fucking breathe again when I'm done with him.

FOURTEEN

Everly

R evealing the truth of what happened to Preacher has to be one of the hardest things I've ever done in my life. Only second to making that phone call to Jimmy to beg for help.

How can he ever look at me the same after knowing what was done to me? What I let be done to me?

Even now, as I sit across from him at the little diner down the street from Jimmy's house, I can feel his bourbon eyes assessing me.

"Stop." His hard word breaks the silence between us.

"What?" I glance up from my menu.

The hard set of his jaw and shoulders reveals his anger. "Stop whatever you're thinking. Because it's not true."

I shift in my seat and concentrate on the menu to avoid his penetrating gaze. "I don't know what you're talking about."

"Yes, you do. Don't play dumb with me, Everly. It doesn't suit you."

Should I be insulted or complimented by that?

I'll prefer to think of it as a compliment because Preacher wouldn't insult me. He's been nothing but supportive since I unleashed my dark revelation.

We both lost our appetites after that conversation, so breakfast went to waste. The emotional upheaval of speaking those words hit me so hard, I had to get away. The fresh air and walk helped, so did the much needed shower. And my spirits were lifted even more when I came back to find Preacher had cleaned the kitchen, taken out the garbage, and even made the bed we slept in last night.

And I do mean *slept* in.

He held me like no one ever has before. In the past, it was always about someone possessing me and showing me I was theirs, but with Preacher, it was about comforting me. About being a safe place to rest my head and close my eyes.

It was the best night of sleep I've ever had. In the arms of a man who looks more dangerous than Axle ever did.

How's that for irony?

I examine him and snort to myself.

His brow furrows. "What?"

"Nothing."

At least nothing I want to admit.

"No." He narrows his eyes on me. "Not nothing. Tell me what's going on in that pretty head of yours."

It's hard to put that into words without losing my shit again. "You're kind of a contradiction, you know that?"

He gives me a little half-smirk. "So I've been told."

"I like it, though."

That sexy smirk returns. "Oh, you do?"

Way more information than I wanted him to know.

It lays it all out there. He knows how I feel and all about the shit in my past. But I guess, if that hasn't sent him running, nothing will.

I bite my lip. "I do."

"That's very good information to have."

Maybe it is, but I still have no idea where *we* stand, especially after everything that's now out in the open.

I redirect my focus to my menu. Now that I've gotten over

the emotional turmoil of my confession, I'm starving. "I kind of want everything on the menu."

He laughs and shrugs. "Then let's get everything."

"That seems like it would be a waste of food."

"I'm used to living with four other grown men, a bulldog, and at least one woman, who happens to be eating for two, plus sometimes another one. We go through a lot of food…fast."

"You live with four other men and sometimes two women?" I raise an eyebrow at him. "There must be some story there."

Preacher's living situation had never really crossed my mind. I assumed he had an apartment or a house just like every other normal human being, but what he's describing is anything but usual.

And with my question, I can practically see him closing off again. It's exactly what happened the other night. Today, I shared a lot with him. Hell, I shared *everything* with him, and he can't even elaborate on a simple topic like who he lives with and why.

His contradictory nature isn't so damn cute anymore. Frustration boils over and prickles my skin.

Am I just wasting my time here?

I set down my menu and push my chair away from the table, but his hand comes down on top of mine, effectively keeping me in place.

"Don't go. I'm sorry." He pulls his hand back and runs it over his beard. "I just don't know how to tell you anything without revealing things I can't or making myself sound insane."

The sincerity in his plea has me sliding my chair back in. "I promise I won't think you're insane."

If anyone is unstable at this table, it's definitely me.

He sighs. "I told you I do security for my friend, right?"

I nod.

"And I do some work for some other people on the side. Well, the guys I live with are my friends, and it's kind of a complicated situation."

Complicated situation.

Those words seem to be his favorite to describe his life and job.

I nod again slowly because I can't quite comprehend that many men living together when it's not a frat house. "And this arrangement works for you guys? Five grown men living together?"

He bobs his head slowly. "I mean, it does for now."

"Will it forever?"

"I don't know."

There's no way that kind of arrangement is viable for very long. People settle down. People want their own space. There must be a lot of testosterone and tension in that place. And there must be a reason why they continue to do it. One he hasn't offered yet.

Our waitress slides up next to the table. "Hi, sorry about the delay. My name is Nicki, and I'll be taking care of you…" she trails off.

I break Preacher's gaze and glance up.

Oh, you've got to be shitting me.

The girl attached to the tramp stamp stares down at us with the same distasteful twist to her lips as when she saw Preacher at the shop.

What are the chances she would work here? And what the hell is her problem, anyway?

She glares at Preacher and me. "It's you two."

Preacher grins at her, completely unaffected by her attitude. "It's us."

I want to say something to her about her behavior, but Preacher gives me a look that tells me to leave it alone.

Who is she to him?

He said he didn't know her, but none of this makes sense if they don't have some sort of history.

Would he lie to me about it?

Something tells me no, but the whole situation with her is uncomfortable and so filled with tension, it makes me want to walk out of here despite my grumbling stomach.

She lets out an annoyed sigh and takes out a notepad and pen. "What can I get for you?"

I clear my throat. "I'll have pancakes, hash browns, orange juice, and a side of bacon."

The girl sneers at Preacher. "And *you?*"

Holy shit. The attitude on this one.

Preacher plasters a smile on his face. "I'll have the trucker breakfast. Eggs over easy, sausage and bacon, and whole-wheat toast."

She jots something down in her notebook and frowns at us. "Is that it?"

"No." I just can't stop myself. If there's one thing I hate, it's fucking rude people, and we've given her no reason to treat us like shit. "I also want to know why you have this attitude toward him." I point to Preacher.

He clenches his jaw—clearly annoyed I've confronted her. But if he wasn't going to do it, someone had to.

She focuses on Preacher and sets her hands on her hips. "You're friends with Warwick Pike, aren't you?" One of her thin, blond eyebrows rises at him, but it's more of an accusation than a question.

Preacher takes a sip of his coffee and practically chokes on it. He darts a look my way and back at her.

She rolls her eyes and waves her hand. "Never mind. It doesn't fucking matter. I'll go put your order in." She stomps away with just as much attitude as she came over with.

"Whoa. What the hell was that about? Who is Warwick Pike?"

He leans back and sips his coffee while he watches her

retreating form. This will be another case of not getting a real answer from him.

His eyes meet mine, and he lifts one shoulder and lets it fall nonchalantly. "Warwick is my employer, technically, but he's also one of my best friends."

"And how does she know him?"

He breaks his focus off her to return it to me. "War and I have only known each other for about six years. Whoever she is, she has to be someone from before that."

"But you don't recognize her?"

"No. Though…" he scratches his chin and watches her from across the restaurant, "she does kind of look like someone I know."

"Yeah? And who's that?"

He chuckles. "Someone you will hopefully never meet."

Ouch.

"That's kind of harsh." I guess it answers the question about where this is going, too.

He waves a hand at me. "I don't mean it like that. He's just about the most terrifying person on the planet."

I laugh and grab my coffee. "I find that hard to believe after everything I've been through."

His eyes soften a little. "You've seen a lot. But he's seen even more. And he's about as deadly as they come."

That shuts me up.

Why is Preacher hanging out with friends who are "deadly?"

It doesn't seem like the type of people a computer nerd would befriend. Yet, it's not my place to ask. He will tell me if he can and if he wants to, which he obviously doesn't.

I bite my tongue to keep the words from falling out anyway. It's a constant struggle to know what to ask Preacher. He shuts down faster than a hooker who doesn't get paid.

Another waitress approaches our table with two over-flowing plates. "Hi, I'm Caitlin. I switched sections with Nicki, so I'll be taking care of you for the rest of the day. Anything else I can get for you?"

Preacher grins at me and shakes his head. "No. We're good."

The waitress disappears, and he leans across the table toward me. "It seems Nicki didn't want to wait on us anymore."

I burst out laughing. "Probably a good thing. She was going to get a shitty tip from me."

"Me too." He winks and digs into his food.

I take my first bite and watch the man sitting across from me.

I'm missing some truly important information about him, and it won't stop eating away at my brain. Computer nerd, pseudo-security worker whose friends are deadly. I'm not quite sure what to make of any of that. And he does not seem inclined to offer me any other information. Maybe over time I can get it out of him, but I don't know how much time we'll have.

My plan for the future is still non-existent.

I can't hold onto the promises he made this morning to protect me. It's not his job, his place, or his business. And I still haven't decided if I'm staying here or not.

It's close to Milwaukee. Far too close to that city and the man who destroyed me. If he ever found out where I was…

I shudder and try to dispel the cold dread climbing up my spine.

A large warm hand settles over mine on the table. I glance up at Preacher.

He squeezes gently, and the tiniest smile touches his lips. "You good?"

I nod, even though it isn't true. This man is making it even harder to figure out my future and where I want to be. After what happened with Axle, making decisions based upon a man, deciding anything for anyone but myself, just seems fucking stupid. And I've done more than enough stupid in my life already.

Staying should only be about wanting to be *here*, not because someone else happens to live in the same place. And I can't make that decision yet. Not when I just lost Jimmy. Not when I would be here totally alone. In this small town so close to a big one that holds someone so volatile and dangerous to me.

If Preacher and I did get together and things ever ended between us, what would I do? Where would I go? Back to Milwaukee, where Axle can so easily get to me? Back to Minneapolis, where I have nothing and no one anymore?

There are just no options that sound good right now.

I need time to think about it, to weigh the pros and cons. I might need somewhere completely new. Miami. Hawaii. Somewhere warm and tropical, where I could reinvent myself and leave behind all the old memories.

"What's going on in that head of yours?" Preacher raises one of his dark eyebrows at me and takes a sip of his coffee.

"What do you mean?" I take a bite of my potatoes and chew.

"You were completely lost just now, staring off into space while you eat."

"Was I?"

I've never been particularly good at lying or playing dumb, and it doesn't seem like he's buying any of this.

"I hope you're not still thinking about that dickbag."

I chuckle and bob my head. He really is a dickbag. "Not really. Well, I was, but not the way you're thinking."

"Then, how?"

How do I say this without sounding lovestruck and sending Preacher running away from me?

The words swim around in my head until they finally settle. "I was just thinking about how different you are from him."

He ponders my words for a minute. "That's a good thing, isn't it? I mean, considering everything."

I turn his question over in my head. "It is, but…"

He sets his silverware down and leans toward me. "But what?"

Here goes nothing. I'll never be able to move forward with my life if I don't know where I'm currently standing. Too many unknowns make me uneasy, and nothing seems certain anymore. "But you're clearly hiding things from me."

He freezes and bobs his head slowly. "I am. But it's not because I don't want to tell you. It's because I can't."

"Why not?"

His eyes dart to the tables around us, and he shifts forward even more, resting his elbows on the table. "For your own safety."

My hand trembles as I set my fork down. "Safety from what?"

His soft eyes harden, and he looks more serious than I've ever seen him. "Trust me, you don't want to know."

"How can you say that?"

Of course, I want to know who he is and what he's involved with. Everything I revealed about my experience with Axle should have told him how important it is for us to be one hundred percent genuine and open about our lives. I had more than an inkling of what was happening at the Devil Brothers' clubhouse, but the things Axle hid from me changed my life in a way that can never be repaired.

I can't go through that again.

Preacher sighs and shifts back. "Because I've seen what happens to people when they get tied up in it. It doesn't end well for a whole lot of them."

"Are you trying to scare me?" The words "doesn't end well" aren't exactly comforting, but it also feels like a deliberate attempt to push me away when that's not what he wants.

He considers me for a moment. "Is it working?"

Yes. No. Kind of.

"No."

He clasps his hands together on the table. "I'm just trying to help you understand why I can't necessarily be as open and honest with you as I might like."

I bite my lip and wring my hands together. He seems sincere. As sincere as anyone I've ever met. But so did Axle, in the beginning. He groomed me. He prepared me to fall in love with him so I'd be ready and willing to do whatever he wanted. So I'd be too afraid to run.

And it worked like a charm. I fell hook, line, and sinker. I won't do that again. I won't go blindly into this thing with Preacher, whatever it might be.

"You know you can't keep me in the dark forever, Preacher. Not if this is ever going to be a thing."

He nods and leans back in his chair, tucking his hands behind his head. "I know."

And something tells me that's precisely the problem.

FIFTEEN

Preacher

I never understood how Cutter could kill so easily, without feeling or hesitation. Not until Everly told me what that bastard and his friends did to her. And now, I can't stop picturing my hands wrapped around his neck, choking the goddamn life out of him.

A bullet would be too quick, too easy of a way out for motherfuckers like that. I want to watch him die. Watch him suffer. The way he made her suffer. I want him to know his death is coming and drag it out as long as I possibly can.

It's not very Christian of me, but neither are a lot of things I've done lately, especially since I've taken up with this band of assholes. Yet, even the guilt can't suppress the desire to vanquish him from Earth.

I shove the door to the warehouse open and storm in. Grace and Warwick look up from whatever they're doing at the table. Probably picking out more baby furniture.

Warwick shoves to his feet. "What's wrong?"

I wave him off. I can't talk about it right now. The feelings warring inside me are too volatile, too intense. Too...unstable.

It took every fucking ounce of restraint I possess not to go off in front of Everly. I wanted to destroy everything in sight. I wanted to rage and smash things since that fucker wasn't within reach. But that wouldn't have served any purpose, and it would have scared the fuck out of Everly. That girl has been through literal torture, and at the hands of a man who was supposed to love her and take care of her. My uncontained wrath would have only terrified her and possibly shown her I'm no better than he was.

That couldn't be further from the truth. I may not be squeaky clean, but one thing I would never…no *could* never do is lay a hand on a woman. And anyone who would doesn't deserve to breathe the same air as someone as sweet and perfect as that girl.

"Something we need to worry about?" Grace's concern freezes me mid-stride.

She's already having issues with the pregnancy. I don't need to be freaking her out now.

I force a smile onto my face while my hands clench at my sides. "No. Nothing like that. A personal issue."

Warwick crosses his arms over his chest. "Since when do you have personal issues?"

Normally, I'd call him a prick for a smartass comment like that—even if it is true. But not today. Not now. Not after that confession. Not when I've been on the verge of a total melt-down for hours and hours.

"Like I said, you don't need to worry about it." I glance over at Grace; she doesn't need to hear the horror of what was done to Everly. "Give me a little time…"

For now, I'm going find out everything there is to know about the sick fucker, and then, he's going to the top of my shit list. I'll make what Valentina did to Arturo look like fucking child's play.

This guy is now my number one priority.

Everything else gets pushed out into the periphery.

Warwick and Grace let me retreat without further questions, and I stomp into my office and plop down onto my chair.

My hands shake as I fire up my databases.

He's a member of the Devil Brothers. He should be easy enough to find.

Those guys all have rap sheets, or they're at least mentioned as associates on someone else's. Hacking the NCIC to access their reports is practically child's play. Their web security is a fucking joke. Back at the CIA, I warned them the vast majority of the nation's systems were vulnerable to even some moderately talented hackers, but those warnings went unheeded. At the time, I was annoyed. Now, I use it to my advantage and for the advantage of the customers who pay me for my skills.

Sorry, Uncle Sam. Better luck next time.

The keys click under my flying fingers, and the information scrolls across my screen.

Darren Rowlands. a.k.a. Axle.

A.k.a. a fucking dead man.

Now that I have his real name, date of birth, and Social Security number, it's time to do some serious digging.

Two prior felony possession with intent to deliver cocaine —plead down to misdemeanor possessions.

Asshole probably had a good lawyer.

Three prior aggravated battery convictions.

This douche wasn't just doing it to Everly.

He's done it to other women before.

And maybe worse.

If this guy is capable of assault and rape, he's capable of murder, too. He's managed to avoid any real prison time other than a short stint for one of the batteries. He thinks he can get away with it. That he's untouchable because of his connections.

No matter. The fucker will get what's coming to him outside of the prison walls.

The DMV database provides exactly what I need to track him down easily. He rides a 2019 Harley Street Glide special with a license plate of AXMAN1 and owns a Dodge Ram HD 2500 truck, license plate AXMAN2, both registered to the address of the clubhouse. That must be his primary residence, which makes sense, given what Everly told me.

Only a douche has license plates like that.

Even if I didn't know what he did to Everly, that alone would have told me all I needed to know about what kind of guy he is.

Time to do a little recon on the building itself.

Dozens of search warrants have been served on the clubhouse in the last decade alone. The building itself sits on an acre near the Milwaukee River. Industrial area. A few residences half a block down, but otherwise, it's desolate. Which means no onlookers. People know better than to get too close to the clubhouse.

That should make getting in and getting to this guy easier.

Every second that motherfucker breathes air is one second too long. One second Everly has to live in fear and I have to simmer in this red-hot anger.

The door opens, and Warwick enters with Cutter, E, and Rion hot on his heels.

Fuck. What do they want?

E takes up his usual spot against the wall. Cutter settles next to him, and Rion and Warwick examine the screen from over my shoulder.

War places his hand on my desk and leans in. "The Devil Brothers? What the fuck are you doing?"

Shit.

The last thing we need right now is another complication. Another conflict that isn't ours but that invites us to do things that could get us tossed in fucking prison or worse. All because I want revenge for something done to a woman who isn't even mine.

I scrub my hands over my face and take a steadying breath so I don't go off on the guys when my anger is directed at the one whose information is scattered across my screens. "I just found out that Everly was beaten and gang-raped by members of the club."

"What?" Rion's hand tightens on the back of my chair until his knuckles whiten.

Cutter pushes away from the wall. "Who the fuck is Everly?" He nudges Rion to the side and leans over to examine the information I have pulled up.

I scratch at my beard. "She's a girl I guess I'm kind of seeing."

Warwick's mouth drops open. "How the fuck did I not know about this?"

I shrug, even though I know why. Because I didn't want anyone to know what was going on with her. Because I knew what they'd all say. Because I knew it was a really fucking bad idea to get involved with anyone with everything going on here.

"She's a tattoo artist and kind of like Jimmy's adopted daughter. He had terminal cancer. She came into town to say goodbye and take care of his business. He died last night."

"Oh, shit." Warwick's hand comes down on my shoulder. "I'm sorry."

He has no reason to be. It's not his fault. None of it is anyone's fault. It's always struck me as strange that we apologize when something tragic happens to someone else, even when it has absolutely nothing to do with us or anything we've done. It's human nature to offer comfort, but it's also human nature to seek relief from guilt that it didn't happen to us.

I saw it every damn day growing up. The way people dealt with death and tragedy. It hasn't changed in thirty years. But I have. I'm more jaded. More realistic. Yet, I still apologized to Everly when she told me the truth. Some things are so ingrained in us, they just never go away.

Shoving Warwick's hand from me, I turn back to the screens so I don't have to look any of them in the eyes while I talk about this. "Anyway, I went to see her last night, and she revealed a bit of her past. I told her I would protect her. Keep her safe from this asshole. She barely got out of there alive."

"Who is this fucker?" Cutter points to something on the screen. "Is that really his license plate? What a shithead. Even if he didn't beat women, he would still be a douchebag."

Warwick sighs, drops his face into his hand, and leans against the desk. "What do you want to do? The Devil Brothers aren't exactly known for resolving issues with calm, rational conversation."

"I know. And I know we have other things to worry about right now and the other upcoming job for Valentina, but I can't just let this go, guys."

No amount of time is going to quench my thirst for vengeance.

Everly deserves to sleep peacefully at night without worrying about whether this guy is going to show up on her doorstep. She needs the solace of knowing he can never hurt her again, and no decision in her life in the future ever needs to be made based on how far away it will take her from the man who utterly destroyed her.

Cutter reaches out and squeezes my shoulder. An uncharacteristic move for him to show support or emotion. "I get it. If anyone ever did anything like this to Valentina…"

He doesn't finish the sentence.

He doesn't need to.

We all know what would happen to anyone who touched his woman. Cutter may have a lot of faults, but he is loyal through and through. He would annihilate the world if it meant protecting Valentina or avenging a wrong done to her.

The light from my screens reflects off his shades. He leans down again and growls at the screen. "We'll take care of it. I'll put a plan together. We need to be prepared."

We.

This is precisely why I never wanted to tell them. I wanted to do this on my own. Not because I love the violence the way Cutter does and want Axle's blood on my hands, but because I don't want them in any deeper than we've already found ourselves on the wrong side of the wrong people.

The Devil Brothers are no fucking joke. This could open a door we can't close.

But before I can protest, Cutter storms out of the room.

Warwick delivers me a sympathetic pat on the shoulder and pushes off the desk. "I need to go lie to Grace about what we've been doing in here and why you acted like that when you came back. Can't tell her truth."

It hurts him to be dishonest with her. Something I never thought I'd say about him. But for the most part, he balances trying to be honest with her with striving to insulate her from what we do. Give her plausible deniability in case she's ever in a position to have to answer hard questions. But it eats away at him.

It's written all over his face now.

He motions toward the info about Axle. "Let us know when Cutter's ready with a plan and what we need to do. But don't let this distract you from your job."

Like I need him to remind me of my duties.

"I know." I scowl at him. "I'm very aware this cartel situation is still looming over us. The last thing we need here is any more surprises."

Rion rolls his eyes. "No shit."

He's been uncharacteristically quiet. Considering he's the only one who has met Everly or even knew about her, I would have expected him to have a whole lot to say.

Warwick saunters out of the room. E watches me for a minute, his tense shoulders pressed back against the wall. He wants to say something. A lot of somethings, but he bites them back and follows War.

Rion drops down on my bed.

"Comfortable?"

He sprawls out, plants his elbow on my pillow, and rests his head on his hand. "I am, thanks." The humor of the exchange fades quickly. "I'm sorry about what happened."

I sigh and recline in my chair. "Yeah, me, too."

What the hell else am I supposed to say?

That learning what was done to Everly has brought out something that was buried so deeply inside me, I hadn't even known it existed? That I'm finally starting to realize why and how Cutter does what he does so easily? That I'm ready to throw away everything I was raised to believe is true for a girl I know very little about and whom I fucked against the wall of a damn dive bar?

Rion clucks his tongue. "You really like this girl, huh?"

What's the point of lying? Would I be this angry if I didn't care?

"Yeah. I do. But..."

"But what?"

I shove out of my chair and wave my hand back toward the warehouse. "Oh, come on. Look at what we do. I can't drag another innocent into this life. Especially after what she's already been through. Being with me, being involved in this world is just as dangerous if not more so than what happened to her at that club."

"You're right." He nods slowly and pushes himself back to a seated position. "This life isn't for everyone. It's dangerous. It's unpredictable. It's frustrating on the best of days. But we aren't going to be doing this forever, even though it might feel like it right now." He climbs to his feet. "We already have our freedom from the Marconi contract. We can do whatever we want. *You* could stop tomorrow if you really wanted to. If you want to be with this girl, we'll figure out the rest without you. Maybe it's time we start looking at getting real fucking jobs."

I bark out a laugh and shake my head. "What the fuck are you and Cutter going to do for real jobs? What's E going to do with his record? Sure, Warwick can go back to managing the fishing company, but is he really going to want to do that? Can you see any of us sitting behind a desk or working the fishing lines?"

He chuckles and glances back toward the hallway. "Not really. I'm just saying, man, it's not out of the realm of possibility." He takes a step toward me and lowers his voice, even though there's absolutely no one to hear us. "But until you make that decision, we need you to be here one hundred percent. I know you. You're going to be thinking about this girl and about what happened to her nonstop until we're able to do something about it, but you can't let that distract you from what is going on, what we need protection from."

Unease burns in my gut. "I know. I got this."

He raises an eyebrow. "You sure?"

I steel my expression and straighten my spine. "Absolutely fucking positive."

Rion's eyes narrow on me in question, but he just smirks and smacks me on the shoulder before disappearing out into the hallway.

My phone buzzes on my desk with an incoming message. I drop back onto my chair and grab it.

Everly.

I just got done planning Jimmy's cremation at the funeral home. Can I see you tonight?

Funeral home.

She should have told me she was doing that. I would have helped. That's not something she should have done by herself. She's probably a mess right now and doesn't want to be alone in Jimmy's house.

I drop my head back and groan.

Shit.

This may not go over very well, but it's not like I can keep her away forever if we're going to keep doing this. And I need to be here to monitor things with our hacker friend.

Sure. I'll pick you up in an hour.

It was a total lie when I said I have this handled. *Nope. Definitely not.*

SIXTEEN

Everly

W hat the hell would I have done if Preacher had said I couldn't see him tonight?

After spending time at the funeral home making arrangements for Jimmy, I just couldn't bear to be alone in his house. Everywhere I looked, I saw him. I felt him in all his things. Smelled him on his clothes and furniture. It was just too much. The overwhelming anguish was consuming me and dragging me into a dark place where bad things seem to live in my head.

I didn't even have to ask Preacher if I could come to his place. He seemed to understand what I needed. Though, he's been quiet the whole ride since he picked me up.

Trees surround us on both sides of the bumpy, gravel road. We're way out of town, in the middle of nowhere, and that's saying a lot considering the town itself isn't exactly a metropolis. The forest finally opens up, and a massive building looms in front of us.

Where the hell are we?

I lean forward and glance up at the monstrosity through the windshield. "What is this place? This is where you live?"

No way.

He gives me a slow smile. "I told you my situation was...complicated."

"Yeah, I just didn't expect you to live in...what is this, a warehouse?"

He shrugs, pulls his truck up outside, and turns off the ignition. "Sort of. You'll understand in a minute."

Understand?

There's not much at all I understand about Preacher. And this place is...odd, to say the least. I scan the woods around the building. The only thing I can tell is we're close to the water.

Really close.

Slivers of moonlight reflect off the water through the trees to our right.

He slides out of the truck and comes around to open my door.

Always the gentleman. Except for when he's fucking you against a brick wall, Everly.

True. But I like that he perceives when to use his gentlemanliness.

Gentlemanliness? Is that a word?

Probably not, but I should make it one. It's the only way to describe him. Despite his size and strength, the man has softness, kindness, and good manners. Someone raised him right.

That makes some of my fear and concern about him ease a little. But he hasn't touched me *that* way since that night at the bar. Which is both appreciated considering everything that's happened and also confusing as hell. Now he's bringing me to *his* place. That only convolutes things more.

Is this him just being a good friend? Is this him wanting more?

We never discussed it at the diner. Nothing has been decided or hashed out. It's enough to drive a girl crazy.

I take his proffered hand and slide from the truck. The motion brings me within inches of his hard, tall, lean body. Heat radiates from him, a welcome relief from the crisp, cool night air all around us. I step into him instinctively and press my cheek against his warm chest. He closes the door behind me, and his arms encircle me, drawing me even tighter to him.

He buries his face in my hair and inhales deeply. He doesn't offer the platitudes anyone else would right now. I can't even begin to explain how much I appreciate that.

After everything I told him, with all he knows, an *I'm sorry* from him right now would burn like acid on my shredded heart. The mix of relief from finally telling him and anguish over wondering how Preacher will treat me now battle in my head as I breathe him in. The strong, masculine scent of musky aftershave and total man envelops me and helps calm my fraying nerves.

His arms are where I need to be tonight. Even if it's only like this. Even if he can never see me the way he did before I revealed my torture to him.

He embraces me tightly then pulls back and peers down at me, the moonlight displaying the concern in his eyes. "You okay?"

I gaze up at him and force a smile. "I will be."

He takes my hand and drags me along toward the building. A massive metal door with a high-tech looking keypad stands in front of us.

Seems like a lot of security for a warehouse...

I bite my lip as Preacher punches in a code and pushes open the door. His large, warm palm presses against my lower back, urging me forward in front of him.

Bright overhead fluorescent lights illuminate the vast space. Two boats roll in the water to my right on boat slips, and to my left, an open warehouse with a massive wooden table and chairs in the center and doors along one wall down a hallway. What appears to be an office sits at the top of a set of metal stairs...

"Wow."

He gives me a lopsided grin. "Kind of an impressive space as much as it is a dump, isn't it?"

"Uh-huh." From the outside, the place looked almost dilapidated and abandoned, but inside, it's evident the outward appearance is intentionally hiding a well-maintained location.

But for what?

He ushers me across the concrete floor toward one of the doors. The space seems deserted and empty.

Where is everyone?

When he said he lived with so many people, I had expected far more activity when we arrived.

Talking and laughing floats through the air from one of the doors.

I guess not so empty.

My stomach churns. I'm about to meet the people Preacher has been so worried about keeping me away from. I don't know whether to be nervous for them or me.

Maybe both.

He moves me toward the first door and escorts me inside an industrial kitchen. Rion leans against a central stainless steel counter, while one other guy and a very pregnant redhead stand at the stove, and a third man rests on the edge of the counter across from us.

My eyes roam over them. Lots of tattoos and muscles and hard looks.

Nervous for me. Definitely for me.

The vibe isn't the friendliest in here.

The redhead's eyes flicker over to Preacher in question then back to me. "Oh…hi." She steps away from whatever she's doing on the stove and moves over toward me with her hand extended. "I'm Grace. Warwick's girlfriend."

Warwick?

That was the guy the waitress asked us about yesterday. A million questions pop into my head.

Which one of these tattooed guys is Warwick? What the hell did he do to that girl to make her so pissed off at anyone who might know him? Does Grace know about whatever he did?

I take her proffered hand and shake. "Hi."

It's all I can manage while I scan the faces of the guys. The clean-cut, boy-next-door one in front of the stove who's tending to whatever Grace abandoned flashes me a half-smile while the one sitting on the opposite side of the counter who has ink scrawled over his hands, knuckles, up his neck and across every exposed inch of his arms inclines his head toward me stiffly. Something tells me that one is Warwick.

Rion flashes a grin as Grace releases my hand. "Nice to see you again, Everly."

"You, too."

Grace waves toward the tattooed guy across from me. "That's Warwick, and the one over there doing all the cooking is Elijah, but we just call him E."

I give a little wave. "Nice to meet you guys."

Preacher's hand pushes at my lower back. "I'm gonna give her a quick tour."

Grace smiles. "Are you guys going to eat with us?"

Preacher glances down at me. "Did you eat?"

I nod. "I already ate, but thank you."

It's a lie. I couldn't eat even if I wanted to right now, but I don't want to impose on what seems like a tight group.

Preacher shakes his head. "We're good."

He doesn't want to eat?

Something tells me his lack of hunger may have something to do with what I told him this morning. I hope I'm wrong, but I saw his face, and even though he tried to hide it when we were at lunch, it shook him deeply. He barely ate anything.

My unease doesn't get any better as Preacher guides me away from the kitchen and down the hallway.

He points toward the staircase. "Up there is Grace and

Warwick's room." He waves to a door on the left. "Cutter's room. And from the sounds of it, he's in there with his girlfriend."

I chuckle. Very distinct noises emanate from behind the closed door.

Preacher points further down the hall. "Down there are Elijah's and Rion's rooms, a small gym, and a closet. And this…" he stops at the next door, "is my room."

He turns the knob and pushes open the door.

Whoa. When Preacher said he was a computer nerd, I never imagined…this.

At least a dozen screens of varying sizes line the walls along two sides of the room, and a massive L-shaped desk occupies the corner. Multiple computer towers stand on top of it, and three keyboards sit in a semi-circle in front of a large, leather rolling chair. Large metal cabinets line the remaining half of one wall, and cords run everywhere. It's like something out of an overdone Hollywood hacker movie. A chaotic jumble of equipment I can't even recognize mixed into it.

Other than a large bed pushed into one corner and a dresser along one wall, you wouldn't even know someone slept here.

"Wow." I turn back to Preacher. "When you said you were a nerd…"

His dark eyes dance with humor, and a low chuckle rumbles from him as he ushers me farther into the room and shuts the door behind him. "I know. But it's my life."

What kind of life is this?

I turn to face him. "Doesn't it…I don't know, get lonely and stuffy and uncomfortable sitting in a room like this all the time and staring at screens all day?"

He runs a hand through his hair and offers an awkward half-smile. "Probably not as much as it should." He shrugs. "I work mostly with these guys, but some friends I made over the years have hired me to take care of some security issues for them as well. So, I'm here ninety-nine percent of the time. It's just kind of always been my life. Even before I came here."

This is the part I've been dreading since I laid eyes on the guys in the kitchen. All the vague statements Preacher has made about his life and the dangers of it swirl through my head, and they come together to one conclusion.

"Would I be correct in assuming that what you guys do here isn't exactly legal?"

He grins at me and steps toward me slowly to take my hands in his. "You could be correct in saying that."

I turn to reexamine his set-up. He's not a computer nerd. He's a hacker. "I see."

And I'm falling right back into the same pattern, just a slightly different version of it. I knew what Axle was neck-deep in when I got involved with him, but I thought I saw something more. Something beneath the front he put up around the guys. I couldn't have been more wrong about him

Now…I know what Preacher is and what he does.

He isn't working in Silicon Valley or for the government doing some sort of high-tech research. He's hacking databases and stealing information and whatever else he can with his skills. And those guys out there are into some shady-ass shit. They may not ride motorcycles, but these guys are just another version of the Devil Brothers.

He sighs and drops my hands to rub his jaw. "I've been trying to figure out how much to tell you before you discover it on your own. It's probably better if you just knew the whole story up front."

Apprehension crawls up my spine and tightens the back of my neck. "Okay."

This is what I've wanted.

I've been asking and waiting for Preacher to open up to me, but now that I have an inkling of where this story might be going, I suddenly want to slam the door on it and pretend I never asked.

He leads me over to the bed and motions for me to sit. I drop down onto the soft mattress and wait while he paces in front of me. The slight limp I've noticed during our time together seems more pronounced here in this small space. Maybe it's part of his story.

I never thought this would be hard for him. His reluctance, I assumed, was always about not wanting me to be privy to the illegal shit he's doing, but this seems like so much more. Like something deeply personal that he's afraid to delve into. Considering what I confessed this morning, I can sympathize with the tension in his shoulders.

He shakes his head. "I'm sorry. It's just that like what you told me about what happened…this is very hard to talk about."

"Okay."

What else do I say?

All I can do is give him the space and time he needs to get it out. I know all too well how painful it can be to relive certain things through words.

"I told you the other night, I grew up in Ohio. Outside Cleveland. I have two older sisters and a younger brother. My parents were…well, still are…strict Catholics. In fact, my dad is a deacon."

"What's a deacon?"

I've never set foot in a church, so the hierarchy and terms go right over my head.

He chuckles. "It's kind of like a junior priest in a lot of ways. They help the priest with certain tasks in the parish, only they're allowed to marry and have children. It's for people who want to commit their lives to the church but also want to have families."

"Wow. Well, that certainly explains a lot."

Like why he's covered with religious tattoos and seems to have a spiritual calm I can only hope to achieve at some point in my life. It explains his good manners and caring nature. The feeling like he truly values people…including me.

"We grew up in the church and went to Catholic school. My brother and I were altar boys and assisted the priest and my father at Sunday masses. I even helped teach Sunday school and Bible study and CCD classes."

The whole organized religion thing was never on my radar. Mom and Jimmy weren't religious by any definition of the word. The idea of being so entrenched so deeply in it like he was is almost as foreign as believing people are exactly who they appear on the surface.

"So…you're a true believer, huh?"

He leans back against his desk. "I believe in God, and I believe in the power of prayer. Though, I definitely have a complicated relationship with Him. Whether I still believe in an organized religion like the Catholic Church is another question."

My eyes skim over the exposed ink on his hands, arms, and neck. "That's a lot of religious tattoos for somebody who's not sure."

He runs his fingers over the ink on his knuckles. "I'm sure enough about the ones that are on me for life."

"And the nickname Preacher?"

"Given my upbringing, I was always the one to say team prayer before a basketball game in middle and high school, and it just kind of stuck."

"You played basketball?"

He chuckles and nods. "Yeah. Why do you seem so surprised by that?"

I point to the array of equipment next to him. "Because nerds aren't usually the most athletic people on the planet."

"Wow." He feigns offense. "Stereotype much?"

I laugh and flash him a grin. "Sorry."

"No, you're not." He beams back at me. "I studied computer science at MIT and got into a little trouble hacking into somewhere I shouldn't have. But instead of throwing me in prison for treason and any number of federal crimes, like they could have, they decided the best plan was to try to use me to their benefit. They sent me to The Farm, and eventually, I joined a special unit of the CIA."

Holy shit.

Everything I thought I had figured out about James "Preacher" Davis just flew away on the wings of three little letters.

"The CIA? Are we talking the Culinary Institute of America or…"

One corner of his mouth quirks up. "The Central Intelligence Agency."

And now he lives in a warehouse and does underhanded things for criminals.

How the hell did that happen?

He waves a hand back toward the door. "You're probably wondering how I went from working for the government to hacking them."

I bob my head but keep my questions to myself. While Preacher doesn't seem to offend easily, the things running through my head could definitely be taken the wrong way.

"My unit helped track terrorist groups and gather intel about them and from locations raided by special forces units. You would think I might be stuck behind a desk my entire career, but I was actually sent overseas several times on joint task force missions."

It's hard to imagine Preacher anywhere but where we are right now. Hard to picture him somewhere bullets flew at him. He's so sweet and caring. A war zone is a direct juxtaposition to everything I know about him…or everything I thought I knew, at least.

"The last time, I was in Iraq with the Rangers and Delta Force." He stares down at his feet and swallows thickly.

Whatever he's about to tell me is serious. His playful demeanor has shut down completely.

"It was an ambush."

Oh, God…

My chest tightens.

"RPGs."

Oh, God…

Tears burn my eyes.

"Only a handful of us survived…including Cutter and Rion."

I try to swallow through the emotion clogging my throat, but I only manage to make a disgruntled animal gasping sound. "Oh, my God. Preacher…"

He glances up at me. "I met them both over there. When you almost die with someone, when you bleed with someone like that, you form a bond that's hard to break. Cutter knew Warwick from way back. That's how Rion and I got roped into this." He spreads his arms wide.

This.

I still don't understand what *this* is really. And I want to ask a thousand questions about what happened in Iraq, but having been in Preacher's position only hours ago, telling a painful story, I understand there are things he won't want to discuss. There are things I held back from him. Some of the things that were done to me. Things I'll never tell another soul on this planet.

So…I won't push him to tell me anything he doesn't want to.

Never.

Preacher's soft, dark eyes plead with me. "I know what this looks like, and I'm not going to lie to you and tell you that we don't do some things that are really unpleasant at times, but what I will tell you is that we are not the bad guys. Not the way the Devil Brothers are."

It's like he can read my mind and already see the road it was going down.

"We might have some illegal connections. We might do some nasty shit that puts us in some very unpleasant places, but we aren't the type who hurt innocent people."

The tears that have been threatening since he started his story spill over down my cheeks. "I want to believe you, but I just don't understand why someone like you does something like this. I don't really know what to say."

"Am I scaring you?" His question is soft and sincere.

I need a second to consider that.

My first reaction is to say no because I feel safe with him, but after meeting those guys and after seeing this, I'm starting to get a clearer picture of what's going on. And it's the same kind of shit I turned a blind eye to when I got involved with Axle. Stuff that should have warned me to walk away from the start.

But I still need to hear it from him. So, I avoid his question and ask my own. "What is it exactly that you guys do?"

His lips press into a firm line. "Don't laugh."

"What? Why would I laugh?"

He grins. "Because it always sounds funny saying it out loud."

"Saying what out loud?"

He pauses for a moment, almost like he's waiting for the perfect moment to drop a punch line. "We're pirates."

A laugh bubbles from my lips as images of Johnny Depp and Captain Hook flit through my head. "You're joking, right?"

He shakes his head. "No. And that's all I'm going to tell you. It's better if you don't know any of the specifics."

"Wow. Pirates, huh?"

Preacher tries to contain his amusement, but it just comes out as a lopsided half-smile. "Yeah, and if that didn't make you laugh, there's more."

"What do you mean?"

"There's a reason I retired after the attack and never went back to the CIA."

"Oh, yeah, why is that?"

"I medically retired."

Medically?

"What do you mean? For what?"

I can't imagine Preacher wanting to slow down for any reason or quitting unless it was absolutely necessary.

He shoves away from the desk and reaches for his belt buckle.

SEVENTEEN

Preacher

"Whoa!" Her hand flies up in a stop motion, and her eyes widen. "What are you doing?"

"It's not what you think."

I'm not trying to bone her. Her reaction would be funny if what I'm about to reveal to her wasn't so fucking painful to talk about, let alone show someone.

She eyes me with apprehension but drops her hand. I slowly lower my zipper and shove down my pants to mid-thigh.

I never anticipated it being this difficult. With everything that's happened and all the people who have seen my injury since I left Iraq—all the doctors and surgeons and nurses and physical therapists—I didn't think it was possible for me to be shy or concerned about someone viewing it.

But this…is different.

This is Everly.

I inch my pants down slowly. At this point, all she can see are the very tops of the scars snaking up my thigh. The worst is yet to come, and I've been dreading this moment since I met her. The inevitable look of sympathy. The feeling sorry for me bullshit.

I've never asked for any of that. I've never asked for anyone to treat me differently because of this, but I haven't *been* with anyone since it happened, either.

Fucking her the other day made me feel like I was no different than before the attack, but this will be the real test. This is full exposure. I owe it to her, though, especially after she opened herself up to me and told me the horrible truth about what happened to her. It makes what I suffered seem like nothing.

Her eyes focus on the scars, and her mouth drops open. "Oh, my God…"

She trails off, and I squeeze my eyes shut and let my pants fall the rest of the way to the floor, exposing the true extent of my injury.

Nothing.

No words. No sounds. Silence.

I slowly open my eyes. Everly's gaze is focused on the prosthetic that starts at the middle of my right thigh. Her mouth opens and closes several times, and she shakes her head.

She's speechless.

Kind of what I was expecting. I'd always wondered how this would happen. How I would reveal this to a girl I was dating. Perhaps dropping trou wasn't the best way to ease her into it, but I wasn't sure how to explain.

Her eyes shoot up to meet mine. "I'm sorry. I just don't know what to say. How did that happen?"

There's another unspoken question there, too. *How the hell didn't I notice that?*

I may have been kind of sneaky and deliberately prevented her from being in a position where she could figure it out. It wasn't the adult way to handle the situation, but I've never had to explain to anyone before. These guys all know, and they're pretty much the only people I've spent any major time with since the attack.

"The RPG attack. They shot several of them at our

caravan and took out a bunch of vehicles, including one I was in. It flipped and burned. A large portion of the chassis landed on top of my leg. Rion and Cutter and two other guys who survived tried to lift it off me, but they couldn't get it."

My hands start to tremble, and I tighten them into fists to keep Everly from seeing it.

The heat of the flames still licks at my skin.

Heavy metal crushes my leg.

Gunfire pops all around me.

The scorching afternoon sun beats down.

Blood trickles into my eyes.

Screams.

Agony.

I grip the back of my chair to steady myself, or I might end up face-first on the concrete floor. Even with my eyes shut, I can feel her gaze on me.

Watching.

Waiting.

Assessing.

Unraveling me.

"The remains of the truck were on fire. It was getting close to the fuel tank. Rion had to amputate my leg right there to save my life." And someone else gave so much more. I breathe deep and slow for a moment, then meet her eyes. "You haven't met Cutter yet, but he got even worse than I did. The flames burned him badly while he worked to save me. But he didn't stop. Not until I was out."

He saved my life and paid the price for it.

"Jesus." A tear slowly moves down her cheek. She wipes it away, but another just takes its place. "I don't know what to say."

"Don't say you're sorry. This has nothing to do with you, and you have nothing to apologize for."

Christ, she said almost the exact same words to me earlier.

I'd rather she didn't say anything, though. I don't want to

hear about her pity for me. I don't want her to ask me for more details. I want to pretend we're back to how things were that night behind the bar before either of us ripped open our wounds to show the other. Before I showed her who and what I am. Because now that she knows it all…it's the first step toward it being over.

I saw it in her eyes. The way she shut down once she realized what we do here. And I can't blame her for that. Not after what she went through. I can't expect her to just pretend we're not doing what we're doing.

But now, she knows everything.

And I have to wait. Wait for her to do or say something. Wait for any sort of reaction. Wait for her to make a damn decision.

She swallows thickly. "I'm glad you showed me. I can't believe I'm going to spend the night with a pirate."

"Why Everly Webster, are you suggesting you're going to have sex with me tonight?"

She bends her head down and bats her eyelashes, peeking up at me coyly.

I laugh, jerk my pants back up, and sit on the bed next to her. "Innocent doesn't really work for you. The ink gives you away."

She smiles and cups my face in her hand. "It's not the fact that I let you fuck me behind a bar?"

I press my lips against hers gently, then tug her hair to draw her head back and into a better position. "Nah." I gently brush my fingers over the small tattoo above her right eyebrow. "Definitely the ink."

Which is beautiful. True art covering her alabaster skin. It's like staring at a fine art gallery. And I want to spend an eternity exploring every inch of it.

With my eyes.

My hands.

My tongue…

She leans into me and drops her forehead against mine. "What are we doing, Preacher?"

I've asked myself that question dozens of times since I met her, and I still don't have the answer.

What I want and what is wise are two different things, and given everything…Everly has every right to feel the same way.

Her warm breath flutters against my lips just before she presses hers to them in a searing kiss. I didn't answer her question, but it seems she made the decision for both of us.

At least, for tonight.

I groan into her mouth and drag her up onto my lap. She straddles me and wraps her arms around my neck, deepening the kiss and grinding down against my growing cock.

The last time we were together, it was rushed. Rough. Harsh. It was everything I didn't want it to be.

That wasn't me. That wasn't how I wanted to be with Everly.

She deserves so much more. So this…now…it's going to be something else. Something different. It's going to be a slow, sensual exploration of each other.

I want to learn her, know her…

Fuck.

I want to make love to her.

That realization tightens a vise around my heart. Because there's no predicting where this is going to lead or if I'll ever be with her like this again.

I roll her onto her back, and her legs open for me. She moans into my mouth and sucks my tongue into hers, rolling her hips up against me. I settle between her thighs and angle in to press my cock against her core in just the right place.

"Preacher! Yes!"

The soft, warm skin on her neck practically melts under my lips as I work my way down it and then over the flow of the top of her exposed breasts. The thin straps holding up the red number she's wearing might as well be nonexistent. I brush my fingers across her shoulders, sliding the straps down and freeing her nipples from the confines of her dress.

They pebble in the cool air of my room, and I take one between my fingers and roll it. She groans and arches up off the bed, pressing herself against me and making it almost impossible to keep my hips from thrusting forward to grind my cock against her wet heat.

Fucking A.

It's like being a teenager fooling around again. Only I'm not going to be satisfied with dry-humping her tonight. Not after experiencing what's it like to be inside her. To experience her coming apart in my arms and shuddering around me.

But there's no rush tonight, and I plan on taking my time to truly experience all that is Everly.

I draw one of her nipples into my mouth and flick my tongue over it. She gasps and digs her nails into my shoulders. The small bite of pain is more than welcome.

It makes me feel alive. It reminds me this is real. That I'm *really* here with her. And I've been dying to do something since the moment I saw her in that shop.

As much as I want to spend the time learning every inch of her body and memorizing every line of ink, I want something even more.

I need to taste her.

I sit back and urge her hips up. She complies and pushes her dress down her stomach, over her thighs, and down her long legs.

My breath catches in my throat. "Holy fuck. You didn't wear any underwear."

She kicks her dress off onto the floor and spreads her legs for me. Arousal glistens between her thighs. "I guess I was expecting to have sex tonight."

I smile and drop down between her legs. "Good."

Because if she decided to walk away right now, I think the

pain would be worse than anything that happened to me in Iraq.

And not just the blue balls. My heart thunders so hard, all I can hear is the rush of blood in my ears. It's like something major is hinging on this. On tonight.

I watch her as I shove down my pants, freeing my aching cock. Her focus drops to my legs, and I bend down and untie my shoes then sit on the bed to remove them and my leg. I glance over my shoulder. Propped up on one elbow, dark hair over her shoulders, her hooded, lust-soaked gaze intent on every move I make, she's a fucking vision.

This exact moment will be etched into my memory for the rest of my life, no matter what happens with Everly.

I drag off my T-shirt and turn back between her spread legs. She reclines onto the mattress and flashes me a sultry grin. Her body is laid out for me like a fucking buffet. I drag just the tip of my finger through her wet folds.

She moans and shudders and fists the comforter in his hands. "Oh, God…"

My finger meets her clit, and her hips fly up. I press my palm down across her hips to hold her in place and drop my face between her quivering thighs.

Her hands find the top of my head, and she pushes down, urging me forward.

Eager. And so am I.

My mouth waters to taste her, but instead, I lightly flick her clit with my fingertip. She bucks and digs her nails into my scalp. I snake my tongue out to taste her. A groan of appreciation vibrates in my throat.

Christ.

"Your pussy has to be the greatest thing I've ever tasted."

She moans and scratches the back of my head. I lick and suck my way across her mound and between her lips. Her hips buck and roll against my face, and I press my hand down to hold her steady.

I'm the one in control, as much as she may not think that is the case. The only thing I want at this moment is to drag out her pleasure and drive her absolutely insane. The same way she did to me the other night.

I slip a finger inside her, and she immediately clenches around it. My cock throbs in response, and I groan against her wet flesh and suck her clit between my lips.

Every muscle in my body tightens, and I slip another finger into her, starting a slow, steady rhythm of thrusts and sucks designed to build her up to a cataclysmic release.

She squirms beneath me, her breasts heaving with every panting breath she takes.

For so long, I wondered if I'd ever be like this with a woman again. And now that Everly is spread out before me, I don't know how I'll ever live without this again. Without *her.*

How the fuck did that happen?

Maybe it was last night…holding her while she fell apart and then slept in my arms. It could have been this morning when she ripped open the wounds Axle left and bared it all to me. Whatever it was that did it, it was like a light switched on and I can finally see what's standing in front of me.

If only the rest of the world's complications didn't stand between us.

But they don't in *this* moment.

Right now, there's only the two of us. No pasts. No futures. Just the buzz of electricity zinging between our bodies and shared looks heavy with lust.

I lock eyes with Everly and withdraw my fingers from her pussy to plunge my tongue inside her. She cries out and shoves my head down, pushing me harder against her.

"More. I need…more…"

I do, too.

I'd love nothing more than to climb up her body and glide into her wet heat, but I need her to come for me first. I need to taste her release on my tongue and experience her thrashing against my face while an orgasm rolls through her.

But I won't drag this out any longer. She needs to come, and I need to witness her falling apart. I slide my fingers back inside her and draw her clit between my teeth. My cock throbs so hard, I might come just from the brush of the comforter against it.

I work Everly up into a frenzy until she's quaking beneath me and hovering just on the edge of oblivion. Then I bite down on her clit and bend my fingers into her G-spot.

Her body stiffens, and then, she explodes.

She bucks and thrashes and tries to back away from the intensity of her orgasm. I hold her down and suck harder, dragging out her pleasure while I move my fingers in time with the clenching of her pussy. My cock aches to be inside her, but the flood of her release into my mouth is the most beautiful thing I've ever experienced.

"Preacher! Please!" She pushes at my head, desperate to break away from my mouth.

I relent, and she collapses onto the bed, panting and trying to catch her breath. A pink flush the color of the sunrise covers her breasts and neck and creeps across her cheeks.

Fuck, she's beautiful.

Her eyes flutter open and meet mine. I crawl over her and lick my lips. She reaches up and threads her fingers into the hair at the nape of my neck, directing me down to press my mouth to hers. The kiss is slow and sweet. Everything we are not.

I tear my mouth from hers and cup her cheek. "Are you okay?"

A grin tilts her lips. "I'm more than okay." She reaches down and grasps my hard cock. "But tasting myself on your lips makes me want this even more."

Christ. That's fucking hot.

I am in so much trouble with this woman. She's too much

for me. Far more than I deserve after everything I've done. Everything I'll have to answer for when I reach the pearly white gates.

She urges me onto my back, and I roll, taking her with me. The weight of her body pressing down on me feels so incredible, I wish we could stay like this forever.

Shit. Did I just think that?

I'm getting a little bit ahead of myself. We barely know each other, but this is where I'm supposed to be.

She climbs up and straddles my hips. Her small hand wraps around my cock, and I watch the tattooed skin on her knuckles as she glides her palm up and down my length. I dig my fingers into her hips, and she rolls them, dragging her pussy along my shaft, coating my flesh in her release.

I close my eyes and grit my teeth. "Christ, Everly."

She giggles, and I open my eyes, not wanting to miss a single second of this. A smug look spreads across the lips that were just plastered against mine, and she shifts up onto her knees and positions the head of my cock against her pussy. Her evergreen eyes lock with mine. She doesn't look away as she lowers herself onto me.

Her nails rake over my shoulders, and when I'm fully seated inside her, she clamps around me and grinds down.

"Oh, sweet *fuck*, Everly." I drop my head back and close my eyes in a desperate attempt to regain control over my body. If I watch her riding me, I might come on the spot.

She rolls her hips and leans back slightly.

"God, yes, just like that."

The slow sensual ride she starts has my balls pulling up tight and ready to release almost immediately. And despite knowing the danger of it, I open my eyes and watch her, head tipped back, mouth slightly parted, gasps of pleasure slipping from her lips as she works me over like she doesn't have a care in the world.

It's incredible. *She's* incredible. After everything she's been through, she can still be like this with me, be completely lost in *me*.

I've never wanted anything so much in my life as to make her happy. To ensure her past disappears in the cloud of fog rolling in off the lake. To guarantee she'll never have to think about or relive those moments ever again because they'll all be replaced by the new ones we've made.

I sit up and drag her mouth down to mine. We wage a war —between right and wrong; love and hate; the past and the future; a war for control over both our lives which seem so completely out of it.

My thumb finds her clit. She mewls and rocks her hips even harder, clamping around me on every downward thrust and grinding against my hand.

Every last ounce of restraint I have disappears, and I arch my hips up to meet her until we're crashing together in a beautiful wave of absolute ecstasy. Her body starts to vibrate. It couldn't come soon enough because I can't hold out much longer.

"God...Preacher." She gasps and then squeezes my cock and falls apart beautifully before my eyes, her hips rolling and jerking, her body accepting mine thrust for thrust, hard and fast through her orgasm until mine breaks.

I come, her pussy milking every last drop from me and completely stealing my heart.

A low groan slips from my lips, and I drop back. She collapses on top of me. Both of us utterly and totally spent.

"God." The word is barely a mumble against the hot skin of my neck. She presses her wet lips there and contracts her cunt around my still-hard cock. "That was..."

"Yup. It certainly was." It's all I can manage to say with my heart racing so hard.

Silence falls over us. I drag my fingers along her spine, and she sighs and snuggles into me even more.

"Oh, shit." Everly giggles and buries her face against my bicep. "Oh, my fucking God."

I push up onto my elbow and roll her onto her back. "What's so funny?"

She covers her mouth with her hand but stares up at me with tears from amusement in her eyes. "I'm sorry…it's just…"

I raise an eyebrow at her. "You know, a woman bursting into laughter after having sex could really bruise a guy's ego."

Her hand comes up to press over my heart, and she flashes a sultry grin. "Not that." She sucks in a breath and manages to contain herself for a moment. "I just realized what you meant earlier when you said if I thought the fact you were a pirate was funny, there was more…" She pushes herself up onto her elbow to fully face me and giggles. "It's the peg leg."

I roll her onto her back, sliding my thigh between her legs. "I was wondering when you were going to catch on to that."

She laughs again and leans up to press a kiss against my lips. "You have a wicked sense of humor, Preacher Davis."

"Is that a compliment?" Because the way she said it could really go either way.

Her tongue snakes out along my lips, urging them to open for her. "Very much so."

EIGHTEEN

Everly

Something jerks me from a deep, amazing sleep. I blink against the harsh light shining from the left side of the room. Preacher stirs next to me and pushes up on his elbow while he runs a hand over his face. He focuses on the lit computer screens.

An alarm blares from the speakers, and red lights flash on one monitor.

"What is that?" I push myself up until I'm sitting and pull the comforter over me.

"Shit." Preacher scrambles to the side of the bed, grabs his prosthetic, attaches it, and walks naked over to the desk to lean over and examine the screen. "Fuck. Fuck. Fuck."

He drops down in the chair, and immediately, his fingers fly across the keyboards.

"Preacher? What's going on?"

Sleep still lingers around the edges of my brain, but literally, alarm bells going off tells me something's going on. Something not good.

He only spares me a passing glance over his shoulder. "Go wake up the guys."

I clutch the comforter more tightly to my naked breasts. "What?"

He can't be serious.

But he just keeps typing. "Go wake up the guys, and get them in here."

It's an order. Short and direct.

"Okay…" Fear coils around my spine and crushes it tightly. I scramble to find my dress in the pile on the floor and slip it on. I peek at his screens long enough to see lines of code zooming past, but it's not anything I can recognize even if I had the time to sit and scrutinize it.

All this is still beyond me. I can turn on the computer, type in Word, use the Internet, but that's about it. This is literally a different language. One Preacher is very fluent in by the looks of it.

He finally glances over at me. "Just go knock on their doors. Tell them I need to see them right away."

"Okay." I duck out the door and into the darkness of the hallway. It's still so unfamiliar…this vast space filled with pirates. God only knows what else is hidden behind these various doors. Men like this must have weapons. They must have all sorts of things I don't want anything to do with. Which is precisely what Preacher warned me about before I knew the truth. Now that I do know…

Goose bumps pebble across my exposed skin, and the chill from the cement floor seeps into my bare feet. The only sound is the slap of them against the floor.

I'll start at the end of the hallway and work my way up.

I jog down to the very end of the hall and knock on the first door.

"Yeah?" The deep voice vibrates behind the door. And it doesn't sound very happy.

"Um. Preacher says he needs to see everyone right now."

I don't wait for a response; I just make my way to the next door. It's slightly ajar. There are so many possibilities.

What the hell is in there?

With my breath held, I nudge it farther open and peek in my head.

A closet.

I was scared of a fucking closet.

"Christ. I'm losing my shit." I shake my head and move to the next door.

This one is closed. I knock lightly. Someone mumbles something incoherent, and a few seconds later, the door opens. Rion rubs his eyes and stares down at me.

I give a lame wave. "Hi. Preacher…" I lose my words. Rion's stark-naked body, covered in nothing but tattoos, stands before me. And he doesn't seem to give a shit that I'm here seeing it. "Shit." I cover my eyes and bite my lip. "Um, Preacher needs to see you. Something bad is happening."

"Shit." Rion closes the door for a second.

By the time I'm to the other end of the hallway outside Cutter's room, E and Rion are already making their way to Preacher's room. I knock on the door where only hours ago, the undeniable sounds of two people fucking had seeped through.

Sure hope they're done now. Or this could get really awkward.

"What?" The growl that comes from the other side of the door is anything but friendly and is barely human.

I swallow and speak to the door. "Emergency. Preacher needs you."

"Who the fuck…?" The door flies open, and another naked man stands before me. Red, pink, and white scars cover his right leg, abdomen, arm, and crawl up his neck and over half his face. A dead white eye stares back at me from one side while a light blue one assesses me from the other. "Who the fuck are you?"

This must be Cutter.

Oh, my God. Is this what happened to him during the attack?

Words suddenly elude me. I open my mouth to speak, but nothing comes out.

His eyes narrow on me, and his knuckles whiten where his hand is tightened around the doorjamb.

"Who are you yelling at?" The accented question comes from a female somewhere in the darkness behind him.

He inclines his head backward. "I don't know who the fuck I'm yelling at, or I wouldn't be asking the question, would I?"

"Um, I'm Everly. Preacher's…" I trail off because I don't know what I am. "He says there's an emergency, and he needs everyone in there."

"Fuck." Cutter reaches back, and the woman who's in there with him hands him clothes. He yanks on a T-shirt and boxers, then holds his hand out again and shoves a pair of aviator sunglasses on before he pushes past me.

Nice to meet you, too.

A gorgeous brunette with striking amber eyes and glowing, softly tanned skin bestows a hesitant smile as she leans against the jamb. "*Ciao.* I'm Valentina." Her accented English is nearly flawless, as is her body from what I can see under the large white T-shirt draped over her. "Have you woken Warwick and Grace yet?"

"No. They are my next stop."

She motions toward the stairs to their room. "Go do that. And ignore Cutter. He has a perpetual stick up his ass."

The wink she gives me helps break through some of the anxiety my encounter with the scarred man had caused.

"Okay." I make my way to the staircase and race up the rough metal steps. They creak under me, the sound ricocheting around the warehouse. I raise my hand to knock on the door, but it's yanked open.

Warwick yanks his shirt down. "I heard Cutter yelling. What's going on?"

"I don't know. Preacher says he needs everybody in there."

He turns back to the room. Over his shoulder, I can just make out Grace sitting up in bed, blinking away her sleep.

"Grace, you and Everly go wait at the table until we figure out what's going on."

She opens her mouth, but Warwick growls at her. "You know why."

The redhead glares at him, her hand resting on her belly, and then half crawls and half falls out of bed to her feet. She sighs. "Well, it looks like your initiation into the club is exciting."

"The club?"

She chuckles softly. "I don't know what else to call it. Come on. Let's go."

Her hand wraps around my upper arm, and I help her down the stairs and over to the table. With a huff, she collapses onto one of the chairs.

I lower myself onto the seat next to her and glance down the hallway toward Preacher's room. "Is this normal?"

Her brows rise. "Is what normal?"

"Blaring alarms in the middle of the night? Secret meetings?" This entire thing seems like it's straight out of some suspense movie. "Who is Valentina, anyway? Why is she in there with them while we're out here?"

It seems a bit odd they'd want to insulate us from whatever is going on but invite her right in.

Grace gives me an amused look. "I guess Preacher hasn't told you everything?"

A flush of embarrassment heats my cheek. "I don't know."

What he said earlier was clearly barely the tip of the iceberg, but he said he was keeping things from me to keep me *safe*.

Who am I to question that?

Warwick's girlfriend offers me a sympathetic look. "What has he told you?"

I consider her for a moment.

What's the proper response to that? Do I let her know what he told me, or was there some secret in there he shouldn't have revealed?

"I don't want to get him in any trouble."

She gives me a knowing look. "He told you something."

I nod and bite my lip. "Um, yeah." I twist my hands on my lap. "He…uh…said he was a pirate."

Her laugh bubbles up her throat and carries through the vast, cavernous warehouse. She massages her hands over her belly. "It's as accurate of a description as there is for these guys."

Soft green eyes examine me for a moment.

I wait for her to say something else. To expand on the comment or explain it better, but she doesn't offer up anything. My gaze drops to her stomach. That baby is coming relatively soon. Which begs the question… "You know what they do…and you're still here?"

Her lips curve up into a tiny smile. "It's a very long story. If we're stuck out here too long tonight, maybe I'll tell you. But I imagine Preacher wants you out here for the same reason Warwick wants me out here."

"Why is that?"

She shrugs like it should be so blatantly obvious. "To keep us in the dark. The less we know, the less of a chance we can be used against them by the police or any of their enemies."

Enemies.

The word conjures so many different images for me. Axle and his friends. Rival pirates on ancient warships battling things out on the high seas.

"They have enemies?"

She shifts in her seat. "How can you not have enemies when you do what they do?"

I don't even know what exactly it *is* they do, but if my assumptions are correct, her statement couldn't be more true.

When I was with Axle, he tried to keep me in the dark, too, about the things the club was into, but I don't think it was to protect me. It was to protect himself and the guys. There are dozens of rival clubs. They were constantly fighting turf wars and getting into each other's businesses. That's why every one of those guys always carried a gun. It's one of the reasons it was so hard to get away from them.

I wrap my arms around myself. The chill of the warehouse seems to be seeping into my exposed skin. Or it might be the knowledge that despite everything we've shared, I still don't know anything about Preacher Davis. And maybe I don't want to know more.

This is precisely the situation I almost lost my life trying to escape, and now, I've walked back into it willingly. Given myself to him again after he told me.

I could have walked away tonight. I could have heard his confession and demanded a ride home and that he never contact me again. He would have honored my request without hesitation. Because he's a gentleman. Which isn't a surprise, given his upbringing.

Why does he have to be such a fucking basket of contradictions?

"Are you cold?" Grace's question breaks through the wall of endless questions haunting me.

"A little."

She holds out her hand. "Help me up."

I jump to my feet and assist her out of her chair.

"Whew. Thanks." She stares down the hall toward Preacher's door. "Fuck it. Let's go." She motions for me to follow her.

"But Warwick said to stay here."

She grins over her shoulder. "I rarely do what Warwick tells me to."

Yikes.

These guys don't seem like the type who appreciate their authority being thwarted. "Doesn't that get you in trouble?"

"Sometimes." She winks. "But, he secretly likes it."

I chuckle. Now *that* I can see. There are men who get off

177

on the back and forth with a strong partner. Maybe I underestimated these guys.

We enter the room to find them all crowded around Preacher.

Grace plants her hands on her hips. "Somebody want to tell us what the fuck is going on?"

Warwick glares at her and growls. "Didn't I tell you two to stay out there?"

Her eyes widen. "Didn't I tell you I don't like being kept in the dark? This seems urgent. Urgent is never good."

Preacher glances over at me before returning his focus to the computer.

Rion turns to us. "Someone hacked into Preacher's system."

"What?" Grace's mouth drops, and she tosses a frantic look between Preacher and Rion. "I thought that was impossible."

The man I was so entangled with only a few hours ago—the one who was so passionate, so caring, so damn giving—snarls like a wild animal over his shoulder. "It was. It is. I mean…" He slams his palm against the desk. "It should be impossible. The guy's been trying to get in for months and hasn't been able to. I don't know how he did it. But I'll have him locked out in another ten seconds."

He slams away at his keyboard for a few moments then drops back in his chair with a heavy sigh. "He's gone."

Warwick drags a hand over his face. "How long was he in the system, and what did he get?"

Preacher frowns. "Long enough to get a lot of shit he shouldn't have."

That isn't good.

Considering what I've been able to piece together. Anything on Preacher's system, a system he thought was airtight, is probably something no one else should see. And anyone trying to get in there is likely up to no good.

"Fuck." Warwick clenches his fists at his sides and bounces his gaze to each of the guys. They seem to share his concern. "Any way to tell what he got?"

Preacher squeezes his eyes shut and pinches the bridge of his nose. "Yeah. I'm going to have to sift through the logs and get this all figured out."

Warwick frowns. "How long will that take?"

"It could be all night."

Shit.

NINETEEN

Preacher

This is a fucking disaster. Of epic proportions. The kind of disaster that could ruin us.

And it's my fault.

I let him in.

He found a hole I didn't think was there. Some minuscule crack somewhere that wasn't even visible. He *found* it and used it to break the whole damn thing wide open. He didn't fall for my trap; instead, he spent his time hammering away until he got what he wanted.

Whoever this guy is, he's better than I could've ever imagined.

I was vain to think my system was foolproof. Instead of spending the last few months hunting this guy, I should've been shoring up my security and retesting it and making sure no one could get in.

Now, I fucked all of us.

And Everly looks like she's about ready to throw up.

Fuck.

I'm such a fucking asshole. We just did *that,* and now I'm sitting here buck fucking naked in my chair with everyone standing around us. I'll need to spend hours trying to figure out what this fucker got from us, and that means completely ignoring the woman who just fucked my brains out even after I told her I'm a two-bit fucking criminal and a cripple.

The words seem so damn inconsequential. "I'm sorry, Everly. But this is gonna take me a while."

Grace loops her arm through Everly's. "Don't worry. I got her."

"You sure?"

Warwick's far better half tosses me an annoyed look. "Of course, I'm sure. We'll go get something to eat. I'm sure E will cook something."

He laughs from the corner, the first anything I've heard from him since he wandered in here half-asleep half an hour ago. "Can I ever deny a pregnant woman?" The words are said with amusement, but the pain in his eyes almost physically hurts.

I give him as much of a smile as I can muster. "Thanks, man. I just need to know what he got. So we know what kind of trouble we're really in."

And how badly I fucking failed.

Warwick leans down to me, close enough no one else can hear him. "I know. Figure it the fuck out."

My hands clench around the armrests on my chair. "I'll get it as fast as I can."

Grace points at Everly. "Also, she's cold."

Of course, she is. If I'd been paying any fucking attention to her, I would have realized it. The warehouse may have a lot of modern amenities and tech, but it's still an old building, and we've almost hit winter.

I really am a dick.

I nod toward my dresser. "Bottom drawer. Sweatshirts."

Everly gives me a tentative smile and walks over to the dresser. She pulls out my old MIT sweatshirt. The thing is about ten sizes too big on her, but seeing her in it fills me with a warm sense of pride I've never possessed before.

Why does it feel so good to see a woman in my sweatshirt like that? There isn't any time to revel in it. I need to get to work.

Warwick waves for the girls to follow him, and Everly steals another look back at me one more time before she disappears out into the hallway. Cutter and Valentina have remained suspiciously quiet about the situation. I glance over at them.

Cutter's shades are firmly in place, but the twist of his lips says everything. He's thinking we're pretty fucked right now. And we might be.

What if they got something that can identify us? Fuck. Fuck. Fuck.

Valentina yanks on Cutter's arm and ushers him out of the room, whispering something to him in Italian.

I need to get this shit figured out. The more time that passes, the longer the hacker has to sort through whatever he managed to steal off my servers.

Time isn't on my side. And I'm the one who exposed *everyone*, so it's not just my ass on the line.

I dive into the code and logs to try to figure out where he was and what information he got away with.

All sense of time vanishes when I'm like this. All that exists is me, the keyboard, and a bunch of ones and zeros. This is my fuck-up, and there's no way to fix it. If he got anything that can identify us, any names, anything personal...

Bile rises in my throat. I swallow it down and prepare myself for hours of mind-numbing work. I could be snuggled in bed with the woman of my dreams, but instead, I'm trying to save our fucking asses.

I really fucked this one up.

I'm going to throw up. The acid churning in my stomach has worked its way up and threatens to end up all over my computers. I've finally managed to work my way through all the files, and it's not good.

Really not good.

"Jesus..." I shove back my chair and push to my feet.

The cool air of the room registers, and I look down. I'm still buck fucking naked.

Shit.

I grab my clothes from the floor and dress before making my way out into the main warehouse. It's probably only psychosomatic, but I swear the scent of Everly still clings to my shirt. I inhale deeply. It might help calm the raging tempest brewing inside.

The crew all looks up from where they sit at the table. Empty dishes scatter the wooden top.

At least they ate.

I slow my approach, trying to delay the inevitable. I have to tell them what I found. The truth of what the hacker got away with. What is making me want to vomit.

Grace and Everly huddle together at one end of the table. It appears they hit it off, which is good because I feel like shit about abandoning her here.

She's a distraction I can't afford right now. The hacker never would have gotten in if I had been paying more attention. But I wasn't. I was concentrating on this woman and what I wanted, not what the crew *needed*. They needed me to be on my game. And I wasn't.

Warwick holds his hands up. "So, what did you find out?"

I drop onto the empty chair next to Everly and do my best not to look panicked. "It isn't good."

"Shit." War's fist slams onto the table. "What did they get?"

I sneak a look at Everly. Her wide eyes hold more

concern than I've ever seen in them. I can't drag her into this anymore then she already is. "Everly, I think you need to head home."

She freezes and watches me for a second. Her bottom lip quivers slightly, but she recovers fast and nods.

This *is* for the best. I don't care if she's offended by the brush-off. She has to understand I'm doing this to protect her. It has nothing to do with not trusting her. It's because I care that I have to send her away.

E shoves his chair back and stands. "I'll take her. You guys can fill me in when I get back."

It's no surprise he's the one who volunteered, but I still have to ask. "You sure?"

He inclines his head toward me and offers a look that tells me he completely understands why I'm doing this. Given his history, it would be shocking if he *didn't* understand and agree with my motives one hundred percent.

"Thank you." I climb to my feet as Everly stands and avoids looking at me. I take her face in my hands and angle it up. The hurt in her eyes stabs a knife into my heart. "I'm sorry about all this."

She wraps her arms around herself and gives a smile that doesn't quite touch her gaze. "I know you are. That's what makes this even harder."

Shit. What the hell does that mean?

There's no time to question her or what's happening between us now. I'll have to figure it out later because there's more danger looming than me just potentially losing this woman.

"I'll call you later, okay?" I brush my thumb over her bottom lip.

She nods, and I lean in and give her a soft kiss.

Uncharacteristically, no one makes any lewd comments. The silence is deafening. Probably because they know this could be the last time I see her face.

185

I'm keenly aware this lifestyle isn't for everyone, and exposing her to it is just about the most selfish thing I've ever done. If she doesn't make the decision to end this…I should.

She pulls out of my arms and walks away with my heart and my favorite sweatshirt.

Fuck. I really fucked this up.

It would be bad enough if this only affected me, but this affects everyone in this room. Even the unborn one.

I turn back to the table. All eyes are on me.

"What did they get?"

That was Warwick's question. And now, I have to tell him, and everyone else, the bad news.

"He got a lot." I spread my palms across the top of the table and stare down at the rough wooden top rather than face the people I've failed so badly. "I stopped him before he could do any more damage, but it's enough that we should be worried, especially you." I point to Valentina.

Cutter's jaw tightens, and a muscle there tics. Valentina's amber eyes darken, and she presses her lips together tightly while her hand continues to scratch Milo's back, where he rests on her lap.

"This is cartel connected. If it was their drugs Arturo took, and their men we killed, they're not just coming for us. They're going to come for you as the new head of the family."

This is something I'm sure everyone has considered since Valentina took over the Marconi empire. Arturo managed to fuck up things and destroy what *Il Padrone* had built. And he pissed off a lot of people. People who won't give a shit that he's gone. Their beef will be with the Marconis, regardless of who sits behind the desk at the estate.

"It's not going to matter that it wasn't your doing, Valentina. These aren't the kind of people who take something like that into consideration."

She scowls, and Cutter clenches his jaw so tightly, I can practically hear his teeth cracking. It's one of the few times I'm glad he's wearing his glasses because I don't think I could meet his eyes knowing how much danger I put his woman in.

Valentina places a hand on Cutter's forearm. It's intended to cool him off. Though, I doubt it will do anything of the sort. "I'll double my guards and my security at all of our asset locations. I'll make sure I'm not ever alone."

Cutter growls and turns toward her. "You think I'm letting you go back to Chicago? I'm not letting you out of my fucking sight. We can defend this place a lot better than you could defend your house. You're not leaving my side until whatever this is gets resolved."

She opens her mouth to argue with him, but he leans over to her and gets in her face.

His lips almost brush hers. "Don't make me remind you of the deal we made, *principessa*. Remember that when you're with me, you're not the one with all the power."

She huffs and crosses her arms over her chest, defiantly. Milo's head pops up, and he glances between Cutter and Valentina before letting it fall back onto his paws. He's unimpressed with them and unshaken by their attitudes.

Those two use their power struggle and bickering like foreplay. They'll be fucking within the next half an hour.

Warwick drums his fingers on the table. "What *exactly* did they get, Preacher?"

My breaths come short and shaky. "All of my research and planning for every raid we've done over the last eighteen months or so. Phone logs that can point them directly to the Marconis as who we were working for."

"Fuck. Can they find us?"

I shrug because I have no fucking idea. Theoretically, no, because all our phone numbers are listed to blind LLCs and connected to off-shore accounts. But I've already been surprised by what this guy can do.

"Shit." War scans around the table. "No one goes

anywhere alone. Until this all gets worked out, no one leaves the warehouse unless absolutely necessary."

Rion and Cutter both nod their agreement. I just stare at the door that Everly just disappeared out of.

Grace chews on her bottom lip. She shouldn't have been here for this, and I'm shocked War didn't order her to their room when Everly left. Maybe he thought this was something she *needed* to know.

Warwick reaches out and pats her arm. "Try not to worry. It's not good for you or the baby."

She takes a deep breath and releases it slowly. "I know. I'm trying not to."

The last thing I wanted to do was cause any more stress for Warwick and Grace. Now, I've not only done that; I've also destroyed any chance I had with Everly.

I push off the table and run a hand through my hair. "There's one good thing that came from this."

Warwick raises a dark eyebrow at me. "Yeah? What's that?"

"I know exactly who hacked the system."

TWENTY

Everly

Normally, the buzzing of the tattoo machine in my hand and pushing ink into someone's skin relaxes me. The constant, repetitive motion. The familiar sound drowning out my own thoughts and the entire world around me. Completely losing myself in my art…

But not today.

Not fucking today.

The one day I *really* need it. Desperately crave it. It fails me.

And it isn't my client's fault.

The guy in my chair has been awesome to work with. He let me have almost free rein of his design, and his skin is taking the color beautifully. This is going to be one majorly badass piece. But even four hours in, I still can't buck the unease over what happened with Preacher even almost two days later.

I can't stop what I learned from running through my head at a million miles a minute, on an endless loop worse than "The Song that Never Ends."

He's a pirate. A goddamn real-life pirate.

If he hadn't told me and I hadn't seen those guys and that

set-up with my own eyes, it would be laughable. But it's very real. Those guys are straight-up criminals. They are the MC of the water.

And therein lies the problem.

After the way Axle destroyed me, I promised myself I would never be with a criminal again. I would never be with anyone where there was any question about the goodness at their core. The logic I've worked up in my head over the last several months has been that anyone willing to commit crimes to make a living could easily do other bad shit, too.

Bad stuff to me.

Yet, I didn't run when Preacher told me the truth. Instead, I slept with him. It didn't send me the opposite direction. I fell into his arms. We made love over and over that night. Almost like we somehow knew it might be our last night together. Which it very well might be.

I can't do it.

Can I?

I can't be with someone like that again. It's just opening myself up for the same kind of heartbreak and pain I've already suffered too much of.

Except Preacher isn't Axle, and those guys aren't the Devil Brothers. They seemed...I don't know...almost friendly, not like angry, violent criminals. Well, except maybe Cutter. That guy is definitely angry. Far more angry than most of the men I've ever met in my life.

But Valentina, whoever she is, seems to feel safe with him, she has to trust him to be romantically involved. Most women wouldn't do that if the guy scared her. And he doesn't scare her. That much was obvious.

She must have balls of steel to deal with him.

The hours I spent waiting with them, waiting for Preacher to come out from his cave, gave me a glimpse into their lives and the rapport that exists in the group. They truly mesh together, even with their obvious differences. And after going through what they have together, I can see why. But it doesn't absolve them of their sins, of what they do day in and day out.

I examine the tattoo on my client's arm. There's only a small section left to color, but I don't even remember doing most of this work. I moved into the zone while my mind wandered around Preacher and the crew.

Endlessly…

I'm overthinking all this. It's all irrelevant anyway since I'll be leaving soon. There are only a few more clients on the calendar. Only a few more sessions forcing me to stay. As soon as I finish packing up Jimmy's house and get it sold, there'll be absolutely nothing keeping me here. And with the money I have from the sale of the house, I could go just about anywhere and do anything I want.

I could disappear and start over without the memories of Axle and what was done to me, or Preacher and what might have been, haunting me. I could live without constantly checking over my shoulder. But I can't leave without saying goodbye to him. I can't end things like this, with nothing decided and no real good-bye.

That's not fair to either of us.

I have to see him again. I have to explain. The thought of disappearing without Preacher ever knowing why, without having the chance to say his peace too, just feels wrong.

It likely won't matter. He'll hear what I have to say, say he understands why I have to go, and he'll walk out the door without a look back at me. It's what men do. But maybe, just *maybe*, for once, someone will choose me.

Other than Jimmy, no man has ever made me a priority. No one ever loved me enough to just *be* with me and offer me somewhere to rest my head.

Could he walk away from that life? His friends?

I try to push the decision I have to make out of my head to finish this piece. The client deserves my full attention right now, and he doesn't have it. The work still turned out amazing, but my heart isn't in it.

It's miles away in a warehouse on Lake Michigan.

"You okay, Everly?"

My eyes connect with those of Tom, the guy on my table. I force a smile. "I'm good. And we're finished."

He glances down at his arm and grins. "It looks great. Jimmy was right when he said you were talented." His lips fall into a frown. "I'm so sorry. When is the funeral?"

I fight the tears. "I'm not having a formal one. He wanted to be cremated and his ashes scattered along Route 66."

Tom shakes his head and laughs. "That's amazing and so Jimmy."

It is.

He didn't want to be buried and become a place where I went to cry and miss him. He wanted to be part of the world he loved forever. It's the perfect tribute to the man who gave up that life for Mom and me.

My eyes sting, and I blink away any tears before they can fall.

Not here. Not in Jimmy's space.

I wipe Tom down and tug off my plastic gloves. That went so fast. I guess when your mind is elsewhere, your body can just work by muscle memory to produce something beautiful.

He hands me a wad of cash and surveys the shop where Jimmy spent the last few years. "I hope you decide to stay around. You do nice work. I'll refer you some clients."

"Thanks. I really appreciate that."

But I've made a decision. One that may end up breaking me.

I have to call Preacher.

The moment the door closes behind Tom, I grab my phone and pull up Preacher's information. My finger hovers over the call button.

Why does this have to be so damn hard?"

I press send and hold my breath.

"Everly?" The deep timbre of his voice vibrates through the phone and straight to my core.

How is it possible I already care so damn much about this man?

The connection between us shouldn't exist after only a few weeks. It builds me up and makes me strong again just as much as it breaks me down and makes me vulnerable. It *shouldn't* be there, but it is all the same. It's a very real, very tangible thing. I can almost touch it. It already lives in my soul.

How can I cut it? How can I let it go?

The emotion of what I need to do chokes my voice. "I need to see you."

He sighs, and I imagine him reclining in his chair in front of his computers, rubbing his hands over his beard like he does when he's stressed. "I can't, Everly, not with everything that's going on. Warwick made us all promise no one would leave. We have to try to sort this thing out. The only way to do that is with me here at the helm."

Ouch.

The rejection stings even though it's not the first time he's done this to me. I massage the ache in my chest. I should've seen it coming given everything that's happened. I should've anticipated he wouldn't be able to leave, that he wouldn't choose *me.* Yet, the thought of not seeing him again, of leaving in the next couple of days without explaining why makes my breath catch. He showed up when I needed him so badly last time.

Maybe he will again.

"Please, Preacher. I…I just want to talk for a little while."

"Shit." He grunts, and something bangs in the background. "Okay. I'll be there in a few hours. Your house or the shop?"

"The shop. I have another client coming in a little bit. But that shouldn't take too long, and I should be done by the time you get here."

"Okay. I'll see you soon." He ends the call without another word.

That might be for the best. I sit and stare at my phone. Tears blur my vision, and I wipe them away and sniffle. Things shouldn't be this hard. And it's only going to get harder in the next few days.

Am I making the right decision?

A stronger person wouldn't care what anyone else thinks about the situation, but I need someone to tell me what I'm doing is right. Someone to agree that it's worth giving up the possibility of finding my forever to protect myself from future harm. That in this case...the risk isn't worth the reward, even when that reward is a guy like Preacher.

It's time to make adult decisions based upon what's *best* for me, not based on reckless emotions. That's gotten me nowhere.

I stare down at my black phone screen. Liz's name appears. The timing couldn't be any better. I need to know she's onboard and she agrees with me. "Liz. I'm so glad you called. I was just about to call you."

A sob comes through the phone, then muffled noises I can't quite make out.

"Liz? What's wrong? Are you okay?"

Another sob and a sniffle send goose bumps shooting over my skin.

"I'm so sorry, Ev."

Icy fear floods my veins. I tighten my fingers around my phone with a shaky hand. "Sorry about what? What happened?"

"I... I...He...I didn't have a choice."

My stomach clenches, and bile rises in my throat. "He who? Liz, what happened?"

So many scenarios race through my head.

Did someone break in? Her ex?

She releases a shaky breath. "He was in my apartment. He was waiting for me when I came home." She gives a little hiccupped sob. "He told me he was sick of playing the fucking games. He told me it was time to bring you home."

Oh, fuck. Axle.

"Axle?"

No. No. No. No.

I push to my feet and squeeze my eyes shut. "Liz, what did he do?"

She sobs again, and every awful thing he ever did to me that he ever encouraged others to do to me slam into the forefront of my brain. Things absolutely no one should have to endure.

"He wasn't alone, Everly. They…"

"Oh, my God. Liz, don't move! I'm going to come get you. Did you call the police?"

"No." The word is sharp and clear. An order. "You need to leave now. He made me tell him where you were. He knocked me out. I don't know how long I was unconscious. He's probably already on his way there."

Oh, God.

I whip around to face the front of the shop and scan the windows. Darkness has fallen. Aside from a few streetlights, there isn't any sign of life outside. The rest of the shops in the strip mall closed hours ago. I'm totally alone here.

"Everly, did you hear me? You need to leave! I'm okay. I'll be okay."

She won't be, though. He'll come back for her if he can't get to me.

"Liz, no." But it's too late. The line is dead.

My knees quake as I climb to my feet. Hopefully, she knows to get the hell out of there before he can return.

He knows where I am.

He's coming here.

He's coming for me...
I need to get out of here. I need to get...
My phone buzzes to life in my hand.
Liz?
I glance down, but the message isn't from Liz.
My worst nightmare stares back at me from the screen.

You look as beautiful as ever, Evermore.

TWENTY-ONE

Preacher

R ion peeks at me from where he sits in the passenger seat
of my truck. "You sure you should be driving?"

"I'm fine." I tighten my hands on the wheel and stare at the road straight ahead.

It's a lie. One I hope he won't call me out on.

"You don't seem fine. You seem pretty fucking upset right now."

I am. And I could do without discussing it with Rion.

After talking to Everly and hearing how distraught she was, I felt like shit having to tell her I couldn't see her. The ability to deny her completely escaped me. Then, I had to fight with Warwick about leaving.

Usually, the testosterone-fueled arguments that happen at the warehouse dissipate quickly, but not this time. He was fucking pissed and was ready to restrain me by force if he had to. I finally told him I didn't give a fuck if he wanted me to go or not and stormed out with Rion hot on my heels. He wasn't going to let me go alone if I *was* leaving. Which is probably a good idea.

The lingering anger over Warwick and this entire fucking

197

situation still has my heart thudding wildly. But Rion's over-reacting.

I can fucking drive.

"We're almost there, anyway." Only a few blocks separate me from Everly. Only moments until I'll be forced to face the repercussions of my choices.

Rion shrugs and stares out the passenger window as we travel down Washington Street. Most of the shops are in the process of closing or have already shut down for the night, but Jimmy always left his place open 'til eight or nine. I can't imagine he had a lot of walk-ins. But tattoo shops tend to stay open later, so I think it was just a force of habit for him.

The lights glare from inside, and Everly's car sits at the end of the otherwise vacant lot. I pull up and park in front.

Rion turns to me. "You want me to come in?"

I shake my head. "No. I need to have this conversation with her alone."

"You sure?"

"Yes. I don't need a fucking babysitter."

He holds his hands up. "I meant more as moral support."

"You would do more harm than good."

"Ouch." He clutches his hands over his heart with a grin. "That hurts, bro."

"I'll leave the car running for you, so you don't suffocate."

He barks out a laugh.

I climb out of the truck and make my way up to the door, scratching at my jaw. I didn't think saying goodbye was going to be this hard, but I'm pretty sure that's what is about to happen. It didn't sound like she was calling to tell me she loved me and wanted to be with me.

Shit. Love? That's impossible.

We've only known each for such a short amount of time. Falling in love doesn't happen like that. Yet Everly bowled me over like a freight train. She decimated everything I thought I knew about myself and what I wanted with her quick smile and humor, with her strength and perseverance. With her damn touch and kiss.

And now…it's over.

I grab the door and tug it open. The bells above it jingle.

Maybe Warwick and Grace and Cutter and Valentina are proof love *can* happen that fast, but I think it's the exception, not the rule. And given what Everly already endured, I can't expect her to choose this life even if she did have those feelings for me.

"Everly?" I scan the shop I've spent so much time in over the years.

It's deserted. She must be in the bathroom or in the back storage area. I make my way around the counter. Her phone lies on the floor next to her station chair.

Something's not right.

Dread sits heavy in my stomach. I grab her cell off the floor and flip it over. The cracked screen raises even more red flags.

Fuck.

"Everly?" I make my way toward the back. The emptiness of the bathroom and storage room matches the feeling in my heart right now.

She's not here. I swipe at the broken screen on her phone.

"Shit." It's password protected.

I storm around the counter to the front door and throw it open.

Rion's eyes meet mine through the passenger window. He reaches over, turns off the truck, and jumps. "What's wrong?"

"She's gone."

"What?" He meets me at the door. "What do you mean she's gone?"

"I found her phone on the floor with a broken screen. Her car is right there." I point to the end of the lot. "But there's no sign of her. She wouldn't leave without her phone."

"Shit." Rion follows me back into the shop.

This isn't my area of expertise. "Look for anything out of place, any sign of what might've happened." I don't need to tell him that, but the feeling of helplessness that's settled over me won't let me stop even for a second.

"No security cameras?" He inspects the shop.

"No, Jimmy never needed them around here."

Which makes sense. There's very little crime here. Everyone knows each other too well, and the vast majority of people carry guns, which helps deter petty criminals from doing stupid stuff.

I return to the other side of the counter, and a flash of red draws my attention to it.

Shit. Shit. Shit.

Her purse rests on one of the shelves of the front counter, a wad of cash visible sticking out of the top. If this had been a robbery, that would be gone. So would her phone.

Rion squats down next to her chair. Her tattoo machine lies on the floor with two different colors of ink spilled across her work station. "Someone took her. It was a struggle."

"Fuck." All the air rushes from my lungs, and the room starts to spin. I grip the counter and grab my phone. There's only one person to call. One person who can accomplish what needs to happen. One person I can trust with helping me get her back.

Cutter answers on the third ring. "What?"

"Somebody took Everly."

"Shit. Are you sure?"

I wish I weren't.

"Yes. There was a struggle. She left her purse and phone, and the screen was broken. The shop was unlocked and wide open, and her car is still outside."

Cutter mumbles something under his breath. "Any idea who it was?"

I search the room as I wrack my brain. Rion wanders

around, checking every corner of the place for anything that might help us pinpoint what happened or who took her.

Axle. That fucking douchebag.

"Her ex. He sent her a text message recently. Maybe he found her."

"Let me know exactly where I need to go."

There's no hesitation. Cutter will destroy anything in his path to get to her. That's not even a question.

But neither is what I have to do. "I'm coming with you."

He growls low into the phone. "That's not a good idea, Preacher. You need to be at the warehouse."

"Don't even start with me, Cutter. If it were Valentina, do you really think you would let me go without you."

"This is different, Preacher. I'm a trained covert operative, and—"

"And I'm a former fucking CIA agent. I've been to The Farm. I know how to handle a weapon. I can take care of myself, and if you so much as fucking mention my leg, I will deck you the next time we're in the same room together."

Cutter is the most lethal and best trained of any of us, but if he thinks he's going to stop me from going after her, he's fucking insane.

Rion watches me from across the shop. I'm sure he agrees with Cutter, that my personal feelings here may get in the way of thinking clearly about what needs to happen, but he's smart enough not to say it. Perhaps because he's right in front of me and within fist distance.

Cutter sighs. "Fine. What do you want to do?"

"Go to the Devil Brothers' clubhouse."

"Fuck."

We only had a chance to sketch out a preliminary avenue of attack on the compound. We hadn't anticipated going in this early. We thought we had time to get everything else figured out and let things calm down with the hacker situation before we went after the bastard who hurt Everly.

If we have to do it now, we have to do it partially blind.

I run a hand over my jaw and examine the evidence of Everly's situation. "I know it's not ideal. But we don't have a choice. Tell Warwick and E what's going on. Bring everything we need. I'll meet you in Milwaukee."

Rion approaches as I end the call and slide my phone and hers into my pocket.

He nods at me. "So, we're going in?"

I bob my head. "We're going in."

Nothing is going to stop me from bringing her home.

———

Cutter parks his SUV behind my truck a few streets over from the Devil Brothers' headquarters. The dark, mostly industrial area gives us a modicum of cover. There shouldn't be anyone around to see us preparing to go in.

Rion and I climb out of my truck and make our way back as Cutter, E, and Warwick move to meet us at the rear of Cutter's SUV. He opens the tailgate and starts handing off all the tools we need to infiltrate the clubhouse.

He passes me a Glock. "Let's go over the plan one more time."

We would've preferred a lot more time to plan this. Our missions are laid out to the last fucking detail. Every crack and crevice of that place and everything about everyone in it would normally be ingrained in the memories of the guys.

But sometimes, fate forces your hand. Sometimes, you have to rush into things a little faster than intended.

This guy fucking pushed me. I cannot...I *will not* let them hurt her again. I would rather die than let that happen.

Cutter turns to face all of us. "Based on my recon, there will be anywhere from ten to fifteen club members in the clubhouse at any time. Not to mention any girl who may be hanging around."

"How are we going to handle bystanders?" The question comes from Warwick, but it's one we all have been wondering about.

If these girls are anything like Everly, they might not be there by choice. "We can't hurt them just because they're there."

Cutter nods. "Agreed. Don't engage anyone who is female or not wearing a cut unless they engage you first or they're armed. We aren't taking any chances." He opens the blueprints for the building I printed earlier when I still thought we'd have time to plan this properly. He lays it across the tailgate. "Two entrances. One at the back. One at the front."

I lean over the blueprint and point to the back door. "Everly told me when Jimmy went in to get her, he used the back door. Apparently, it was damaged and never properly repaired."

We all look to Cutter. He's the one in charge of this op.

He looks at the blueprint. "That might've changed after the Jimmy incident, but I still think it's our best way in."

Rion snorts. "And these guys don't seem too bright. My guess is they're too stupid to shore up their defenses, even though an old man did manage to come in."

That gets a chuckle from everyone, which cuts a little bit of the tension in the air but not mine. I can't find any humor in anything right now. Not when Everly is in the hands of that man.

Cutter leans over to point at the blueprints. "I'll lead. Rion bring up the rear. Preacher and I will take the hallway to the left. Warwick, E, and Rion, you guys take the one to the right. They both circle around back to the main area in the center. We'll meet you there if we haven't found her." He hands all of us the earbud radios. We pop them in then grab the NODS goggles from the case on the tailgate. "I'll cut the power, and then we go."

We all pull on the goggles. The benefits they offer in the

dark night don't only help Cutter. They give us a leg up we'll definitely need.

The walk to the clubhouse is the longest of my life. He's had her for hours. Who knows what he's been doing to her, what *they've* been doing to her…

I shudder as we approach the back of the one-story building. Cutter hustles to the power box and cuts the line to the house. The building was mostly dark, anyway, but a few random lights go out on the exterior.

Cutter readies us at the door. A janky old lock is the only thing that separates us from the interior. And given the marks on the wooden jamb, it's been broken open more than once. Rion passes Cutter a crowbar, and the door easily gives way.

Christ. That was almost too easy.

Rion was right. They are too stupid to fix their weaknesses.

We step inside. The eerie silence of the building settles over me. It's almost three in the morning, so it isn't unexpected, but it leaves me uneasy.

How are we going to find her? Please, God, if you're listening, let her be okay. Give me guidance to locate her and get her out of here safely.

Rion, E, and Warwick split off to the right, and Cutter and I move to the first room on the left. The door stands ajar. We peer inside, the NODS giving us a tremendous advantage in the darkness.

One male sleeping with a naked female draped over him.

Not Everly.

Dammit.

The door to the next room is closed, but Cutter points above the jamb.

Jesus, these assholes have their names above the doors like a fucking college dorm.

It's pathetic as shit, but it may be exactly what we need to find her without unnecessary bloodshed. The way Everly described it, there are some good guys in the club, guys who would never have let what Axle was doing to her continue. I'd hate to see them pulled into this when they had no idea what was going on behind their backs. As for the other fuckers who participated in her torture, I'll have to deal with them another time.

We move down the hallway—one door, two doors, three doors—and turn the corner.

Pay dirt.

The name *Axle* is scratched into the wall above the door in front of us.

Cutter grabs the doorknob, turns it, and we push inside. The creaking door hinge has the guy in the bed bolting upright and shaking his head.

He rubs his eyes and squints into the darkness. "What? Who? What's going on?" His hand reaches for his nightstand.

Not gonna happen.

Cutter puts a bullet straight through his palm. The suppressor on the gun helps muffle the sound of the shot, but in these tight quarters, someone could have heard it. Which means, we don't have a lot of time.

"Fuck!" He clutches his injured hand to his stomach and tries to reach his gun with his other one, but Cutter races forward, grabs him by the throat, and drags him from the bed.

I scan every inch of the room. Fear tears at my stomach.

No sign of Everly.

Where the hell is she?

I shove open the door to the attached bathroom, but there's no sign of her in there, either.

No. No. No.

The crying and blubbering from Axle is bound to wake the rest of the guys eventually.

We don't have much time, but this bastard must have stashed her somewhere else.

Cutter hands him off to me. I return my gun to the holster at my hip and shove him against the wall, my hand tightening on his throat. As much as I want to strangle the life out of him right here, right now, I need to know where she is.

"Where the fuck is Everly?"

His eyes widen, and he grabs at my wrist with his unin-jured hand. I release enough pressure for him to speak.

"What the fuck are you talking about? I don't know where that bitch is."

My fingers curl against his trachea, restricting his airway. "Oh really? Because the text messages you sent her say otherwise."

He gulps against my hand, his body shaking. "Who...the fuck...are you?"

I get into his face, so close, I can smell the fear bursting from him. "I'm the guy who's going to make you pay for what you did to her."

Despite my hand secured around his throat, he chokes out a laugh. "You're a fucking...dead man. The guys are going to wake up and blow you the fuck away."

Shit.

He's not wrong.

I glance at Cutter, where he stands near the door.

He nods at me. "We need to make this quick."

I jerk Axle from the wall and slam him back against it. "I know you took her, so tell me where the fuck she is."

His fingers dig into my wrist again. "Okay. Okay. I drove up to some shit little town in Wisconsin she was supposed to be crashing in. Went to the tattoo shop. She wasn't there."

My heart sinks into my stomach. "What do you mean she wasn't there?"

I release a little of the pressure.

He gasps for breath and shakes his head. "The place looked deserted. I waited for like half an hour. I figured she would come back for something because her phone and purse were there, but she never showed, so I drove to the house where she was supposed to be staying, but she wasn't there either."

Fucking hell.

I release him, and he slumps against the wall.

Axle massages his throat. "We had a party here tonight I needed to make it back for, so I decided I would go back up there for her tomorrow. I sent that message before I left. I was just fucking with her."

"Motherfucker!" I return my hand around his throat and slam him against the wall again. "You fucked with her, and now, I'm going to fuck with you. You think it's fun to beat and rape women?"

He sputters and gags. "She wasn't innocent. She fucking asked for it."

My fist connects with his face, and blood splatters on the wall next to him. "You want to say that again, Axle?"

He coughs, and blood trickles from his mouth. He sneers at me. "I see she's got you wrapped up in that venus fly trap of a pussy. Well, you can have the dirty slut. I don't want her anymore, anyway."

My fist connects again, sending his head back into the wall with a sickening crunch.

Fuck.

As much as I want to believe she's here so I can take her home with me, this asshole is telling the truth. If she were here, there's no reason she wouldn't be in this room with him. He wouldn't go through all that trouble to make up a lie to cover if he had her.

Fuck. Fuck. Fuck.

I pull my gun from the holster and press the barrel against his temple. "If you're lying to me and she's here, I'm going to rip you apart limb from limb to give you the most agonizing death possible."

He shakes his head and groans. "No, man, I don't have her."

Excited yells float from down the hall. Shouts of warning.

Cutter motions toward the sounds. "We'll have company soon."

The pop of gunfire erupts from the other side of the building.

"Shit." I glance at Axle. He may not have her, but he's still a fucking monster. "You're coming with us."

Worst case scenario, I can use him as a bargaining chip to get the fuck out of here. The Devil Brothers won't shoot one of their own if I'm using him as a human shield.

I drag him from the room and into the hallway behind Cutter. The radio in my ear crackles. "Headed your way. Four guys on us. Rendezvous at the door."

Cutter heads back down the hallway toward the exit. I drag Axle behind me. A guy who's stupid enough to stick his head out of his room earns a shot from Cutter to the head. He crumples to the floor, and we blow past him without a look back.

There's no time to ponder the life Cutter just took or the moral ramifications of what we're doing. All that exists is rage and urgency to find her.

E, Warwick, and Rion rush toward us from the other wing of the clubhouse.

Rion focuses on Axle. "Where is she?"

I grit my teeth. "Not here."

"Are you sure?"

I give a bleeding Axle a once-over. "Yeah. He doesn't have her. I don't have a fucking clue where she is."

A bullet hits the wall behind us, and everyone returns fire almost simultaneously.

Everly said, not all the guys in the club would've condoned what Axle and his buddies did. Some of these guys who are shooting may be innocent of the worst of it, but they still aren't anyone I'll feel bad about putting a few holes in anymore. Not when they start throwing bullets at us.

We make it to the back door, and everyone files out, leaving Cutter, Axle, and me.

I stare down the man who so brutally abused Everly. "You don't deserve to live."

Thou shalt not kill.

The words have been drilled into my head for so many years by so many people. It's one of the basic tenets of the Catholic faith. One of the things I thought was so cut and dried only a few years ago.

Oh, how things have changed.

Wrath burns inside me, so hot, fire licks across my skin. He's a monster. He tortured her. He let his friends torture her. This is the type of demon who needs to be sent back to hell.

He sent upon them His burning anger, fury and indignation, and trouble. A band of destroying angels.

The verse sends a calm over me. Determination to do what must be done. If anyone on this planet deserves what's coming to him, it's this man. We are doing God's work by taking this fucker out of circulation. We *are* that band of destroying angels. We're on a mission, not just to find Everly, but to ensure what happened to her doesn't happen again.

I push him against the wall next to the door. "A quick death is more than you deserve." Far more. He deserves to suffer just as much as he made Everly suffer. "I don't have a choice, though."

My hand tightens around the gun. I raise it and press the barrel to his forehead.

Forgive me, Father, for I am about to sin.

But for the best reason of all.

Love.

I pull the trigger.

His brain splatters against the wall, and his body crumples to the floor. Blood pools at my feet almost instantly.

The righteous will rejoice when he sees the vengeance; he will bathe his feet in the blood of the wicked.

A strange mix of relief and anguish floods my body. I'm frozen in place, staring down at Everly's tormentor.

Cutter grabs my arm and drags me to the door before I can consider it further. If he hadn't, I might have stayed there forever, looking at what I just did.

We rush out into the cool night air. Bullets fly around us.

Running on my prosthetic is definitely something I would love to avoid. I hit the treadmill at the gym in the warehouse with my running prosthetic occasionally, but this one isn't designed for this.

Uneven ground. Rocks. Little lighting out here. An artificial knee joint that doesn't work the way my real one does. The very real threat of ending up face-first on the ground looms with every step I take.

My thigh aches. I stumble and right myself, and I grit my teeth through the pain. We return fire before darting behind a building for cover. The dark shadows along the wall help conceal us until we have to move across the street to the vehicles.

Rion climbs into the driver's seat before I can object. "Any idea where else Everly might be?"

I shake my head. "I don't have a fucking clue."

Who the hell else would've taken her?

None of this makes sense. The truck roars to life, and Cutter fires up the SUV behind us. My phone rings in my pocket.

I scramble to get it out as we tear away from the curb.

An unknown number? Everly?

"Hello?"

"Hello. To whom do I have the pleasure of speaking?"

The heavily accented voice is calm and smooth over the line, but completely unfamiliar.

Who is this guy?

I glance at Rion. "This is Preacher."

"Ah, Mr. Davis, just the man I was hoping to reach. I have something that belongs to you."

TWENTY-TWO

Everly

Darkness and cold.

Those two things have encompassed my entire existence for hours.

I have no idea what these assholes want, but their guns made it crystal clear when they came into the shop that they wanted me to go with them.

There wasn't any time to run, and I couldn't even get off a text to Preacher. The messages from Axle were enough to make me rush to the door to try to lock it. But before I could even get around the counter, the bells jingled. They were the harbinger of my doom. Only instead of Axle, it was three heavily armed goons straight out of a movie nightmare.

There was no escaping them then. And there's no escaping now.

Not when I'm sitting in this freezing cold, pitch-black room, tied to a damn chair.

I twist my wrists against the rope restraints for what must be the hundredth time. They bite into my skin, and I wince and sag back against the chair to ease the tension. No amount of fighting is going to set me free. These assholes know what they're doing, at least when it comes to tying up helpless women.

Not the most comforting thought in the world.

Though very little is comforting now, except knowing I'm at least not in the hands of Axle again. These guys may be the unknown, but given what I *do* know about the other option, I think I'm happier with even a sliver of hope of getting out of this intact, physically and emotionally.

I just wish someone would tell me what the fuck is going on…

A door flies open, letting bright light stream in from a hallway. I squeeze my eyes shut against it. Another light flips on above me. Footsteps echo off the concrete floor.

"Ms. Webster, my apologies for the way you were treated." The smooth, accented voice sounds almost kind.

What the hell?

I open my eyes and blink against the light for a moment. Once they adjust, I examine the man standing before me.

Dark eyes assess me from an incredibly handsome, tanned face. A soft, welcoming smile graces his lips, and the perfectly tailored blue suit wrapped around him is more fit for a business meeting than a kidnapping. He's handsome. And undoubtedly deadly.

It's a mask.

He moves closer, stopping only a few feet from me. His hand slips into his pants pocket, and he pulls out a switchblade.

Oh, God. No!

He flips open the blade, and I cringe away from him and tug at the ropes. It doesn't matter that the skin is probably tearing open.

I'm not letting this asshole cut me.

His hands fly up in surrender, blade in one. "I mean you no harm, Ms. Webster. I'm just going to cut the ropes."

Cut the ropes?

My heart settles a little while I examine him. He seems sincere enough.

Should I trust this guy?

He *did* kidnap me, which doesn't exactly put a checkmark in the "trust him" column, but it's not like I have much choice right now. Not with my hands and feet tied to a damn chair, no answers, and while I'm at this man's mercy.

My life is literally in his hands. He steps closer slowly, waiting for me to respond to his approach. He squats and cuts the rope from around my ankles.

This is my chance.

I immediately kick out. My right foot connects with his shoulder, knocking him off-balance.

But my victory is short-lived.

He rights himself, grabs my feet, and holds them steady. Something sinister flashes in the depths of his almost-black eyes. "Now, now…promise you won't try to run or do anything stupid, or I won't release your hands and will re-tie these, too."

I force myself to nod my agreement.

Play along, Everly.

No ropes will open up all sorts of possibilities I won't have otherwise.

The man eyes me, assessing whether to accept my response. "I can be a reasonable man, Ms. Webster, but I expect people to be reasonable with me, too."

Reasonable? Is he fucking serious?

He releases my legs and wanders around the back of the chair to free my hands. The cool metal of the blade slides between the rope and my wrist. He holds it there for a second. No doubt a reminder of how easily he could take that blade across an artery if I don't comply. Then, with a flick of the blade, the bindings are gone.

I jerk my hands to my lap and knead the raw, red skin on my wrists. At least they aren't bleeding. I'll take that as a win in this situation, but I just can't bite back the words that tumble from my mouth. "What about this is reasonable? What the hell do you want from me?"

Insulting your captor then demanding answers. Smart, Ev. Really smart.

But it's too late to take it back.

The man circles back around and delivers a cold smile, one that screams that he's capable of things I can't even imagine. "You see, Ms. Webster, your boyfriend and his friends took something that belongs to me, and I would very much like to get it back and seek…other reparations."

My boyfriend? He can't possibly mean Axle. That's been over for six months. Unless…

"This is about Preacher?"

Eyes that hold a strange mix of danger and compassion narrow on me. "What did you think this was about?"

"I…I didn't have any idea."

At first, I considered that perhaps Axle had sent someone for me. But it's not his style. He likes to get his hands dirty. I never considered this could be connected to Preacher.

How would this guy even know we're involved?

A grin splits his face. "Do you have any idea what it is Mr. Davis and his friends do, Ms. Webster?"

Shit. Oh, shit. Shit. Shit.

This is precisely what Preacher has tried to protect me from. This is exactly what Grace warned me about. They keep us in the dark for these types of moments.

He was right. They do have enemies.

I gulp and shake my head. "I don't know anything. He doesn't tell me anything. I'm not even his girlfriend."

Because I'm not. Not really.

The man smirks and folds his knife. He returns it to his pocket and crosses his arms over his chest. "Ms. Webster, Mr. Davis and his friends stole over sixty-million dollars in heroin from me."

No.

Heroin?

This guy is insane. There's no way Preacher and the guys would be dealing with drugs. That doesn't sound like them at all. I always suspected Axle and the Devil Brothers were involved in drugs somehow, either selling them or running them, but Preacher? It just can't be true.

I shake my head. "You must be mistaken."

"I'm not, Ms. Webster. And not only did they steal almost one-hundred kilos of pure heroin, but they also killed thirteen of my men on one of the ships transporting it."

Any warmth remaining in my body after being in this room seeps out of my skin. The chill leaves goose bumps over every inch of me.

They killed thirteen people?

My chest tightens. Air won't fill my lungs. The room spins despite being seated on this damn chair.

It can't be true. Preacher would never...

The man squats to my eye level again. Sympathy softens his gaze. "This may be a shock for you, Ms. Webster, but it is the truth. I have no reason to lie to you. And I've done my homework." He pushes back to his feet. "It wasn't easy to track them down. Mr. Davis has quite a sophisticated system protecting them. But I have a secret weapon, and once we got inside, we had all the information we needed to confirm they were behind this and to locate you from Mr. Davis' phone records."

The hacker...

This is the guy who was behind that.

Well, shit.

Preacher was right to be worried. He knew they were in trouble. Only *I'm* the one who was kidnapped at gunpoint and tied to a fucking chair. Not them.

"What do you want from me?"

I don't understand what I have to do with any of this.

There's absolutely nothing I can offer him by way of information about the crew.

Why didn't he just go after the guys?

He beams at me. "I already have it. I contacted Preacher and his friends in an effort to end this."

End this doesn't sound good. Not good at all.

"End this? End it how?"

"I think you know, Ms. Webster. I can't let this go. There must be repercussions. I'm sorry that you got involved. I'm sure Mr. Davis never intended to drag you into his mess. But he shut us down before we could pinpoint his location. Yours, however…" He *tsks* and gives me a sad smile. "You know I can't let anyone go. Even you. When they arrive, it is going to be an unfortunate end for everyone involved."

My breath catches, and tears burn my vision.

I'm the fucking bait.

And once the guys arrive in an attempt to rescue me, I'm going to die because of Preacher Davis.

There were times I thought Axle might kill me. He and his friends went far enough that I truly believed it would happen on at least half a dozen occasions. The things they were capable of would shock even the most depraved people. Yet, Preacher, a man I trusted and believed in, dealt in heroin and murder.

And I'll lose my life because of it.

A sob slips from my lips, and I bury my face in my hands.

No.

I jerk my head up and stare the man down. I'm not going to show how weak I am. What I need is a plan. A way to get out of here and warn Preacher before they do something stupid like come in here with guns blazing to attempt a rescue. This guy isn't playing around. It will be a slaughter.

I clear the emotion from my throat and try not to look threatening. You attract more bees with honey, after all. "Can

I ask for a favor, Mr.…" I raise an eyebrow at him as if he's really going to tell me his real name.

"You can call me Mr. Rose."

How about Mother Fucker instead?

"Well, Mr. Rose. Would it be possible for me to use a bathroom?" I flash him the sweetest, most innocent smile I can muster. It's been a long time since I've tried to appear innocent. And as Preacher so aptly pointed out, the tattoos don't help with the illusion.

He grins at me. "Of course, Ms. Webster. I wouldn't want you to be uncomfortable. As I said, I apologize for the way my men handled you. They can be…a little overzealous at times." He waves to one of the men standing just outside the open door in the hallway. "This is Rafael. He will see you to the bathroom."

This may be my only chance to get away from these guys. I'm no master of espionage or escapes, but I've watched enough true crime television to learn a thing or two about how to get away with your life. I may have failed to save myself once, but I'm not about to go down so easily now.

Rafael grabs my arm and jerks me up from the chair. Mr. Rose clears his throat and glares at his goon. The man doesn't want me harmed but plans to kill me anyway.

Talk about ironic.

I laugh to myself. This whole situation is so fucking insane.

Rafael ushers me down an empty hallway with cracked paint and plaster falling from the walls and ceilings. Wherever we are, the building is old. Probably abandoned. We pass two closed doors before he directs me inside a small, single-stall bathroom. One tiny rectangular window lets in a stream of moonlight.

He glances up at it, then shuts the door behind him.

I immediately dart to the wall to check it out. No wonder he seemed unconcerned about a possible escape out the window. Even if I weighed fifty pounds, I couldn't have fit through it. And even if I somehow managed to get out, all that's visible are a vast, empty, cracked parking lot and a forest of trees surrounding it.

Where the hell are we? And how the hell do I get out of here to warn Preacher?

After they nabbed me, they tossed me into the back of a van with no windows. I couldn't see anything about where they took me, but it seems like we drove around for a while. That doesn't give me much to work on for creating an avenue of escape. Not even a direction to head that might lead toward a town and people who could help.

My legs wobble as I move away from the window and to the toilet stall. If I don't actually use the bathroom, my buddy Rafael out there may get suspicious.

The door to the bathroom opens, and I exit the stall to wash my hands.

I force a smile at Rafael. "Can I help you?"

He glowers at me. "Hurry up."

His eyes follow my every move. I wash and dry my hands, and he grabs my arm again and ushers me back to my room where Mr. Rose occupies the chair I had been sitting in.

He rises and sweeps his arm over it, indicating I should take a seat.

I do what I'm told. There's no reason to take any chances until I have a way out. And I have yet to see anything that offers that as an even remote possibility.

A phone rings somewhere in Mr. Rose's jacket. He reaches into an inside pocket and beams as he inspects the screen. "Excellent timing. Here's your boyfriend now."

Preacher!

He presses the screen and brings the phone to his ear. "Mr. Davis, so nice to speak with you again." He listens to something Preacher says and chuckles. "Of course, Mr. Davis. Have you given our earlier conversation any more thought?"

His gaze holds mine.

This man doesn't mind staring down the woman he just kidnapped and plans to murder. Talk about cojones.

"Well, Mr. Davis, let me just say this. I've seen what you and your crew are capable of on the *Marcella Marie*. Don't think you'll be able to storm in here and rescue Ms. Webster. Believe me when I say, I came well-equipped and well-prepared."

I have no doubt that Rafael is only the tip of the iceberg when it comes to Mr. Rose's goon arsenal.

The guys don't stand a chance. And neither do I.

TWENTY-THREE

Preacher

———————

F*uck. Fuck. Fuck.*
    I believe Rose when he says he's ready for anything we can throw at him. Especially after what we did on the *Marcella Marie*, he's going to be heavily gunned and will shoot first and ask questions later. They aren't called The Blood Rose Cartel because they're known for being forgiving and kind to their enemies.

Even if we somehow did manage to get in there and get Everly out, which was my first inclination when I got his call earlier, that won't end this. The cartel will come after us, over and over again. We'll be looking over our shoulders for the rest of our lives with massive targets on our backs until they kill each and every one of us, likely in the most violent way possible.

Whoever sheds man's blood, by man his blood shall be shed…

We took his heroin. We killed his men. That's not something you walk away from unscathed when you're dealing with someone as deadly as the Roses. There's no way to resolve this where everyone leaves happy.

Unless…

I glance at the guys where they stand around at the back of my truck. The moment I got the call from Mr. Rose and realized who had Everly, I started trying to formulate a plan. But only one idea keeps popping up. Only one potential avenue holds promise. And it's the one that will piss off a lot of these guys. And someone else even more important.

But it's the only way I can think of getting out of this with our lives. Rose's warning only solidifies that this is the only way.

First, I need to confirm Everly is okay. "Mr. Rose, can I please speak with Everly to make sure she's all right?"

"Of course, Mr. Davis. I'm placing you on speakerphone now."

"Everly?"

"Oh, my God, Preacher!" Her voice comes through the phone, tight and panicked, not at all how she normally sounds.

"Are you okay? Did he hurt you?"

If he did, I will tear that motherfucker limb from limb and make what I did to Axle look like nothing.

"I'm okay. But he's going to kill all of you and me. Don't come. It's a trap—"

Fuck.

Mr. Rose laughs into the line, and the background noise disappears, letting me know he took it off speakerphone. "That's quite enough, Ms. Webster. You're very brave to attempt that."

Brave and stupid. What was she thinking?

The woman is being held hostage because of us, and she's still risking her life to warn us of Rose's intentions. I suspected as much, but hearing her confirm my worst fears gives me the clear path I need to take to try to resolve this.

He needs to know none of this was our choice. If he understands what we were dealing with, he might have even a modicum of compassion for our situation and be willing to negotiate an end other than all of us in shallow graves. "Mr. Rose, I understand your anger at the loss, but please know, we were forced to make runs for Arturo. We weren't in any position to question his orders, not when Warwick was so far in debt to the Marconis and they'd made threats against our lives."

He considers my statement in silence for a moment while I pace behind my truck. Rion, E, Warwick, and Cutter all watch me anxiously. Waiting for a response from Rose is like waiting for the other shoe to drop.

"I know you were working for him, Mr. Davis. It took quite some time to unravel everything that was going on. At first, I thought the theft of my shipment from *Neptune's Daughter* was one of our Mexican or South American rivals. I prepared the next shipment carefully. My own boat. My own men. But still…I lost the product and much more."

The *Marcella Marie*. It was an absolute bloodbath. But now we know it was the cartel waiting for us, not a set-up by Arturo.

"But once I learned that Arturo Marconi had stepped into power right around the time my shipments went missing, it wasn't hard to put two and two together. The Marconis always resisted our efforts to expand our territory into Chicago, and it was well-known in certain circles that Arturo was looking to get into the drug game, despite his uncle's wishes."

Something we all wish we had known. It might have saved us a lot of trouble. We could have taken Arturo out well before any of this clusterfuck came crashing down upon us and might have been able to make arrangements with *Il Padrone* that would have gotten us out from under the debt contract.

But something tells me Rose doesn't give a shit about our plight. It doesn't stop me from trying, though.

"Mr. Rose, we never would have acted if we had a choice. Arturo didn't give us one."

"That's all well and good, Mr. Davis, but it doesn't bring

back my drugs. It doesn't bring back the thirteen men your crew killed in cold blood. It doesn't mend the relationships that were strained by not having the product we had promised. Unfortunately, nothing can make me whole again. At this point, all that's left is vengeance and retribution."

Exactly as I feared.

He's going to kill all of us, no matter what happens when we try to go get Everly. There *is* no making deals with these people. At least, not under normal circumstances.

But we can offer something no one else can. Something so big, so valuable, Rose will *have* to give us at least a moment of consideration.

Shit. Here it goes.

"What if we could make it up to you?"

He chuckles. "What could you possibly offer me that I can't already take on my own?"

I suck a deep breath and prepare myself for the decking I'm probably going to take from Cutter. The guys still stand rapt, waiting for some sort of indication what we're about to do. I meet Cutter's stare, even though looking away might be wise. "The Marconi territory."

Cutter snarls, and Rion and Warwick pull on his shoulders to hold him back.

A laugh floats over the line, deep and rich, just a twinge maniacal at the edges. "There are a few problems with that suggestion, Mr. Davis, the least of which is it's not yours to offer."

He's absolutely fucking correct.

It's not.

But I pray to God Valentina won't fight me on this after what we did. If it weren't for us, she wouldn't have control of the Marconi family. She'd have nothing and would have been deported back to Italy. She *owes* us. And it's time to cash in.

I clear my throat and turn my back on the guys. Cutter's

already angry enough. I don't need to be looking at him while I say this. "No. It isn't mine. But I can guarantee Ms. Marconi will be amenable to any agreement we come to."

He chuckles again. "How could you possibly guarantee what Valentina will do?"

I cringe and turn to face Cutter. "Because she's a personal friend. She's the girlfriend of one of my best friends."

Probably a former best friend…

There's no way Cutter is going to let this slide. He'll see it as a betrayal, no matter what I say.

But it's worth it if Rose takes the bait and Everly comes home safe.

Rose's silence has my fists clenching, and I close my eyes, but then he *tsks*. "Well, well, well, maybe you have something to seriously consider after all."

I heave out a sigh of relief, but once I see Cutter's face, even with the glasses blocking his eyes, he might as well have already stabbed his knife straight into my heart. It would be less painful than anticipating what's coming from him.

"I think we should meet in person, Mr. Davis. To hash out all the details of this agreement. Of course, Ms. Marconi needs to be in attendance. As much as I would love to blindly trust you and your statement that you can negotiate on her behalf, I've been burned in the past and am not willing to risk it this time around. You can't really blame me for that, can you?"

Smart.

Smarter than I gave him credit for. I don't have any authority whatsoever to make decisions for Valentina. I can't even make decisions for the crew. But I have to believe, once she hears what's happened to Everly, she won't leave her in the hands of this monster to destroy her…and us.

It wouldn't end well for anyone. She has to see that. I have to *convince* her of it. I have to convince *all* of them.

I yank at my hair with my free hand. "Where should we meet?"

"County Highway KK and Town Line Road. The abandoned mill. Oh, and Mr. Davis?"

"Yes?"

"I suggest you don't attempt anything stupid. I would hate to see Ms. Webster suffer for your sins."

The soul who sins shall die. The son shall not suffer for the iniquity of the father, nor the father suffer for the iniquity of the son. The righteousness of the righteous shall be upon himself, and the wickedness of the wicked shall be upon himself.

This is on *me*. I can't let Everly pay for my bad deeds and suffer for my sins. This is *my* doing. My burden to bear. My pain to take. And I deserve all of it.

The line goes dead, and I drop my phone onto the tailgate of the truck. My hands tremble, and my vision blurs. "I'm sorry, Cutter. I didn't have a choice."

"You had a fucking choice." He throws the words at me like daggers. "You didn't have to drag my woman into this. You offered to open her organization up to the fucking Rose Cartel. Are you fucking insane?"

I shake my head and grapple for anything that might appease Cutter. "I'm sorry. There was no other choice."

"No other choice?" He slams his hands against the side of the truck.

Warwick and Rion both step in between us.

Cutter snarls at me. "You *did* have a choice. We could have regrouped and figured out a plan that didn't involve letting a fucking cartel deal drugs in Valentina's territory."

There *is* no other plan. Even with Cutter and Rion's skills, we can't take out all of Rose's men and the entire cartel he has back home, which would be the only way to truly end this. When Warwick suggested it what feels like so long ago, it sounded insane and so off the wall, I had brushed it off. But now, it's our only hope.

"You know as well as I do that the longer I leave Everly there, the less of a chance we have of getting her out alive."

"You're willing to sacrifice what isn't yours to offer for a girl you're fucking for a couple of weeks? You're offering up Valentina. After what I did for you? After what *I* sacrificed for you? You're going to treat someone I love so callously?"

Shit.

It's the first time I've ever heard him say he loves Valentina. We all know he does, but those aren't words that come out of the mouth of a man like Cutter very often. If at all.

"I'm sorry. I understand why you're pissed, but we don't have a lot of time before we need to get to the meet."

He smashes his fist against the tailgate. "Fuck you, Preacher. Everly isn't the only consideration here."

"I know that!"

"Sure doesn't fucking seem like it."

Warwick pushes on Cutter's chest, forcing him to walk backward toward his SUV. "We'll meet you at the warehouse and get this figured out with Valentina. Rion, ride with Preacher. E is with us."

E, as usual, hasn't interjected a word during the showdown between Cutter and me. He prefers to be the neutral party whenever possible, but he still gives me a sympathetic look before turning to climb into the SUV behind Cutter and Warwick.

I slam the tailgate closed and slide into the driver's seat. Rion climbs in next to me and stares at me while I dig into my pocket for the keys.

This is such a clusterfuck.

And it's all my fault for being selfish and pursuing something with Everly instead of keeping her safe from all the danger in my life. I drop my forehead onto the steering wheel and squeeze my eyes closed.

Rion snatches the keys from my hand and shoves them into the ignition. "We need to go."

I know.

But my entire body is frozen. Fear has wrapped around me like a cocoon. Stealing my breath and any ability to move forward.

"I fucked this up so badly."

"I hate to agree, man, but you could end up losing your friendship with Cutter over the decision you just made. And we may lose the sweet deal we have with the Marconis because of this, too. This doesn't affect just you anymore. This could change things for all of us."

Shit. He's right.

I just put everything we've worked for all these years on the line. We're finally in a position to choose our jobs, to choose our exit strategy. And I just put it all in jeopardy. I put Valentina on the chopping block when she had no hand in what Arturo did.

Fuck.

This is a royal fuck-up.

God, guide me down the righteous path.

It seemed right at the time. What I was doing. What I offered to save Everly. But now…the price may be everything I've worked for.

I fire up the engine and pause with my hand on the gearshift. "I really fucked this up, didn't I?"

He snorts as he buckles his seat belt. "You sure did, buddy. And while I may not agree with the decision you made, I do hope this works for everyone's sake. And I'll kick your ass later for the position this puts me in if it doesn't."

I nod at him. "Fair enough." I peel away from the curb and jump on the highway toward the warehouse.

Convincing Valentina is the next step. The guys will have to restrain Cutter again while I talk to her, but it's been laid out for Rose now. There's no going back.

Rion taps his knuckles on the center console. "You know you're going to have to tell Valentina what you did."

"I know."

"She may kill you before Rose has a chance."

No shit.

TWENTY-FOUR

Everly

I don't know what Preacher said after Mr. Rose turned off the speakerphone, but whatever it was, it sure changed my captor's entire attitude like a switch had been flipped. The smile he sported no longer held that underlying sinister edge.

It was genuine. It made him seem almost human.

Other than that it has something to do with Valentina, I didn't get much out of Mr. Rose's side of the conversation.

What could Valentina possibly have to do with any of this?

There are so many things I don't understand, so many things Preacher didn't tell me. While he said it was for my own good, maybe being left in the dark is more dangerous than knowing the truth. At least if I knew everything, I could understand what I am up against and might figure out how to fight it.

But I'm blind. Totally, utterly, completely, unequivocally blind. And it's the shittiest feeling in the world. I've been here before, and I swore I would never be back. At the mercy of someone else. Someone who intends nothing but harm.

Mr. Rose waves at the plate in front of me. "Aren't you hungry?"

After he hung up with Preacher, he ushered me into

another room where a table was set with a white tablecloth, fine china, and a meal that was clearly prepared at a fancy restaurant.

I stare down at the lasagna, of which I've taken one bite. My second bite still sits on the end of my fork, abandoned. I push the plate away slightly. "I'm sorry. I don't seem to have much of an appetite, given the circumstances."

Like your wanting to kill my friends and me if whatever Preacher suggested doesn't pan out.

He reaches forward and grabs his glass of red wine. I haven't touched mine. I don't want to dull my senses in case I need to make quick moves or decisions.

His eyes never leave mine as he takes a sip. "I guess I can see how this situation would be upsetting if you're not used to it."

Not used to it? Is he for real?

"This is something you get used to?" I raise an eyebrow at him.

He grins and offers a slight shrug. "I guess it just doesn't seem to faze me anymore."

"What doesn't?"

His hand comes up nonchalantly. "Life and death situations."

"None of this bothers you?"

He can't be serious. That's impossible.

"Preparing to kill people *doesn't bother you?* What you do *doesn't bother you?* You deal drugs. You put *drugs* in the hands of people with families and ruin their lives."

He sets down his drink and shakes his head, though he doesn't seem angry by my outburst. More amused, if anything. "They make their own choices. I'm simply providing something they would find elsewhere if it weren't coming from me."

What a fucking self-centered way of thinking about the world.

"Maybe, but you make it easier for them to get it. Maybe

if it weren't in such supply, there wouldn't be so many drug addicts and overdoses. How many people lose members of their family to a disease like this?"

He considers me for a moment. "You have a soft heart, Everly. It probably makes you a good person, but it also means you're easily hurt and easily taken advantage of."

His words couldn't be more true.

Am I that fucking transparent?

I've placed my heart in the hands of only two men in my life, and both times, it's led to catastrophic repercussions. And Mr. Rose saw that after only a few hours with me.

"Is it that obvious?"

He swirls his wine and watches the red liquid in the glass. "Personal experience makes me capable of recognizing it in others. I've been with many women who thought they could change me. Who thought they could take the bad boy entrenched in the cartel world and turn me into the perfect husband and father. The perfect man. They thought I would somehow walk away from the danger in the lifestyle for them. That never happened."

"Why not? Don't you want love and affection? Someone to spend the rest of your life with?"

"Of course, I do." He sips his wine, then dangles the glass from his fingertips. "And I can have that. I just have to find a woman who is as dedicated to the life as I am and who is willing to accept me for who I actually am, not what she wants me to be."

"You can find that? A woman who's going to accept this?" I swing my arms out. "Who will accept that you're a man who is willing to kill me, a complete innocent, and Preacher and his friends."

"But they're hardly innocent, Ms. Webster."

"They're not. But they're not bad people. And you're willing to wipe them from the face of the Earth for what…a few million dollars?"

He chuckles dark and low and leans back in his chair. "You say that like it's not a lot of money. And in the grand scheme of things, in my business, it's not, but it put a major crinkle in my operations here for the last six months. Pissed off a lot of my customers. It harmed relationships I will have to spend a long time mending. So, although the monetary value may not be a lot, the cost is great."

I'll never understand men like this or their world. Yet, this is the world Preacher is a part of. He may not deal drugs. He may not run a cartel. But he's involved. He's part of this. He *is* a criminal, even tucked away behind his screens. He plays a role. A big one. The crew couldn't operate without him, and who knows what else he's doing for his other "clients" behind closed doors.

Even if he manages to get me out of this alive, it's not the kind of life I can condone. It's not the life I want. I had already made the decision to leave, but this cements it. Even if walking away from him might break me.

I finally found someone who makes me happy, who makes me whole again, and I'm still going to have to cut him out of my life. If I still have one.

"Don't look so distressed, Everly. Preacher and his friends will be here soon, and the goal is to come to a resolution that lets everyone walk away happy."

That may be the goal, but will it ever happen?

I'm not so sure. Even if it does and they both get what they want, I can't "walk away happy." Not when I can't have Preacher.

Mr. Rose takes several more bites from his plate before pushing it away. He drains his glass of wine and plasters on a knowing smile.

I might almost like him if we'd met under different circumstances.

Christ, I am such a shitty judge of character.

One of his men approaches the table. "They're here, sir."

My gut twists, and I clench my fists under the table. I eye the knife next to my plate. Hopefully, I won't need a weapon, but it would be easy to slip it into my pocket without anyone even noticing.

Mr. Rose clears his throat and eyes the knife.

Or maybe not.

"I appreciate your tenacity, Ms. Webster, and your willingness to call me out on things you disagree with, even though you're very much at a disadvantage here. It takes guts and spunk. In a different place, in a different time, you might be exactly the type of woman I'm looking for."

I scowl at him. "Except, I would never ever get involved with a man the likes of you."

He pushes to his feet and presses his hands over his heart. "That wounds me greatly, Everly. Now, let's go see about coming to an arrangement that everyone finds satisfactory."

I follow him out and down into a large, open space that was once a factory of some sort, under the watchful eye of my buddy Rafael. Massive machines line one wall, and piles of tangled metal occupy the space across from them.

Sitting at dinner with Mr. Rose and the hours I've spent in captivity prior to that convinced me leaving Preacher is the right thing to do. But the second he and his friends walk through the door, everything my head decided flies out the window and my heart takes hold.

He looks like shit. His thick, dark hair, usually slicked back, is disheveled like he just rolled out of bed or has been running his hands through it a hundred times. The dark rings under his eyes and hard set of his shoulders tell me all I need to know about how worried he's been.

This is destroying him.

Our eyes meet, and every fiber of my being longs to run across the room and throw myself into his arms, but Rafael's grip tightens on my upper arm. Preacher's gaze narrows on Rafael, and his lips twist into a sneer.

Mr. Rose smiles next to me. "Now, Ms. Webster, we can't have you running over to your friends until we get what we want."

I should've known it wouldn't be so easy. They couldn't come in firing. It would have been a bloodbath for both sides. Whatever it is Preacher thinks he has to negotiate with, it better be something good.

Valentina enters the building last, right behind Cutter. But it's not the same woman I saw at the warehouse the other night.

Holy cow.

This one wears a tight, knee-length black dress that shows off every curve with a plunging neckline that leaves nothing to the imagination. Her long, dark, sleek hair runs down the middle of her back. She's polished. Put together and powerful. And the hard look on her perfect face says she's not fucking playing around.

Mr. Rose's grin spreads when he sees her. "Miss Bianchi, or do you go by Marconi now?"

She offers him a cool smile and walks to the center of the room where Preacher, Rion, E, and Warwick already stand. Cutter stays glued to her side.

"I'm sure you've done your research, Mr. Rose."

Her English is just as immaculate as it was the other night, only now, I detect a hint of Italian. She did say *ciao* the night we met, but it never clicked before.

Italian…

Marconi…

No, it can't be.

The welcoming smile she held falls as she stares down the man who holds our lives in his hands. "You know exactly what to call me."

"A thief?" Mr. Rose raises his dark eyebrows at her.

"No, Mr. Rose, I've taken nothing from you. My belated

cousin, on the other hand…" She shrugs slightly. "All I can do is apologize for his behavior."

"Apologies don't replace the millions of dollars that I've lost or appease the angry customers who did not receive their product due to your family's actions."

Jesus. She is *part of the Marconi crime family from Chicago.*

I might not even recognize the name if it hadn't been spoken around the clubhouse when I was with Axle. And it sounds like the Marconis were the ones Preacher and the guys were working for when they stole Mr. Rose's drugs.

The connections are starting to make sense now.

But what is she doing here with the guys? How is this going to get me out of the situation alive?

She shakes her head, her dark hair swirling around her shoulders. "No, it will not. But I can offer you something else by way of reparations."

Preacher takes a step forward. "I told you I would get her here and that she would agree to what we discussed. Give Everly to me."

Mr. Rose spreads out his hands. "I have not heard Ms. Marconi agree yet. How do I know this isn't some ruse to get Everly that will be rescinded as soon as she's in your hands?"

He makes a good point. One that has bile rising up my throat.

They don't have anything to offer him. Not really. The kind of money they're talking isn't something that can so easily be turned over in a matter of hours. And there's no way that amount of heroin is still sitting around to be returned to him.

Valentina takes another step forward. Cutter growls and grabs her arm. She glares at him over her shoulder, and he releases her with his lips pressed together in utter contempt for what's happening. He's trying to protect her, but she's pissed. Watching them war for superiority, even in circumstances like this, almost has a smile hitting my lips.

She casts Cutter one last look before she turns her attention to Mr. Rose. "I have something I can offer you as a sign of good faith."

Mr. Rose opens his arms again. "I'm all ears."

So am I. What does she have that can save all our asses?

TWENTY-FIVE

Preacher

Everly's bottom lip quivers, and I clench my hands at my sides to keep myself from lunging across the distance between us and beating the shit out of Mr. Rose and then taking her in my arms and never letting her go.

But once she's free, I'm going to have to let her.

There's no way she'll stay with me after this experience. After she was brought into this type of danger simply by knowing me and because she means something to me.

We've made a lot of enemies over the years; the Rose Cartel is just one of the dozens if not hundreds of people we've pissed off. They were just the ones smart enough to find us.

If what Valentina is offering doesn't work, there's no plan B. Not really. They searched us for weapons before we ever entered, and even though I know Cutter has at least one hidden somewhere on him, even he couldn't work the miracle necessary to take out Rose and his half-dozen men and get Everly away safely without some of us sustaining injuries. If not worse.

And then, even if we took them out, we would just be

facing retaliation from one of the most powerful cartels in the world, which puts us in no better a position.

Valentina nods to me. It's time to show Rose what we have to offer. I pull a set of keys from my pocket and hold them up.

Rose switches his attention from Valentina to me. "What are those?"

I take a tentative step forward. "An offer of good faith. And I hope enough to keep Everly alive."

Mr. Rose eyes the keys.

I follow his gaze and grip them tighter. "When Arturo had us take the second shipment from the *Marcella Marie*, we had already put things into action to remove him. We had no intention of delivering the product to him if we didn't have to."

"That was almost two months ago. I assume the product has been sold at this point."

Valentina shakes her head. "The Marconis don't sell drugs. Every ounce that was taken from that ship is currently in storage at one of my warehouses. The keys to which Mr. Davis is holding."

Mr. Rose's eyes light up. They glitter with what can only be interest, and a smile spreads across his face. "Well, this is a pleasant surprise. But again, it does nothing for me regarding the first shipment or the angry customers. What do you plan to offer me to assuage this wrong?"

I glance over at Valentina. She gives me a dirty look, one that says she's going to kill me later if we survive this. It isn't unexpected, though. When we got back to the warehouse and told her what I had offered Rose, she lost her shit. One thing *Il Padrone* refused to get involved with was drug dealing. And his daughter wasn't happy about the idea, either.

But one thing about Valentina…

She may be as tough as nails. She may have the backbone and drive of a man ten times her size. But she also has a heart.

One I was able to pull the strings of when I told her what they would do to Everly if we didn't cooperate.

Valentina may not know Everly well, but she won't let an innocent woman, one I care about more deeply than I probably should, suffer. "I would be lying if I said I like the idea of having drugs sold in my territory. My father worked very hard to keep that shit out of the hands of the people who live there. But…" her eyes dart over to Everly, "Everly is a friend, one I'm not willing to risk the life of simply because of some lofty morals. I am willing to give you permission to deal within the boundaries of my territory in Chicago, to make up for the shipment that was lost."

Mr. Rose presses his hands together in front of his lips and watches all of us for a moment. "I'm sorry I'm not leaping for joy at this moment, Ms. Marconi, but something tells me this offer comes with some stipulations I may not be so thrilled to accept."

I close my hands around the keys so tightly, the metal digs into my palm. The pain is welcome. It helps me stay focused on what I need to do right here, right now, instead of what I want to do.

Just take the damn deal, Rose. Take it and end this.

Valentina is just as steady as she was the moment she walked in. A true head of the family. "Mr. Rose, I do not believe my three stipulations are anything we can't both live with. First, any product you bring in must be okayed with me. If you're going to be selling in my territory, I don't want to hear stories about laced heroin killing people or drugs being cut with other products that cause death."

Rose drops his head back and laughs, the sound echoing around the space. The goon holding Everly's arm just stares straight ahead.

"So, one of your stipulations is that I sell a pure product?"

"Not necessarily pure, Mr. Rose. I understand enough about how the business works to know that isn't feasible, but it will be tested to ensure it's as safe as possible for those ingesting it."

As safe as possible.

We're talking about drugs here.

Heroin, cocaine, and dozens of others I haven't even thought about yet. This conversation seems so asinine. There's nothing safe about any of it. But I can't be righteous now, not when Everly's life is at stake. And neither can Valentina.

I'm sure I'll pay for this with her later.

Rose regains his composure and circles his hand for her to continue. "What are your other stipulations?"

"Well, you may sell within my territory, but you're not to engage in any other enterprises. Everything else remains under the purview of the Marconis. If I learn of anything else going on, our deal is invalidated and I'm free to take whatever action necessary to remedy it."

The veiled threat makes Mr. Rose smile. "The third stipulation?"

Valentina sets her shoulders. "This is a limited time offer. You have two years."

He snorts and waves his hands to stop her. "No. No. No. If we are going to do this, it will be a permanent arrangement."

She steps forward, her long, tanned legs slipping out of the slit in her dress, the four-inch stilettos on her feet clicking against the cement floor. Cutter moves with her like white on rice.

"Let me make myself clear, Mr. Rose. While you may hold Everly, I hold the largest territory of any organization in Chicago. Offering you this opportunity and an untapped market will not be unlimited. Two years is more than sufficient to make up for what you lost and then some. By that point, I'm sure your territory will have continued to grow as well."

Mr. Rose runs his fingers along his chin for a moment.

Shit, Valentina.

The expiration tag was not part of what we discussed

before we got here. Putting a limit on the deal could be the very thing that prevents it from happening. The thing that keeps me from bringing Everly home safely.

Rion senses my frustration and places his hand on my shoulder. He's trying to keep me from lashing out. And that's a good thing.

Because right now, I'm on the edge of losing my ever-loving shit.

I never thought anyone would get under my skin this way. Other than the guys, I haven't been close to anyone for so long; I was confident it would never happen. Now that it has, it's like my whole world is coming apart.

And there's nothing I can do to stop it.

Mr. Rose stares at Valentina and me for a moment. His eyes dart from the keys clenched in my hand to her stern look of distaste for him.

God, please don't let her fuck this up. I'll do anything. I'll go back to church. I'll become a better Christian. I'll do whatever it takes.

The problem is, you never know what it will take. And I know enough to understand that God doesn't barter. That's not what He's about. But it's human nature when in these types of situations to beg and make deals with the big guy upstairs. Even I'm not immune to it.

Everly pleads with me from her green eyes, begging me to end this. To make everything okay.

Fuck, I wish I could, baby.

Every second of silence that lingers in the air between Valentina and Rose might as well be an eternity. My hand clenches around the keys again. I don't even care if blood trickles between my fingers.

Let me bleed. Let me suffer. I deserve it for dragging her into this mess.

Mr. Rose finally extends his hand to Valentina. "We have a deal, Ms. Marconi."

She steps forward and places her small palm in his. He

grabs her hand and jerks her toward him until their faces are almost touching. Cutter lunges and wraps his arm around her waist. He tries to tug her back, but the head of the cartel is stronger than he appears.

He holds Valentina firmly against him. "If you try to fuck with me in any way, everyone in this room, anyone someone in this room has ever cared about, anyone someone in this room has even looked at, will pay the price. Do you understand me?"

Veins throb in Cutter's neck and at his temple as he fights against the desire to rip Rose apart limb from limb with his bare hands. I feel bad for the guy. Cutter's not used to being told he can't do something. Especially when it comes to protecting someone he cares about.

It's what he does best. What we rely on him for. This must be utter torture for him as much as it is for me watching that goon with his hand around Everly's arm.

Valentina gets right into Rose's face, showing no fear, exactly what I would expect from her. "When I make a promise, I don't break it. But bear in mind, Mr. Rose, this is a two-way street. If you try to fuck over any of us, if you threaten any of us, if you try to touch any of us, I will unleash a hell on you that you could never imagine."

And she will.

As Grace so aptly called it when she joined our little merry band, letting Cutter go is like releasing the Kraken. Once he starts, there's no stopping him.

Rose releases her and takes a step back, holding up his hands. "I'm glad we could come to an arrangement." He holds out his hand toward me. "The keys and address of the warehouse?"

I step forward and drop the keys into his hand. "Between McKinley Park and Back of the Yards, along Pershing between Ashland and Western."

"Obviously, I'm going to need to retain some sort of collateral until I see that what you say is in that warehouse is actually in my hands."

I anticipated as much. "Me. I'll go with you. Release Everly to them."

"No." Everly jerks against the hold of the man next to her, and a single tear trickles down her cheek.

Valentina holds up a hand. "Cutter and I will accompany you to Chicago. I need to head back there, anyway. Is that enough collateral for you?"

Rose grins. "That should do nicely, Ms. Marconi." He turns back to Everly and his goon. "It's been a pleasure getting to know you, Ms. Webster. Mr. Davis is one lucky man."

He motions to his goon holding Everly, and the man shoves her forward. She stumbles and drops to her hands and knees on the concrete. I close the distance between us in a second and scoop her up into my arms.

She sags against me and buries her face in my neck.

Complete and utter vulnerability.

That is what I have in Everly.

She didn't deserve any of this. Especially after what she's already been through with the MC. This is what I feared could happen but prayed never would.

And now, I'll lose her forever.

I nod to Cutter and Valentina before I turn and make my way toward where we parked the truck. Rion stays hot at my heels and slides into the driver's seat so I can take the back seat with Everly. I climb in and shift her onto my lap. She nuzzles down into me deeper like she can't get close enough.

God, I wish that could last…

But once the adrenaline from what just happened wears off, she'll be running for the hills, and I'll be left alone again.

And it's all my fault. It's the price I need to pay for my sins.

TWENTY-SIX

Everly

E verything after the moment Preacher scooped me up into his arms is nothing but a blur.

Hazy memories.

Muffled voices and sounds.

Bright lights and then darkness I welcomed.

Because I didn't want to look at it. I didn't want to acknowledge what was happening around me. If I didn't see it, hear it, feel it, I could pretend it was all a shitty nightmare.

But now that I'm awake, lying here in the warmth and comfort of Preacher's arms and bed, I can no longer ignore the reality of the situation.

And God, is that situation ever complicated.

The man I should despise right now, the one who got me into this mess and put my life at risk, is instead offering me comfort in the violent storm. Somehow, in the tempest my life has become in the last few months, Preacher Davis has become my refuge. My safe harbor. The place I feel sheltered and protected enough to sleep despite every reason not to.

He shifts behind me and pushes up onto one elbow. I roll onto my back and peer up at him.

The only light in the room coming from the moonbeams,

streaming in through the open blinds in the one window, casts an ethereal glow on one side of his face.

The massive banks of computer monitors are off—the first time I've seen them like that. I imagined they were always on and he was always at the keyboards—watching, waiting, hacking, and making moves. Like his own version of the Great Wizard, only instead of a curtain, he hides behind the digital worlds.

I guess a near-death experience is a special occasion that calls for it to be shut down, for *him* to be shut down to *it*.

Preacher brushes a strand of hair off my forehead and leans in to press a kiss against my temple. He drags his head back with a question in his eyes. Maybe he was expecting me to recoil, to push him off me, to run, but I don't have the energy to fight the pull, the need I have for the comfort of his arms.

If I didn't have this right now, I don't know where I would be or how I would manage to hold myself together.

His thumb gently strokes my cheek. "Are you okay?"

As far as I can remember, they're the first words he's said to me since we escaped Mr. Rose's clutches.

He doesn't wait for me to answer, though. "I'm so sorry for everything. This is all my fault. I should never have dragged you into this, exposed you to the insanity of my life."

I press my finger over his lips to silence him. Every word he said has already been through my head a hundred times in the few minutes I've been awake. I don't need to hear him apologize. I don't need to hear him tell me how sorry he is.

I've heard empty apologies before. From men like Axle and men before him. Preacher didn't even have to say a single word, and I knew how much he regretted everything that's happened and how guilty he feels just by the way he looks at me.

Because at his core, Preacher is a good person.

He may do bad things.

A lot of them...

But he's not bad, not really.

Which makes the whole situation even more confusing.

"Don't apologize, Preacher. I don't need your apology. What I need is an explanation."

"What do you need to know?"

So damn much. But we'll start with the obvious.

"Why all this happened. I think I have a right to know, don't I?"

He sighs and lies back, dropping his arm over his eyes. "You do. I just hate exposing you to this information because it puts you at so much risk."

I snort. "How can I possibly be at any more risk than what happened already?"

His arm shifts enough for him to glance over at me from under it. "Good point. First, there's something you need to understand about all of...this." He waves his hand around. "None of us chose this. Not really. At least, not in the beginning."

How does one accidentally become a pirate?

"Warwick took a loan from the former head of the Marconis years ago, to save his family fishing business after his father's death. He OD'd on heroin when War was in college."

I freeze. And I thought I was confused before.

In debt to the mob...

A shudder rolls through me, and I shift closer to Preacher, pressing my face against his chest and my body along the hard lines of his.

"Anyway, he took the money, and in order to pay it off, he agreed to transport cargo for the Marconis. At least, that's how it started. He knew he couldn't do it alone, so he brought in Cutter, who he had known for years, and eventually, Cutter brought Rion and me in once he realized the Marconis were essentially setting them up to be their on-call piracy business."

"What about E?" He's always so quiet and reserved.

Watching and analyzing without saying anything. By far, the most serious of the group from what I've seen.

The corner of Preacher's lip turns up. "Elijah found his way to us when he got out of prison."

Prison?

I don't even want to ask what he was in for. I don't want to know. Imagining the possibilities is enough for me when it comes to that.

"E knew Warwick from some time they both spent in a local jail over some piddly shit. Apparently, Warwick told him if he ever needed a job to try to find him, and that's exactly what he did. We knew what we were doing was illegal, but we were doing it to help Warwick dig himself out of this hole. It didn't start out as anything malicious."

Now, that, I can believe. Preacher is good. Deep down. He's *really* good. The other guys, I'm not so sure about. Yet, if Preacher believes in them and loves them, I can't, in my heart, think they are bad people, either.

His hand brushes along my arm. "We were all struggling to find a place in the world after ours imploded. We were willing to hurt people but only as a last resort. And thankfully, we rarely have to." He releases a deep sigh. "Just seeing all of us coming aboard and the threat of a gun is usually enough to keep things peaceful."

Yet, Rose said the crew had killed thirteen of his men. That doesn't sound so peaceful to me.

I lightly drag my fingers across his pecs. "So, what happened?"

"Arturo Marconi happened." His free hand tightens into a fist. "He was the nephew of *Il Padrone*, who had controlled the Marconi family for decades. But Arturo wasn't content to wait until his uncle stepped down. He had his sights set on becoming head of the family. But first, he ordered us to take some cargo from a ship. It went south, and only half the shipment got to him. He almost killed us over it, but we managed to save our asses by essentially offering him *more* unfettered access to our ships and others. And then, he took out his own flesh and blood without hesitation."

There's so much evil in the world. So many things I never knew existed. So many people I *hoped* didn't exist. Axle was my initiation into the real world, and now, after my experience with Mr. Rose, I don't think I'll ever be able to remember a time where things were simple.

"After that, Arturo stepped up as the head of the family. We were in the process of trying to take him out when he ordered us to raid another ship. That one was a clusterfuck. I'm not going to go into details, but suffice it to say, what happened there would put us all away for a very long time."

So would everything else they've done.

But coupled with what Rose told me, the "clusterfuck" he's talking about must have been when they killed Rose's men. That could get them a hell of a lot more than "put away."

I shudder again. The weight of the day's events and Preacher's words finally begin to press in on me.

His arm tightens around me. "Valentina used to be *Il Padrone's* bodyguard, and no one knew it, but she's also his daughter."

What?

I jerk up onto my elbow. "No! So, that's how she became the head of the family?"

He nods. "We basically helped to get her there without even knowing it. And once she took control, we were no longer forced into doing jobs. We could say no, but we rarely do because she's not Arturo. The type of things we do for her are a lot easier to live with and sleep with at night."

I can see that. She seems like a decent person, despite her position. If she was willing to step up and do what she did today for someone she doesn't know, I can only imagine what she would do for friends.

He rolls onto his side again and stares down at me. "You

have to understand that this life…it may seem stupid to you, and it may seem like I'm being dumb by being involved with this, considering the skills I have, but these guys are my family. Rion and Cutter saved my life, and Warwick gave us all purpose when we were adrift and needed a direction. I don't think I can walk away from it." He sucks in a deep breath and brushes his thumb across my bottom lip. "Even for you."

I bury my face against him, and strong arms wrap around me.

It's exactly what I thought he would say when I knew I had to leave him. He would choose them and this life. Even a day ago, it would have made me angry to be his second choice, but now…I understand it.

And accept it.

"I would never ask you to change who you are. I can't say the thought of what you do makes me happy. And after what happened with Rose tonight, I would be smart to turn tail and run." I pull back and meet his eyes. "But you make me feel safe despite all this. It's something I haven't felt in a very long time and never thought I would again."

Preacher captures my face between his hands and tilts it up. "Please say you're going to stay. Axle…" He pauses and considers his words, and something dark flashes in his eyes. "He can't ever hurt you again."

He doesn't say the words, but they hang there between us all the same.

Oh, my God. He killed him.

I don't know whether I should be revolted or relieved.

Axle is gone.

It's like a giant shadow that's been following me around all this time has finally been vanquished by the sun. But another has settled over Preacher. I can't see it, but it's there.

For someone like him, with his upbringing, his beliefs, taking a life is the ultimate sin. And he did it.

For me.

Nothing makes sense anymore, and what I'm about to say is probably the wrong answer. Anyone in my position would be smart to say no and never look back. Anyone who has suffered what I've suffered wouldn't think twice about disappearing and escaping this world.

But I've never been smart. I've never made the right decisions. My past has proven that.

So why change things now?

Bad decisions brought me to Preacher, and Preacher is a risk I'm willing to take. "I'm going to stay here. I'll keep the shop open. The rest is up to you."

The rest…

Like us. Like where *we* are going.

Waiting for his response feels like standing and waiting for the firing squad.

Is all this too much for him? Me? All my baggage and fears? Is he going to be able to concentrate on his work while I'm here and do what he needs to in order to protect the guys?

His eyes shimmer with unshed tears. The man who is so damn strong, so damn smart, has a soft spot that just burst open. "Jesus, Everly. You really know how to break down a firewall."

I chuckle at his nerdy play on words, and he leans down and presses his lips against mine in a slow and passionate kiss. Even though it's not the words I wanted to hear, it's an answer, nonetheless.

He's in this. With me.

He pulls away and wipes the tears from my cheeks. Love shines in his gaze, something so tangible I can feel it seeping into my bones.

"I can't promise the world to you, Everly. But I do promise I will always, always, always come for you. Forever."

Epilogue

PREACHER

TWO MONTHS LATER

The screen in front of me blurs, and I rub at my eyes for the thousandth time today. I've been in here too long, at this for what feels like an eternity. But I'm not going to walk away until I'm absolutely sure.

The Blood Rose Cartel managed to get in—though I still don't know how—and I'm not going to let that happen again.

Two months of work, and I'm still not fully satisfied with the safeguards I've put in place. The only way to test them was to invite some of my hacker friends to try to bust in.

There are only two I trust that much, and neither has been able to access our server, even after extensive attempts. That should give me confidence, but instead, it only makes me wonder who else out there is better than me. Better than them.

Who the fuck did Rose use to hack us?

All I found was a screen name. *REDROSE.*

And then…poof. Nothing. He disappeared into the ether of the net.

I'll track him forever if I have to, and I'll work myself to death to protect my family.

My door opens, and Everly sticks her head in. "Hey, babe, we need you."

I glance over at her and grin. She's the best damn thing in my life. I don't deserve her, not at all, but she's managed to settle into life as part of this motley crew despite knowing the kind of things we do.

Thank you, God, for answering my prayers.

"What's going on; can it wait?"

She shakes her head, and any amusement disappears from her lips. She looks over her shoulder and steps inside. The door clicks shut behind her, and she leans back against it.

Uh-oh, this doesn't look good.

"You're freaking me out here, Ev. What's going on?"

She bites her bottom lip. "I'm not totally sure. All I know is Valentina got a call, and now, she's ranting about something in Italian to Cutter."

I chuckle to myself more than to her. When Val gets really worked up, she slips into the mother language, and while Cutter can understand her, the rest of us are totally in the dark. The Latin I learned growing up helps me catch bits and pieces, but it's not enough to completely comprehend her.

"No idea what it's about?"

She chews on her lip. "No."

I stare at my screen and run a hand across my beard. "I guess this can wait." It's waited two months already. "All right." I shove to my feet, walk over to her, and drag her up against me to press my lips to hers. "What time do you have to leave?"

She peeks down at her watch. "I have a client in an hour."

Perfect timing.

I won't have to deal with the death glares from her about staying away while we discuss business. She understands it's for the best and that it's only for her protection, but it doesn't stop her from feeling like she's being excluded from a major part of my life.

Which she is. For her own good.

What happened with the Rose Cartel cannot happen again. The security cameras I installed at the shop that link to my system help give me a modicum of comfort knowing I can at least keep an eye on her, but we'll never be one hundred percent safe, not as long as I live this life. The tentative peace and arrangement Valentina brokered have relieved some of the fear, but there are other enemies out there, lying in wait.

I back her into the door and deepen our kiss.

She pulls back her head. "If you're looking for a repeat of our first time together, I don't think we have time or that the guys want to wait for you."

"Fuck the guys."

She laughs and kisses me again, circling her arms around my neck. I lift her up to wrap her legs around my waist.

Bang. Bang. Bang.

The pounding vibrates the door behind her.

"Get the fuck out here, Preacher." Cutter's voice cuts through the wood and is like a cold bucket of water on my libido.

That fucker.

This is payback for when I interrupted Valentina and him a couple of months ago.

I groan, and Everly releases her legs from behind my back and drops her feet to the ground. She presses one final kiss to my lips before turning, grabbing the door handle, and jerking it open.

Fuck.

My cock strains against my pants, and I reach down and adjust it away from the zipper.

I follow her out into the warehouse, where everyone is gathered around the giant table. Everyone except Grace that is. She's back on bed rest, and no one's taking the risk of exposing her to anything that could upset her.

Valentina flashes Everly a smile, and Everly grabs her purse off the table.

"Bye, guys. I have a client."

Everybody waves. Except for Cutter. He just can't find it in his heart to be friendly to anyone. Especially the woman who led to me throwing Valentina under the bus.

At least, that's the way he sees it. Who knows if or when the tension between us will snap…

The douche.

As soon as Everly slips out the door, I take my seat.

Valentina remains standing. She presses her palms flat on the table and meets all of our eyes, one by one. "We have a problem, and I need your help with it."

This doesn't sound good.

Warwick sighs. "Whenever you have a problem, we end up getting shot at."

The corner of her mouth curls up in amusement. "I can't promise you won't get shot at this time, either. But I promise you this is for a good cause."

He grins back. "Oh, yeah, what's that?"

"What do you guys know about the Albanian mob?"

I hope you enjoyed reading *Safe Harbor*, the third book in The Inland Seas Series. The fourth book, *Anchor Point*, is available at all retailers.

ELIJAH

Life outside the walls of my prison cell is far harder than the time I did inside.

There, I had my misery to keep me company.

Out here, I'm forced to face the reality of

everything I've lost.
Nothing can repair the gaping hole in my chest.
Yet, a broken woman wrapped in chains threatens to unravel
the tangle of excuses I use to keep everyone
at arm's length.
But letting Evangeline into my world means exposing her to
the real threat.
Me.
And all the terrible things that come along with that.

EVANGELINE
Taken.
Enslaved.
To be sold to the highest bidder.
The monsters who stole me away from my life
have no conscience.
I'm not so sure the man who rescues me is any different.
He's an ex-con and a pirate— not to be trusted.
But the dark veil of anguish that shrouds him can't hide the
truth of who he is at his core.
Elijah isn't the enemy.
He may be broken and tormented…
And exactly what I need.

Elijah and Evangeline.
Agony and regret.
Faith and acceptance.
This anchor may pull them both down...

AVAILABLE NOW: books2read.com/AnchorPoint
Sign up for Gwyn's newsletter to stay up to date on
releases and other news: www.gwynmcnamee.com/newsletter

About the Author

Gwyn McNamee is an attorney, writer, wife, and mother (to one human baby and two fur babies). Originally from the Midwest, Gwyn relocated to her husband's home town of Las Vegas in 2015 and is enjoying her respite from the cold and snow. Gwyn has been writing down her crazy stories and ideas for years and finally decided to share them with the world. She loves to write stories with a bit of suspense and action mingled with romance and heat.

When she isn't either writing or voraciously devouring any books she can get her hands on, Gwyn is busy adding to her tattoo collection, golfing, and stirring up trouble with her perfect mix of sweetness and sarcasm (usually while wearing heels).

**Gwyn loves to hear from her readers.
Here is where you can find her:
Facebook:**
https://www.facebook.com/AuthorGwynMcNamee/
Twitter:
https://twitter.com/GwynMcNamee
Instagram:
https://www.instagram.com/gwynmcnamee
Bookbub:
https://www.bookbub.com/authors/gwyn-mcnamee
FB Reader Group:

https://www.facebook.com/groups/1667380963540655/

Website:

https://www.gwynmcnamee.com

OTHER WORKS BY GWYN MCNAMEE

The Inland Seas Series (Romantic Suspense)
Squall Line (Book One)

WAR

Out on the water, I'm in control.

I don't make mistakes.

But the fiery redhead destroyed my plans and

left me no choice.

I had to take her.

Now I'm fighting for my life while battling my growing attraction for my hostage.

Grace may have started my downfall, but she could also be my salvation.

GRACE

The moment he stepped foot on my ship, I knew he was trouble.

He took me, and now, my life is in his hands.

But things aren't what they seem, and Warwick isn't

who he appears.

The man who holds me hostage is slowly working his way into my heart even as greater dangers loom on the horizon.

War and Grace.

Dark and light.

Love and hate.

This storm may destroy them both...

Rogue Wave (Book Two)

CUTTER

Complete the mission.

It's what I was trained to do—no matter what.

But when things go to shit right in front of me, my objective gets compromised by a set of fathomless amber eyes.

This isn't a woman's world.

Yet, Valentina refuses to see how dangerous the course she's plotted really is.

How dangerous I am.

VALENTINA

The man who saved my life is just as lethal as the one trying to take it.

Maybe even more.

While he may have rescued me, in the end,

Cutter is my enemy.

The one intent on destroying everything I've striven for.

But the scars of his past draw me closer even though I know I should move away.

Cutter and Valentina.

Anger and desire.

Fight and surrender.

This wave may drag them both under…

Safe Harbor (Book Three)

PREACHER

When it comes to firewalls, no one gets

through my defenses.

For the past five years, protecting this band of f-ed up brothers has been my mission.

But Everly pulls me from my cave and does the one thing no one else ever has...

She makes me believe there's a life outside the world

on my screens.

Too bad actions have consequences, ones that threaten everything and everyone around me.

Including the beautiful tattoo artist who has managed to etch herself onto my heart.

EVERLY

The emotional upheaval of the last six months would be enough to break anyone.

And I can already feel myself cracking.

A tall, sexy, tattooed bad boy is the last thing I need thrown into the mix.

All I want is to keep my head down and pour my pain

into my art.

But Preacher walks into my life and offers me safety in a world where I thought there was none.

Until our pasts finally catch up with us…

Preacher and Everly.

Fear and loss.

Hope and heartbreak.

This harbor may be their salvation.

AVAILABLE AT ALL RETAILERS:

books2read.com/SafeHarbor

Anchor Point (Book Four)

ELIJAH

Life outside the walls of my prison cell is far harder than the time I
did inside.

There, I had my misery to keep me company.

Out here, I'm forced to face the reality of

everything I've lost.

Nothing can repair the gaping hole in my chest.

Yet, a broken woman wrapped in chains threatens to unravel the
tangle of excuses I use to keep everyone

at arm's length.

But letting Evangeline into my world means exposing her to the real
threat.

Me.

And all the terrible things that come along with that.

EVANGELINE

Taken.

Enslaved.

To be sold to the highest bidder.

The monsters who stole me away from my life
have no conscience.

I'm not so sure the man who rescues me is any different.

He's an ex-con and a pirate— not to be trusted.

But the dark veil of anguish that shrouds him can't hide the truth of
who he is at his core.

Elijah isn't the enemy.

He may be broken and tormented…

And exactly what I need.

Elijah and Evangeline.

Agony and regret.

Faith and acceptance.

This anchor may pull them both down…

AVAILABLE AT ALL RETAILERS:

books2read.com/AnchorPoint

Dark Tide (Book Five)

RION

There is no black and white in this life.

The line between right and wrong blurs.

I'm constantly crossing it.

Saving a life is just as easy as taking one.

And I'm damn good at both.

Finding a woman who can survive in this world was never on the
radar.

But Gabriella pulls me from the bottom of a bottle and touches me in a way no one else can.

Too bad secrets and lies have a way of catching up with everyone.

GABRIELLA

How did I end up here, slinging drinks at a dive bar in the middle of nowhere?

The choices that brought me to this were never even a glimmer of possibility only a few years ago.

How things can change so fast…

And now, my path puts me on a collision course

with Orion Gates.

His bigger-than-life size and personality should

be a warning.

The profession he's chosen should be the ultimate

final straw.

But instead, I find myself unable to resist his pull.

A decision that could lead to the end of all of us.

Rion and Gabriella.

Lust and lies.

Betrayal and ruin.

This tide may drown everyone…

AVAILABLE AT ALL RETAILERS:

books2read.com/DarkTide

The Hawke Family Series

Savage Collision **(The Hawke Family - Book One)**

He's everything she didn't know she wanted. She's everything he thought he could never have.

The last thing I expect when I walk into The Hawkeye Club is to fall head over heels in lust. It's supposed to be a rescue mission. I have to get my baby sister off the pole, into some clothes, and out of the grasp of the pussy peddler who somehow manipulated her into stripping. But the moment I see Savage Hawke and verbally spar with him, my ability to remain rational flies out the window and my libido takes center stage. I've never wanted a relationship—my time is better spent focusing on taking down the scum running this city— but what I want and what I need are apparently two different things.

Danika Eriksson storms into my office in her high heels and on her high horse. Her holier-than-thou attitude and accusations should offend me, but instead, I can't get her out of my head or my heart. Her incomparable drive, take-no prisoners attitude, and blatant honesty captivate me and hold me prisoner. I should steer clear, but my self-preservation instinct is apparently dead—which is exactly what our relationship will be once she knows everything. It's only a matter of time.

The truth doesn't always set you free. Sometimes, it just royally screws you.

AVAILABLE AT ALL RETAILERS:

books2read.com/SavageCollision

Tortured Skye (**The Hawke Family - Book Two**)

She's always been off-limits. He's always just out of reach.

Falling in love with Gabe Anderson was as easy as breathing. Fighting my feelings for my brother's best friend was agonizingly hard. I never imagined giving in to my desire for him would cause such a destructive ripple effect. That kiss was my grasp at a lifeline —something, anything to hold me steady in my crumbling life. Now,

I have to suffer with the fallout while trying to convince him it's all worth the consequences.

Guilt overwhelms me—over what I've done, the lives I've taken, and more than anything, over my feelings for Skye Hawke. Craving my best friend's little sister is insanely self-destructive. It never should have happened, but since the moment she kissed me, I haven't been able to get her out of my mind. If I take what I want, I risk losing everything. If I don't, I'll lose her and a piece of myself. The raging storm threatening to rain down on the city is nothing compared to the one that will come from my decision.

Love can be torture, but sometimes, love is the only thing that can save you.

AVAILABLE AT ALL RETAILERS:

Books2read.com/Tortured-Skye

Stone Sober (**The Hawke Family - Book Three**)

She's innocent and sweet. He's dark and depraved.

Stone Hawke is precisely the kind of man women are warned about — handsome, intelligent, arrogant, and intricately entangled with some dangerous people. I should stay away, but he manages to strip my soul bare with just a look and dominates my thoughts. Bad decisions are in my past. My life is (mostly) on track, even if it is no longer the one to medical school. I can't allow myself to cave to the fierce pull and ardent attraction I feel toward the youngest Hawke.

Nora Eriksson is off-limits, and not just because she's my brother's employee and sister-in-law. Despite the fact she's stripping at The Hawkeye Club, she has an innocent and pure heart. Normally, the only thing that appeals to me about innocence is the opportunity to taint it. But not when it comes to Nora. I can't expose her to the filth permeating my life. There are too many things I can't control, things completely out of my hands. She doesn't deserve any of it, but the power she holds over me is stronger than any addiction.

The hardest battles we fight are often with ourselves, but only through defeating our own demons can we find true peace.

Building Storm (The Hawke Family - Book Four)

She hasn't been living. He's looking for a way to forget it all.

My life went up in flames. All I'm left with is my daughter and ashes. The simple act of breathing is so excruciating, there are days I wish I could stop altogether. So I have no business being at the party, and I definitely shouldn't be in the arms of the handsome stranger. When his lips meet mine, he breathes life into me for the first time since the day the inferno disintegrated my world. But loving again isn't in the cards, and there are even greater dangers to face than trying to keep Landon McCabe out of my heart.

Running is my only option. I have to get away from Chicago and the betrayal that shattered my world. I need a new life-one without attachments. The vibrancy of New Orleans convinces me it's possible to start over. Yet in all the excitement of a new city, it's Storm Hawke's dark, sad beauty that draws me in. She isn't looking for love, and we both need a hot, sweaty release without feelings getting involved. But even the best laid plans fail, and life can leave you burned.

Love can build, and love can destroy. But in the end, love is what raises you from the ashes.

Tainted Saint (The Hawke Family - Book Five)

He's searching for absolution. She wants her happily ever after.

Solomon Clarke goes by Saint, though he's anything but. After lusting for him from afar, the masquerade party affords me the anonymity to pursue that attraction without worrying about the fall-out of hooking-up with the bouncer from the Hawkeye Club. From the second he lays his eyes and hands on me, I'm helpless to resist him. Even burying myself in a dangerous investigation can't erase the memory of our combustible connection and one night together. The only problem… he has no idea who I am.

Caroline Brooks thinks I don't see her watching me, the way her eyes rake over me with appreciation. But I've noticed, and the party is the perfect opportunity to unleash the desire I've kept reined in for so damn long. It also sets off a series of events no one sees coming. Events that leave those I love hurting because of my failures. While the guilt eats away at my soul, Caroline continues to weigh on my heart. That woman may be the death of me, but oh, what a way to go.

Life isn't always clean, and sometimes, it takes a saint to do the dirty work.

AVAILABLE AT ALL RETAILERS:

books2read.com/TaintedSaint

Steele Resolve (The Hawke Family - Book Six)

For one man, power is king. For the other, loyalty reigns.

Mob boss Luca "Steele" Abello isn't just dangerous—he's lethal. A master manipulator, liar, and user, no one should trust a word that comes out of his mouth. Yet, I can't get him out of my head. The time we spent together before I knew his true identity is seared into my brain. His touch. His voice. They haunt my every waking hour and occupy my dreams. So does my guilt. I'm literally sleeping with the enemy and betraying the only family I've ever had. When I come clean, it will be the end of me.

Byron Harris is a distraction I can't afford. I never should have let it go beyond that first night, but I couldn't stay away. Even when I learned who he was, when the *only* option was to end things, I kept going back, risking his life and mine to continue our indiscretion. The truth of what I am could get us both killed, but being with the man who's such an integral part of the Hawke family is even more terrifying. The only people I've ever cared about are on opposing sides, and I'm the rift that could end their friendship forever.

Love is a battlefield isn't just a saying. For some, it's a reality.

AVAILABLE AT ALL RETAILERS:

books2read.com/SteeleResolve

The Deadliest Sin Series (Dark Romance)
WRATH (Book One)

All I see is red.

Blood.

Pain.

Rage.

It consumes me.

The moment he took her, wrath invaded my soul.

I only have one purpose.

End him and take back what's mine.

Love isn't always clean, and wrath is the deadliest sin.

AFTER WRATH (Book Two)

They took something from me.

Something that can never be replaced.

They destroyed something.

Something that can never be repaired.

Only one thing can appease the burning rage in my soul.

Unleashing my wrath on those responsible.

The Dragon will rise.

Death will reign.

Because wrath is the deadliest sin.

SURVIVING WRATH (Book Three)

I fled into the night and didn't look back.

I grieved.

I loved.

Then he appears.

Dark.

Dangerous.

I never thought wrath would find me again.

But you can't run from it.

Not when wrath is the deadliest sin

The Slip Series (Romantic Comedy)

Dickslip (A Scandalous Slip Story #1)

One wardrobe malfunction. Two lives forever changed.

Playing in a star-studded charity basketball game should be fun, and it is, until I literally go balls out to show up my arch nemesis. When I dive for the basketball and my junk slips out of my gym shorts, I know my life and career are over. There's no way the network can keep my kids' show on the air after I've exposed myself to millions of people. I don't know how Andy, the new CEO, can go to bat for me with such passion. I also never anticipate how hot she looks in a pair of high heels.

Rafe's dickslip has made my new job even more stressful. It's hard enough being a woman in a man's world without dealing with sex organs being publicly displayed when someone is representing the company. But he's an asset to the network, not to mention hot as hell. I can barely keep my eyes off him or his crotch during our meetings. Defending him to the board puts my ass on the line as much as his, but it's worth it. So is risking my job to fulfill the fantasies I've had about him since he first set foot in my office.

Things may have started out bad, but… some accidents have happy endings.

AVAILABLE AT ALL RETAILERS:
www.Books2read.com/Dickslip

Nipslip (A Scandalous Slip Story #2)

One nipple. A world of problems.

I own the runway. Until my nipple pops out of my dress during New York Fashion Week and it suddenly owns me. Being called a worthless gutter slut by a fuming designer is the least of my problems. My career is swirling around the toilet like the other models' lunches. Until smoking hot Tate Decker steps in with a crazy idea about how his magazine can maybe salvage my livelihood.

It's less than two feet in front of me. Perfect and perky and pink. And the woman it's attached to looks absolutely horrified. I need to help her, and not just because she's beautiful and has a perfect rack. Using my position in the industry to expose the volatile nature of our business puts my career in jeopardy in an attempt to save Riley's. I'm willing to risk that, but falling for her isn't part of the plan.

When love and tits are involved... Things can get slippery.

AVAILABLE AT ALL RETAILERS:

www.Books2read.com/Nipslip

Beaver Blunder (A Scandalous Slip Story #3)

One brief mistake. A world of hurt.

No panties. No problem. At least until I slip on the wet floor and go heels over head in front of my colleagues and half the courthouse. Returning to consciousness can't be more awkward, until I find out who my sexy, argumentative, and bossy knight in shining armor really is. My career may not survive my beaver blunder, and my heart might not survive Owen Grant.

Madeline Ryan tumbles into my life on a wave of perfume and public embarrassment. She falls and exposes herself in front of me, and I find myself falling for her despite the fact she fights me every chance she gets. Being a woman in a good ol' boy profession demands a certain brashness, but it definitely has me thinking, maybe litigators shouldn't be lovers.

With stressful jobs and big attitudes, going commando has never been so freeing.

AVAILABLE AT ALL RETAILERS:

www.Books2read.com/BeaverBlunder